PRA… E

"The first boo… Budewitz has created a b… Erin Murphy, who uses… sheet of Suspicion to catch a killer. The supporting cast of characters, from Erin's mother, Fresca, to her cat, Sandburg, are charming. I'm looking forward to my next visit to Jewel Bay."

—Sofie Kelly, bestselling author of the Magical Cat Mysteries

"Clever, charming, and completely yummy. Leslie Budewitz cooks up a delectable mystery! A tempting concoction of food, fun, and fatalities that will have you racing through the suspenseful pages . . . then heading for the kitchen to try out the irresistible recipes. More please!"

—Hank Phillippi Ryan, Agatha, Anthony, and Macavity award-winning author

"An intriguing sleuth who loves gourmet food, family, and her hometown, plus recipes to die for distinguish a delectable mystery."

—Carolyn Hart, national bestselling author of *Dead, White, and Blue*

"Small-town charm and big-time chills. Jewel Bay, Montana, is a food lover's paradise—and ground zero for murder! A dizzying culinary delight with a twisty-turny plot! I'm totally enamored of Leslie Budewitz's huckleberry chocolates, Shasta daisies, and Cowboy Roast coffee."

—Laura Childs, *New York Times* bestselling author

Berkley Prime Crime titles by Leslie Budewitz

DEATH AL DENTE
CRIME RIB

Death al Dente

Leslie Budewitz

BERKLEY PRIME CRIME, NEW YORK

THE BERKLEY PUBLISHING GROUP
Published by the Penguin Group
Penguin Group (USA) Inc.
375 Hudson Street, New York, New York 10014, USA

USA | Canada | UK | Ireland | Australia | New Zealand | India | South Africa | China

Penguin Books Ltd., Registered Offices: 80 Strand, London WC2R 0RL, England
For more information about the Penguin Group, visit penguin.com.

DEATH AL DENTE

A Berkley Prime Crime Book / published by arrangement with the author

For information, address: The Berkley Publishing Group,
a division of Penguin Group (USA) Inc.,
375 Hudson Street, New York, New York 10014.

ISBN: 978-0-425-25954-2

PUBLISHING HISTORY
Berkley Prime Crime mass-market edition / August 2013

PRINTED IN THE UNITED STATES OF AMERICA

10 9 8 7 6 5 4 3 2 1

Cover illustration by Ben Perini.
Cover design by Rita Frangie.
Interior text design by Kelly Lipovich.

ALWAYS LEARNING **PEARSON**

For my mother, Alice, and my husband, Don

Acknowledgments

The Merc could not have sprung to life without inspiration from my friends and neighbors. Many thanks to all of you for understanding that while Jewel Bay looks a lot like our real town, it's not. I've renamed streets, created tensions, and messed with other details for my own mysterious purposes. Still, I've tried to paint a true-to-life picture of Northwest Montana, a truly delicious place.

A squillion thanks to Peg Cochran aka Meg London, Daryl Wood Gerber aka Avery Aames, Krista Davis, and Janet Bolin for their encouragement and advice. Peg, you are this book's fairy godmother. And thanks to the Guppies chapter of Sisters in Crime, where we all met—the best writers' group anywhere.

I deeply appreciate the work of two women well-named for their professions, Faith Black at Berkley Prime Crime and Paige Wheeler at Folio Literary Management. My instructors and classmates—all friends—at the Breakout Novel Intensive, aka BONI-HR 2012, laughed and learned with me in the rain. Thanks to you all for making this a better book.

Thanks to Jody Fisher, a fantastic, real-life jazz guitarist, for playing at the fictional Gala; to Greg Naive at The Computer Place in Kalispell for setting up Erin's computer system; to Stephanie Mills at Bigfork Drug for explaining pharmacy procedures; and to Keith Nelson at Kalispell Glass for—well, no spoilers. Karen McMullen and Bob Marsenich, owners of the Treasure State Mercantile, aka The Merc, in Polson, inspired the name and business model of my Merc. Thanks to Karen for the feng shui lessons. Karen, Bob, and Ron Brevik shared stories of the modern world of retail. One place in Jewel Bay does closely resemble its real-life counterpart; thanks to Mark "Mister" Langlois for letting me borrow the Garden Bar, rename it, and well, I said no spoilers! Wally Lind and the Crimescenewriters online group answered my questions—and other writers' questions prompted even more ideas. Of course, I made the mistakes all by myself.

My brother and sister-in-law Tom and Kathy Budewitz gave me the sweatshirt I wear on difficult writing days—the one that says, CAREFUL, OR YOU'LL END UP IN MY NOVEL. I hope you don't mind that I took the slogan literally.

My mother, Alice, has waited a long time to see this book; your confidence in it, and me, mean the world.

The quote in Chapter 19 on knife wounds is from *Murder and Mayhem: A Doctor Answers Medical and Forensic Questions for Mystery Writers*, by D. P. Lyle, M.D.; every writer should have a copy. My fictional herbalist relies on *The Forest Farmacy*, by Thomas J. Tracy, of Swan Valley Herbs, Bigfork, Montana. For other medical info, I am grateful to my husband, Don Beans, R.N., L.Ac., Ph.D., and other initials which are very helpful to a mystery writer, including M.R.—Mister Right.

Mercantile: A system of commerce designed to foster the economic interests of a community; promote agriculture, manufacturing, and tourism; and nurture a sense of stability and well-being.

Glacier Mercantile, Jewel Bay, Montana: A purveyor of high-quality, whole and natural foods, grown and prepared with love by your neighbors. Your Destination for the Taste of Montana.

· One ·

"Who put these huckleberry chocolates on the front counter?" I grabbed the stack of purple boxes crammed with gooey huckleberry-filled chocolate wannabes swathed in purple foil and shoved them onto an open shelf on the side wall, next to the herbal snoose.

"I did, honey," my mother said. "Our customers love them."

"Our customers," I said, "buy one for seventy-five cents and walk around the store, so preoccupied with unwrapping it and indulging their sweet tooth that they can't fathom buying Montana-made goat cheese, or buffalo jerky, or your pastas and sauces. Then they grab a napkin that costs us five cents apiece to wipe purple goo off their fingers, and half of them drop it on the floor. There goes our profit."

My mother scowled. "Erin, what on earth has gotten into you? Why do you hate huckleberry chocolates?"

"I don't hate huckleberry chocolates. I love huckleberry chocolates. But we can't rebuild this business on fake food and chemical sugar."

She picked up the boxes I'd just moved and carried them

back to the cash register. "We have always had huckleberry chocolates right here, where the customers can see them."

"Mom, you hired me to run the place, remember? To shake things up."

"Some things shouldn't be changed."

"Mom, we agreed. The Merc will die if it's just another knickknacky gift shop. But an artisan market for local and regional foods—"

"Those are local. They're made five miles from here, by a woman you've known half your life."

"With high-fructose corn syrup and milk chocolate that tastes like rancid Hershey's. If we find a vendor using fresh berries, real sugar, and high-quality fair trade dark chocolate, sixty percent cocoa solids or better, I will build the Great Pyramid of huckleberry chocolates right here." I jabbed at a spot on the oak floor, ten feet inside the Merc's front door, little changed in the hundred years since my great-grandfather Murphy built the place and opened the town's first grocery. "I will worship at her kitchen stove. I will put an ad in the paper and a post on Facebook offering a free huckleberry truffle to everyone who walks in that door. And if they aren't wrapped in purple paper, I will even consider raising the price split."

My mother stared as though she didn't recognize me. Not for the first time since I'd returned to Jewel Bay, Montana, the hometown I couldn't wait to leave after high school, fourteen years ago, to take over her struggling business so she could focus on building her own product line.

And not, I was sure, the last.

"But Erin, chocolate isn't local. Neither is sugar." Tracy, my shop clerk and sole employee, cocked her head, her thick chestnut hair swaying. One elaborately beaded earring brushed her plump shoulder.

"That's not the point." I reshelved the chocolates. Poor things. Not their fault they represented the worst of the specialty food market. Overprocessed and overpriced, they were nothing more than overhyped M&Ms that melted in your hand, and gummed up your mouth. "Our mission is to sell high-quality natural and organic food. Real food. Sustainably grown." We'd been over this, and my mother had agreed, knowing the Merc desperately needed a change in direction to survive. But while she'd turned over the reins, she hadn't quite given up control. "We showcase the local, but we won't sacrifice quality for proximity. We are selling a vision—the natural taste of Montana."

"If it's made in Montana, it must be good." Tracy repeated our new slogan in a singsong voice, her earrings swaying like a drunk failing a field sobriety test. She squeezed her Diet Coke can. Its metallic twang made my brain hurt.

"I think you're taking this Festa too seriously," my mother said. *Like you always do*, I heard in her tone. "Why don't you eat something? Slice up some tomatoes and fresh mozzarella, with basil and that yummy herbed olive oil."

I groaned inwardly. The two women who ran Rainbow Lake Garden had brought us incredible Early Girl tomatoes and heavenly Genovese basil from their greenhouse. Perfect for Caprese salad, the dish the angels serve when God needs a snack.

"Mom, thanks. You go ahead and eat, but I've got too much to do. We still have to decorate." The Merc, formally known as the Glacier Mercantile, backed onto a small courtyard. Our next-door neighbor, Red's Bar, sported a larger courtyard. Tonight, we were throwing open the gate between the two and hosting the kickoff dinner for the First Annual Jewel Bay Festa di Pasta. Tracy and I had decorated our space that morning. But Old Ned Redaway—aka Red—didn't want us to "doll the place up" until his Friday burgers-and-beer lunch crowd had cleared the door. Which meant ignoring my gurgling tummy until every table was set and the last lights strung.

Meanwhile, we had a store to spiff up. For the next hour,

we filled shelves and displays with goods our vendors and producers had delivered, and worked with the smattering of midday customers. I helped my mother—Francesca, aka Fresca—refill the coolers and shelves that held our signature products and biggest sellers: her handmade pastas, both fresh and dried, and a dozen varieties of sauce and pesto. That done, she restocked wine from Monte Verde Vineyard: Chardonnay, a red blend, and cherry wine with the peppery vibrance of a young pinot noir. She cradled a bottle of prize-winning Viognier, admiring the label my sister had designed.

I paused to read over my mother's shoulder. "Looks great, doesn't it? Chiara turned Jennifer's scribbles into a brand with a simple, attractive message."

"Yes," she said. "It says 'drink me.'"

I laughed and kissed her cheek. Working with—for—my mother wasn't always easy, but we were still the Murphy girls.

On the surface, the Merc looked like any other specialty food shop. In reality, we were more like a co-op, with nearly two dozen regional growers and producers consigning their food and drink for sale in a single space. I wanted to prove that even a small mountain town with long winters and a short growing season could do a lot to feed itself, while sharing local bounty with our thousands of summer visitors. In the two months since I'd been back in town, we'd redefined our goals and realigned our product mix. The Festa—a village-wide event I'd conceived to celebrate the start of summer—was the big test. After all, we called ourselves The Food Lovers' Village.

I helped Tracy unpack cartons of jams and jellies, lining them up on the shelves and in the open drawers of an antique Hoosier cabinet: cherry, strawberry, black cap, wild chokecherry. And the crème de la crème, the King, the Queen, the Champion of jams, wild Montana huckleberry.

One eye on the clock, I made sure the sidewalk produce

cart was full, then headed for the back door, where crates of decorations stood ready. The front of the Merc houses the retail shop, while a certified commercial kitchen fills the back third. Fresca cooks here, and so do half a dozen vendors. We sponsor cooking demonstrations, and plan to offer regular classes this fall.

On the long stainless steel counter dividing the kitchen from the shop, I spotted a handmade ceramic platter bearing a bit of paradise. I slid to a stop.

"Smell that Genovese basil, darling." My mother—I'm still getting used to thinking of her as Fresca, now that we're in business together—closed her eyes. "Isn't it heavenly?" She breathed deeply, the few lines in her lovely, oval face disappearing as she closed her nearly black eyes in an expression that could only be called rapture, a few strands of silver in the straight, dark hair that brushed her slender shoulders. Her secret for looking youthful at sixty-one?

If it worked for her . . . I plucked a stack of tomato, mozzarella, and basil off the platter and savored the pepperysweet smells before taking the first bite, my other hand cupped to catch any stray juices. "Mmm. The taste of summer."

"*Mangia, mangia.* But sit. You know women gain weight when we eat on the run."

"Can't." I'd inherited my late father's "black Irish" fair skin and dark hair along with enough of my mother's good genes to avoid most weight problems. We're about the same height—five-six—and I've got a few pounds on her, but not enough to worry me. Still, being a grocery manager and the daughter of a woman whose idea of hello is a plate of something tempting, I know the risks. "Time to decorate." I took another anyway.

"Festa di Pasta," Tracy said, sliding onto a stool and picking up her own Caprese appetizer. "Don't you love the name?"

"I still think you need a saint in there somewhere," Fresca

said. "Festa di Pasta di San Pietro or Tomaso or San Somebody."

I laughed. "No saints in this town."

"To be authentically Italian—"

"Mom, the point is to be authentically Jewel Bay. And to show off the new Merc." Jewel Bay is not what people expect in a Montana town. Cutting-edge art and lip-smacking restaurants instead of cow pies and shoot-outs on dirt streets. But we have our belly-up bar, and plenty of cowboys, with farms and ranches nearby. And even a real live dude ranch, giving guests from around the world a taste of the old Montana and the new.

Out back, I opened the wooden gate between the courtyards and paused, soaking up the early afternoon. By six, when guests arrived, temperatures would be perfect, dinner smells mingling with the scent of sun-warmed fir and pine. A jazz quartet—the winemakers Sam and Jennifer Krauss and two friends—would harmonize with the rushing Jewel River a few hundred yards away, as locals and visitors toasted another sparkling summer in Jewel Bay.

But now, there was work to be done. As promised, Red's staff were cleaning the picnic tables and benches, and the outdoor bar, cut from old-growth pine decades ago, glistened.

Old Ned, seventy if he was a day, white apron around his ample waist, stood tall behind the bar, ruffling what was left of his once-red hair. "'Bout time, girlie. Let's get this glorified spaghetti feed of yours going."

I'd known Ned all my life, and his gruffness never bothered me. Red's courtyard buzzed with activity during good weather, but ours had stood dormant for years. Next spring, I plan to invite the local nursery to bring in potted flowers, herbs, and vegetables.

Ned's "boys," as he called them, made quick work of the setup, stringing white Christmas lights along the walls and through the tall shade trees. Red and white—the school colors—are a Friday tradition in Jewel Bay, so we added green for the Italian touch. Fresca and I arranged candle lanterns in strategic locations, amid terra-cotta pots filled with red and white geraniums and spikey dracaena.

We spread checkered oilcloth over the tables. She set out centerpieces: handmade red willow baskets stuffed with goodies donated by village vendors and flying small flags from America, Italy, and the state of Montana. One lucky winner at each table would take home a taste of Jewel Bay.

I consulted the list on my iPad, making sure we hadn't missed anything. I'd given the caterers a diagram, and all was in place: steam trays, grills, stacks of white china plates. "Drinks at the bar," I said. "Stuffed mushrooms and the grilled fennel and prosciutto there." I gestured toward a round table. "And the pasta and vegetable buffet there," at a long table. Dessert would be served at the tables: grilled peaches with a red wine-balsamic reduction and cookies. "Perfect."

"Talking to yourself again, Erin?"

I spun toward the deep voice. I hadn't seen Ted come in. "The only way to be sure of intelligent conversation."

"I'm kinda hard to miss." At six-two and maybe two-sixty, with a sandy beard and a bulging belly, that was an understatement. As usual, Ted Redaway—Edward, like his father, Ned—wore jeans and a denim shirt with a black leather vest and motorcycle boots. We'd known each other since kindergarten, when the teacher sat us—the only two kickers—across the table from each other. He nodded at the sandwich board reading FIRST ANNUAL JEWEL BAY FESTA DI PASTA. "Bit early to call it the First Annual."

"Call it optimism," I said.

He laughed. "I like big thinkers."

Old Ned appeared in the doorway. "About time you got here."

"Thinks he can put me to work 'cuz he owns the place." Ted winked. "I'm coming, old man."

"Ted." We all turned at the sharp note. "I hear you've been talking about me." Fresca gave him The Glare I knew so well. "You've been telling people I stole Claudette's recipes and fired her to make room for Erin."

His face flushed as red as the bandanna knotted around his neck.

"Why would you say such things?" she demanded. "You know I'm a professional chef. And she ran off to Vegas on her own, chasing Dean Vincent."

"I'm only repeating what she's been saying herself."

"I don't believe it. We've been friends for fifteen years."

And it had been that long since I'd seen my mother's hands shaking or heard such hurt and anger in her normally calm voice.

"Just ask Claudette." He tried to hide a smirk. "She's back."

· *Two* ·

"What? When? Where is she?" My mother voiced my thoughts.

"Ted," I said. "What's going on?"

He looked around—not, I thought, for Claudette, but for someone to rescue him. Even for something to do, if that would get him out of the heat. "The Elvis thing didn't work out, I guess. Dean's reopening his office, and Claudette . . ." He flushed again. "Well, I don't know what she's planning. She don't have much to come back to, thanks to you."

Mom's dark eyes flared, then she turned to me. "Why didn't she call?"

"Why on earth a grown man would dress up as somebody else and prance around in gold lamé"—Old Ned pronounced it "luh-mee"—"is beyond me."

Claudette Randall running off to Las Vegas with Dean Vincent last spring had been Jewel Bay's biggest scandal in ages. No one had expected Dean—"I'm a tribute artist, not an impersonator"—to close his chiropractic clinic and take his dreams on the road. Especially not his wife, Linda.

They'd been separated, again, but everyone assumed they'd reconcile, again. Claudette, my mother's oldest friend, had managed the Merc the last couple of years. With business way down, Fresca had urged me to come home and take over. "Use your skills and experience where they're appreciated," she'd said. "Let Claudette focus on the customers. She's good at that." I'd loved city life: the art, the music, the food. The buzz. But my job as an assistant buyer at SavClub, the international warehouse chain headquartered in Seattle, wasn't going anywhere. Then an elderly friend died and left me a cat my landlord hated. When Claudette took a hike, it seemed like a sign.

So far, so good. But if Ted was right . . .

"She must be devastated. What will she do?"

"Mom, don't cry for her. She gave you less than twenty-four hours' notice, after all the time you'd worked together. And remember your fights?"

She frowned. "We never fought, Erin. We just had different ideas about what was best for the shop. She's still my friend."

I shrugged. It hadn't sounded that way in her calls asking my business advice and hinting—not so subtly—that I come home.

"Besides, Claudette would never tell lies about a friend."

For a moment, Ted's green eyes seemed to twinkle, as though he were enjoying himself. But the shadow of a branch waved in the breeze, and I realized it was just the glint of the afternoon sun. "Maybe you two weren't such good friends after all," he said.

Old Ned glowered. "You stop that BS." He draped one arm around Mom's shoulders and the other around mine. "Different ideas is par for the course in business. Don't let it bother you none."

"Thanks, Ned," I said.

"You coming back's been good for the town, by jingo.

Shake things up a bit, bring in new customers." He winked. "Folks get dry when they shop."

"Ned, we couldn't ask for a better neighbor." Mom stretched to kiss his cheek and I followed suit. She took my arm and we headed back to the Merc, leaving Old Ned Redaway blushing.

Inside the shop, Tracy busied herself with more displays—hoping, no doubt, to avoid questions. Claudette and Tracy had been good friends, though at thirty-four, Tracy was a good ten years younger. Both about five-two, Tracy was nicely rounded, with a softly pretty face, while Claudette was all angles and energy. When Claudette left, Tracy had lobbied hard for her job. My first act as manager had been to give her a raise and ask her to stay. The Merc needed continuity. Plus I'd been an assistant long enough myself to understand her disappointment.

I climbed the stairs to the loft office, where my mother sat swiveling the desk chair. "Mom, what was all that about? Where did you hear those rumors?"

"Heidi thought I ought to know before the Festa dinner tonight."

Heidi Hunter, my mother's best friend, the goddess of cookware. Gourmets trekked from half a dozen states and provinces to visit her shop, Kitchenalia. Hold your wallet tight in there. "Hard to believe Heidi and Ted are gossip buddies."

"Apparently it's been all the talk for days, and not just from him. Small towns are like that."

I pulled up an antique mahogany piano stool. "You don't think people talk more in small towns than in cities, do you?" The gossip I'd heard at SavClub would make a habanero sweat. The bigger the office, the slimier the politics.

"Maybe not, but with fewer people, rumors spread faster

and everyone hears them." She reached for her coffee cup, a hand-thrown model from our stock, and saw that it was empty. "Though I hadn't heard a word."

"So? Just shrug it off and get back to work." Funny to hear yourself channel your parent's standard advice—especially to your parent.

But my mother didn't budge. "Claudette didn't say any such things. She knows those were my recipes, many from your noni and papa. She helped me adapt them for production level, and expand the market. The Merc was my baby, part of the family. But it hurts that she hasn't called."

"Maybe Ted's right, that she wasn't the friend you thought."

Fresca shook her head, a few silver strands catching the light. "She needed to make a change. She just had to figure out what she wanted to do."

"Sounds like she still does."

She stroked my cheek with her long, slender fingers. "Some people drift forever, darling. But others know they're right where they belong."

I'd been making lists and gathering supplies for weeks, but it wouldn't hurt to have more votive candles for the lanterns. On my way home to shower and change, I detoured to the grocery store on the highway to rustle up a few.

After buying all their white and yellow candles, I headed to the drugstore to check their supply. If all went well, there would be more Festas to come, and candles keep.

And if it went badly—

A dynamo in a riotous sundress darted out of a doorway and across the sidewalk in front of me. The splashes of orange, purple, and green against a white background looked like a bird of paradise in flight. "Claudette!"

She slammed to a stop, long light brown curls flying, face hot pink.

"You're back! We just heard."

She jerked a thumb at Dean Vincent's chiropractic clinic, tucked into a small space beside the drugstore. "After all I did for him . . ."

"What's wrong? What happened?"

"I gave up everything to help him pursue his dream. And all along . . ." Her rage steamed the air between us. "Nothing but a ruse to make his wife jealous."

I pulled her to a bench outside the drugstore and made her sit.

"He talked me into going to Las Vegas so he could study Elvisology. I thought he loved me, and we were starting over together somewhere new." More sobbing. Blubbering. "But he never meant any of it."

I rummaged in my bag for a clean tissue and slipped it into her tiny, trembling hand.

"I am mortified," she said, her voice high and strained. "What will people think?"

"That Dean's a jerk."

A small laugh. "And that I'm a complete fool who can't do anything right."

"Well, I know that feeling."

Her eyes widened. "You? You've got to be kidding."

Dare I ask? Just dive in. "Claudette, I've been hearing . . ."

She stopped crying. "What? What are you hearing?"

"That you've been telling people . . ." *Erin, that bad taste in your mouth is your foot. But you're in this far—keep going.* "That my mother stole your recipes and forced you out to make room for me."

"What? That's ridiculous. I never said anything like that." She blew her nose, turning it red. "Who said that? Oh my gosh, Fresca must be furious with me."

"She doesn't believe it." But before I could suggest she tell my mother herself, a male voice broke in.

"Claudette." Dean Vincent didn't look much like Elvis

today, in his khakis, sky blue button-down, and L.L. Bean mocs, though he had the height and the dark, full hair. The Casual Friday look in cities; everyday garb for small-town professionals.

His eyes barely registered me. "Claudette, be reasonable."

She rose. "How dare you call me unreasonable?" She'd perfected the short woman's trick of looking up with only her eyes, keeping the rest of her face level and her voice sharp but steady, intimidating with presence instead of size.

"I never meant to hurt you." He sounded like he actually believed himself.

"No. Just string me along and make me look like an idiot."

Time to say good-bye. I glanced at the drugstore entrance, surprised to see Chef James Angelo, my mother's sauce-making rival, watching from the doorway.

"Claudette, honey." Dean took a step forward, one hand extended. "Can't we talk?"

She stiffened. "Don't you touch me."

He raised both hands in defeat. "Okay, okay. I just wanted to say I'm sorry." He backed away and slipped inside his clinic.

Claudette sank back onto the bench. "All my plans ruined."

"There's always Plan B," I said.

She sighed. "Too late for that."

"Come to the Festa tonight. We're kicking off summer with an Italian dinner at the Merc—all local ingredients, wine, music. Everyone will be thrilled to see you."

A spark lit her hazel eyes. "Really? You think your mother wouldn't mind?"

"Mind? She'd be furious if I didn't invite you. The courtyard, six-ish."

That would quell the gossip.

· *Three* ·

I pushed the hand-carved front door shut behind me and kicked off my flip-flops. Home, though not for long. The time spent comforting Claudette had cut my schedule to the bone.

"Hey, Mr. Sandburg." A sleek, sable Burmese, the deep espresso brown of an Italian roast, the cat stood in the entry, in his "you can pick me up if you want to" stance. I dropped my keys and bag on the table, and scooped him up on my way to the bedroom.

"No time for love, buddy. I can't be late, not tonight." I plopped him on the bed, where he circled three times, still meowing, though his cries quieted as he settled in, the soft down comforter poofing up around him.

If the locals thought I'd walked into a sweet deal with my job at the Merc, I could imagine what they thought about the cabin. The caretaker's place on the lakefront property of our family friends, Liz and Bob Pinsky, it had come vacant last spring. My timing had been perfect—the Pinskys offered it to me, free and clear. It sat high above the main house, with peekaboo views of the lake, windows draped with lacy branches of Douglas fir and mountain birch. They'd refinished the ponderosa pine log walls and plank ceilings, reusing the original doorknobs and locks that regularly gave me fits. Best of all was the perfectly planned bed-and-bath addition.

Inside the slate shower, I fumbled for the shampoo—a lavender-chamomile tester from a potential vendor. While I believed Claudette's denial, Ted's gossip still rankled. Much as I loved being home, the rumors stung. The Festa's success would shut them up.

The shampoo bottle flew out of my hand. I bent to pick it up and smacked my head on the grab bar.

Good going, grace.

My mother had insisted she didn't believe Claudette was spreading rumors, so in theory, she would welcome Claudette back with open arms. I'd invited her on the spur of the moment, but she belonged at the party. She was part of the family, and part of the village.

As I dried off, I heard my phone—the default ring, so not my mother or sister, or the shop line. I glanced at the clock. No time to spare.

Good thing my outfit was all ready. I slipped on the skirt I'd chosen weeks ago, a flouncy blue-and-white floral, and a white linen tank. The clasp on my Mexican silver belt balked, but after a few tries, I got it cinched.

Standing on one foot, I managed to get my first sandal on, but dropped the other. *Geez, girl. Take a breath here.* I bent to pick it up, and spotted my red boots in the corner of the closet.

Eureka. I yanked off the sandal and pulled on one boot. Extended my leg and admired the view. Midcalf, ruby red leather, pointed toes, and a riding heel, with white stitching in a tulip and vine pattern. I smiled and slid my foot into the other.

Oh, the magic.

I twirled in front of the mirror, then raised my arms and danced a quick jig. My hair, cut in a bob just below my chin, spun like a dark halo.

I slipped on shiny-bright silver earrings and a pair of silver bangles that danced across the three colored stars tattooed on my left wrist. Rubbed them for luck.

On the bed, Sandburg mewed softly, tail switching across the new Julia Child biography I'd tossed there. I stroked the purr button on his forehead with my thumb.

"Cinderella found the right shoes all by herself," I told him. "And now she's off to throw the best ball this town has ever seen."

All looked just as planned. Almost—I adjusted the angle of the flags in a centerpiece.

Fresca arrived, wearing a knee-length pale coral tank dress and a short stack of Bakelite bracelets inherited from a stylish aunt, an ivory Pashmina shawl over her shoulders. The soft colors complemented her silver-and-black hair and olive complexion. She looked like one of my grandmother's peace roses that still grew on the orchard homestead. The tweets and woofs of the musicians' sound check competed with the rattle and roll of the delivery carts. All the village restaurants had a piece of the event.

I made the rounds with a long-handled lighter and set the lanterns aglow.

At quarter to six, my sister and her husband arrived. Chiara—say it with a hard C and rhyme it with tiara, she likes to say—clapped her hands. "Little sister, it's wonderful."

"Don't sound so surprised." At a glance, we look like twins, with the same dark hair, fair skin, and heart-shaped faces, although I'm two inches taller and she's two years older. Tonight, she'd pulled her hair back and fastened it with a giant salmon pink flower barrette made by one of her gallery partners.

"Like you waved a magic wand," Jason said. With his receding hairline, solid-color button-downs, and khakis, and his career in software and web design, Jason was the perfect foil for my funky dresser artist sister. And the perfect mate. "Even the stale beer smell's gone."

"Masked by tomato sauce. It'll be back tomorrow."

Lights sparkled in the trees, and lanterns flickered on the tables. A small-town beer garden transformed into a festive fairyland. The butterflies in my stomach settled.

Most guests arrived through the bar, although a few trickled in Red's back gate. The Pinskys. Heidi, on the arm of a hunky real estate broker from Pondera. Tony and Mimi George from the Jewel Inn, the historic lodge that anchors Front Street.

"Oh my," my mother whispered with a look at Dean Vincent, in a white bell-bottomed jumpsuit with gold trim, pompadour gelled to a shine, and Linda, in a leopard print number that looked painted on, her platinum hair in a chignon. "Are they back together?"

I swatted away a gnat. "I ran into Claudette outside the drugstore. She was foaming. If I'd known they were coming, I'd never have invited her."

Fresca's dark eyes and coral mouth made perfect echoing O's.

"Looking good, girls." Old Ned sported his Friday afternoon red-and-white plaid shirt, dressed up with a crisp white apron.

Among the mingling guests were the network broadcaster who summered here and her millionaire husband, chatting with the minister's wife who ran the local food pantry—beneficiary of ticket sales for tonight's dinner and tomorrow night's Gala. A retired general and his wife visited with the school superintendent. The bookstore owner and book club ladies, village merchants, even a few new faces, all chatted happily.

Brubek's "Take Five" filled the air. Sam and Jen, vintners

by day and musicians by night, swayed with the beat. They'd looked a little rattled earlier—a missing cord or some other bit of gear, no doubt—but they'd found the groove. Wine flowed, appetizers disappeared. Just as planned.

I headed for the bar and a glass of pinot grigio. "Erin." Tracy interrupted me, a cluster of pinecones and branches bearing the three flags in her hands. "This goes on the back gate. I completely forgot."

After all our prep? "Don't worry." I took the arrangement and wound through the courtyard, pausing to exchange a few greetings. The high wooden gate opening on Red's courtyard was closed, to my surprise, and I muttered as I unlatched it with one hand. Finally, it gave and opened with a loud creak. I stepped into the alley, also called Back Street, passed the communal garbage and recycling bins we'd convinced the Village Merchants Association to install, and turned to look for a good spot to hang the cones and flags.

And screamed. Beside the black garbage bin lay a bird of paradise. Claudette, in her bright sundress, sprawled on the ground.

Footsteps crunched on the gravel as guests emerged from the courtyard. I knelt and reached for her neck, my fingers trembling. But the streak of red running down her dress and the blood pooling on the ground made clear that this hothouse flower would never bloom again.

· Four ·

No matter how prepared you think you are, there's no preparing for murder.

Nothing natural about Claudette's death. Had someone planned to kill her—or seized an opportunity?

The eyes of town bore down on us. My scream seemed to have punched a button prompting everyone at the Festa to pull out a phone and bombard county dispatch.

Gordon Springer, the tall, balding pharmacist, knelt beside me and checked Claudette's wrist and neck. His pursed lips and gray complexion confirmed my diagnosis.

Funny how the mind makes the shift from seeing a woman—a friend—to seeing "a body." "Oh, Claudette," I whispered, resisting the urge to stroke her arm or soft caramel hair, so absurdly out of place against the dusty gray gravel. Beside her, Tracy's pinecone arrangement lay where I'd dropped it, flags flying at broken angles.

"Let me through." A strained baritone pierced my bubble of grief.

"No." I rose to confront Dean Vincent. "Don't you come near her."

"Erin, I'm a doctor. Let me help."

"You're a chiropractor. Who just dumped her."

If he transformed onstage the way he did in Back Street, he'd convince Priscilla herself. It was Elvis himself who stepped within inches of me, shoulders stiff as he leaned in, rage deepening his electric tan. "I—didn't—touch—her."

"Let the EMTs handle this," I said. "They're almost here." With the sheriff right behind, judging from the multiple sirens. The fewer people who touched a crime scene, the better. I knew that much from *Law and Order* reruns.

Not so easy, in the middle of a party in the middle of town.

Dean hovered, but kept a respectable—if not respectful—distance. I heard Gordy tell Ned and my brother-in-law to usher everyone back in and make sure no one left. I stayed put. The minister, a tall, heavyset man with rounded shoulders and a neck that seemed permanently bowed, began a prayer. My mother slipped her shawl around my shoulders, then led Dean inside.

We kept vigil, the minister and I. The sirens' whirl and wail grew louder, almost louder than my heart. How was it that my chest did not explode?

What had happened? Who had done this?

Who had ruined the Festa—and killed my friend?

Erin, for shame. How can you think of the Festa first?

But I did. All our plans and work—for what? So people could remember the Festa and think of murder? Laugh and call it a killer party?

And a flame-out wouldn't harm just me and the Merc. I'd convinced the village merchants—the ruling powers of Jewel Bay—to start a new festival in a town full of festivals. Restaurant owners and retail shopkeepers alike had committed time and money to the idea. Would they blame me for its failure?

Tires on gravel. Doors opening. Footsteps and voices, urgent and solemn.

A hand on my shoulder.

My gaze met that of my old friend Kim Caldwell, now a sheriff's detective. All business, her short blond hair and dark outfit accentuated her slim build and made her look taller than five-eight. She nodded, and I rose, wordless, brushing the dirt from my bare knees. Her turf now.

More vehicles, more footsteps, more voices. EMTs took charge of the body while uniformed deputies took charge of the alley and parking lot, fanning out, searching, eyes watchful, gun hands ready.

Head still bowed, the minister opened the gate, and he and I stepped into the courtyard. Chairs stopped scraping, ice stopped clinking, eighty bodies stopped moving, their faces turned toward me.

"I'm so sorry," I said. "She's gone." My throat felt brittle and dry, full of tumbleweed. "This is such a—a shock. A tragedy. We all loved Claudette." Murmurs of agreement, but obviously someone had not loved her. Was the killer here, among us? I stumbled through an abbreviated version of the speech I'd planned about the Festa, the other weekend activities, and the Food Bank benefit. "We're here, the food's ready. Claudette loved a party, so . . ." I opened my arms in welcome, unable to say more.

"To Claudette," someone said, raising a glass. My hand was empty, my eyes full, but I joined the gesture.

And just like that, the courtyard snapped back to life. Lids came off serving dishes and corks slid out of bottles. Talk fired up as guests migrated to the buffet.

I collapsed into the nearest chair. There were a million things I should be checking, but none of them seemed to matter. Or more accurately, to need me. The apron-clad caterers and bartenders knew what they were doing. Let them.

If only I hadn't gone out to the alley, maybe Claudette would be alive.

Foolish thought, and I knew it.

"What about the music?"

"What?" My mother's question broke my trance.

"The music, darling. The quartet should keep playing, don't you think? Soothing tunes."

At my nod, she beelined for Sam, on lead guitar, her hair fanning out over her shoulders.

Ray from the Bayside Grille slid a small plate in front of me, disappearing before I could speak. Mushrooms stuffed with herbed bread crumbs, shallots, and chopped mushrooms, grilled fennel and shrimp wrapped with prosciutto, olive tapenade on crisp bruschetta.

Ohmyohmyohmy.

Old Ned put a sweating glass of white wine on the table. It looked fragile in his meaty hand.

"Such service. Thanks. Aren't you on guard duty?"

He grunted. "Delegated to Ted. Serves him right, showing up late."

I stood and wrapped my arms around him—or part of him. I'd never hugged a bear but imagined this came close. He wiped away a tear.

Behind him, Dean glared, drops of sweat curling his Elvis sideburns. I felt a twinge of sympathy for Linda, one of those women learning too late that looks weren't enough.

"I didn't kill her." His words, slow and deliberate, held a hint of Memphis that no longer rang true.

Being callous and conceited didn't make him a killer. Or rule him out. Too many people within earshot, so to save myself from saying something I might regret, I picked up a shrimp by the tail and took a bite.

"I told you it was pointless," Linda said. The large diamond on her left ring finger flashed as she grabbed Dean's hand and jerked him away.

I sat and sipped my wine. Pinot grigio, nectar of the gods.

An electronic thump caught my ear. The music had stopped. So did the chatter as we all directed our attention to the bandstand, where Kim tapped the mic. "I'm Detective Kim Caldwell. The sheriff, deputies, and I are sorry for your loss. I assure you we'll do everything we can to get to the bottom of this as quickly as possible."

A pair of deputies in tan-and-brown uniforms emerged from the Merc's courtyard. One gave Kim a swift nod. Our space, it seemed, had been searched and found satisfactory.

"I'd like everyone who saw or spoke to Claudette Randall at any time today to go over there"—she gestured toward the Merc's courtyard—"for brief questioning. If you didn't see her, but you have information you think we should know, that includes you. The rest of you"—she scanned the crowd—"are free to mingle. The alley is blocked, so you'll need to leave through the bar. Make sure you give your name to the officers at the front door. We appreciate your cooperation." She popped the microphone back in its stand and nodded to Sam, who took that as permission to start a soft melody.

A uniformed deputy, who looked like he held black belts in half a dozen martial arts, stood before the back gate, now firmly latched.

"Where can we talk?" Kim asked me, her tone not unfriendly.

I led her to a café table in the corner, on the Merc side. "Can I get you anything?" I said, surprised to hear my voice shake.

"No." We'd met in sixth grade, after her parents moved home to help her grandparents run Caldwells' Eagle Lake Lodge and Guest Ranch south of town. Her extended family was as close as mine, maybe closer. She and I had been best friends all through junior high and high school. Until my father died, winter of senior year. That had been too much for her, and the night of his accident, I lost my best friend, too. Since my return, we'd run into each other a few times, but exchanged only small talk. Why she'd chosen law enforcement remained a mystery. When we were kids, all she wanted to do was ride. She even talked me into competitive barrel racing. She'd dreamed of becoming head wrangler—leading guests on trail rides, taking care of the stock, wearing jeans and plaid flannel, smelling of fresh horse manure.

Now she wore a charcoal linen jacket over a soft gray tee and black knit pants, and I caught a whiff of gun oil.

Something slid down her left wrist and she shoved it back up her sleeve. A bracelet? A memory flashed across my mental screen and vanished.

"I'm sorry to have to put you through this," she said, her voice low, her blue eyes neutral. "Your family means a lot to me."

Right. My family meant so much she dropped me like a rock when my father died. Like it might be contagious. Like I had done something to her.

I nodded. Until I knew what was going on, I needed to be very careful.

She laid a small recorder on the table between us. "Mind?" I shook my head and tucked a strand of hair behind my left ear. "Tell me what happened."

I described the encounter outside the drugstore, then finding Claudette this evening. "I didn't hear anything in the alley. With all the noise in here . . ." My voice trailed off. An argument, a cry for help—could I have saved her? "I wish I'd noticed who came in the back gate. Maybe someone saw something important."

As I spoke, Kim made a few notes with a silver ballpoint pen. She'd developed a great poker face. "I'll need the guest list."

"There isn't one. We didn't keep track of who bought tickets."

"Who sold them?"

"The Merc. Le Panier. The kitchen shop. Chiara's gallery." I ticked them off on my fingers. "Oh, and the Chamber." As an unincorporated town, Jewel Bay had no mayor or city hall. The Chamber of Commerce and village merchants ran the show.

"No ticket taker at the back gate?"

"No. We kept an eye on the front, to keep regular bar traffic out, but we didn't worry about the back." Party crashing hadn't seemed like a big risk. But then, neither had murder.

"Quite the shindig." She stood. Her jacket fell into place, but not before I spotted her gun. "Stick around. I'll need to talk with you again before I leave."

Which meant my questions for her would have to wait.

A few feet away, she stopped. "Erin, I'm sorry. Crappy way to welcome you back to town."

The murder, or her own distance?

"Crappy" did not begin to describe either one.

Notes from the double bass drifted by. Forks clinked, voices rose and fell. A laugh skittered on the air. Normal party sounds, or nervous reaction to tragedy?

All our hard work.

I slipped into the Merc to use the restroom. Closed now, the shop stood quietly, a testament to the sweat and tears that had built it. Mine and Fresca's, yes, but also Claudette's.

A muffled sound. I cocked my head. Took a step forward, then another. "Who's there?"

No response. Then, a sniffle? I hit the kitchen lights. Tracy huddled in the corner, arms wrapped around her knees, head bowed, chestnut hair grazing the floor, her gauzy floral skirt barely visible. A checkered paper napkin lay balled on the floor. She raised her head and blinked, eyes red and puffy, mascara streaked.

"Oh, Trace." I crouched and hugged her.

She hesitated, then relaxed against my shoulder. "Who? Why?"

"I don't know. I can't imagine who hated Claudette enough to kill her."

"Dean." She spat it out.

"He's slime. But that doesn't make him a killer."

Her expression said she didn't agree. She straightened and I sat back, the tender moment gone.

"I told her not to go," she said. "But Claudette was convinced this was their chance to make a life together, that if they stayed, he'd always be caught in Linda's web."

The Vincents had come to Jewel Bay during my years away, and I didn't know them well. Linda had tried to persuade me to carry her chocolates, but I'd found them barely edible.

"She reminded me of my ex that way," Tracy continued, her soft voice heavy with memory. "Always looking for the next best thing. Couldn't see that she might already have it."

"Did you tell Kim—Deputy Caldwell?"

Her earrings swung as she shook her head. "I won't speak ill of the dead."

"If it helps find the killer . . ." My own wariness aside, I knew Kim needed every useful tidbit. Claudette deserved our honesty.

Tracy looked skeptical. "Maybe." She wiped her swollen eyes. "No matter what happens, Erin, the Festa was a great idea."

"*Is* a great idea." I stood and extended my hand. "C'mon. There's a party going on."

For the next half hour, I mingled and chatted. Now that the major interviews had been completed, the guests were free to roam. Though everyone expressed shock and sadness, no one seemed to blame the Festa for the murder—or their temporary captivity. No doubt the food and wine helped.

"Terrific lasagna, Erin," the minister said, his fork full.

"And everyone's very generous to the Food Bank," his wife said, patting her sparkly beaded bag. "Even Deputy Caldwell contributed."

The price of getting people to talk, no doubt.

My mother always says when you don't feel the way you want to, act as if you do, and before you know it, your mood will shift. So I kept moving, smiling, exchanging a few words with each guest.

The party must go on, and all that.

"There you are, darling. Come sit." Looking only a little less fresh than when the evening began, my mother beckoned me to the table she shared with the Pinskys and Heidi and her date. The crowd began to thin. Murder may have made them hungry and generous, but it also made many of them head home early.

My mother motioned to Wendy Fontaine, silent and watchful in her white chef's jacket and bright pants. Her thick black brows and tight ponytail emphasized the severity of her plain features. She brought each of us a balsamic-drizzled peach garnished with a spoonful of honey-vanilla mascarpone and a palmier. My idea, and a tasty one. Wendy could play nicely with others when she chose.

My mother spotted Kim and called her over. "I have to admit," Kim said, her face carefully neutral as she took the extra chair, "I'm surprised you went ahead and served dinner after such a tragedy. Especially considering your history with the victim."

Victim. A chilling word. And what history? Who had she talked to? Well, everyone, obviously.

"We loved Claudette," I said. "And wasting food meant for a Food Bank benefit would be seriously bad karma."

"I'd like to speak with the two of you alone."

"We'll be off then," Liz said as Wendy slid a dessert plate in front of Kim. "See you tomorrow night." She kissed the air around us. Bob waved, and they left, Heidi and her guy behind them.

"What's tomorrow night?" Kim held up the palmier. "And what's this?"

"A concert at the Playhouse, with drinks and hors d'oeuvres in the lobby. That's a palmier—a puff pastry sugar cookie."

"Honestly, Kim," my mother said, wrapping her shoulders in the shawl I'd returned, "Jewel Bay's not such a hotbed of crime that you can't pay a little attention. Maybe get involved with community activities."

Kim reddened slightly, tightening her narrow jaw in a familiar sign of stubbornness.

"Are you in charge of the investigation?" I asked. "What do you think happened?"

"I report directly to the undersheriff. But I can't reveal any details."

"Why not? It happened here. Don't we have a right to know?"

My mother spoke at the same time. "Don't treat us like suspects. We have a right to know."

"You have rights," Kim said. "But that's not one of them." She bit into the palmier and the crunch filled the silence.

I pushed my plate away. "You've still got people working in the alley."

"A thorough crime scene investigation can take hours."

"What about Claudette?" I said. *The body.*

"Hospital morgue overnight. State crime lab in the morning."

The thought of lively, energetic, confused Claudette lying on a refrigerated slab, riding to Missoula in the back of an ambulance, kept in cold storage until the ME could get to her, turned the twinkling summer night into a dull day in November. Kim said it wouldn't take long, though. Not a lot of murder in Montana.

Not a lot of consolation.

"How was she killed? Or are you keeping that from us, too?" my mother said.

Kim's jaw contracted again. She said nothing, and ate her peach. I could feel my mother's anxiety vibrating between us, and wondered if Kim sensed it.

"One more thing, Erin. Why invite Claudette when you knew she and Dean had just had a big fight?"

"I told you already. Plus I had no idea he was coming to the party. Didn't know he was back in town until today."

"Didn't know he'd gone back to his wife," Fresca added forcefully.

"I know people think we hated Claudette for leaving the shop on such short notice." My voice cracked. "But we didn't. And she seemed so miserable—I wanted her to come have a good time."

If Kim meant to goad me into saying more by her own silence, it wouldn't work. I had nothing left to say. I was as empty as the wineglasses scattered across the table.

Finally, she clipped her pen to the notebook, tucked it in her jacket pocket, and stood. "You'll be here in the morning." It wasn't a question.

"We open at ten, but I get in earlier."

Now all the guests were gone, leaving only Old Ned and one bartender. Despite Kim's refusal to reveal details, I suspected no witness had placed Claudette inside the bar, the Merc, or the courtyard—or we'd have been shooed out and crime scene techs would be crawling all over. A few lanterns still glowed, and I blew out the candles.

"You leave that be," Ned said when he spotted me scanning the courtyard, once so festive and now such a mess. "My boys will clean up in the morning."

I kissed his ruddy cheek. "Thanks, Ned. You're a prince."

The musicians and caterers lugged their gear through Red's to Front Street, unable to pull their vans into the alley. I waved good night. Like the food, the music had hit all the right notes.

My car was parked out back, too, so after checking the Merc's doors, I walked down the street, past darkened shop windows, and turned the corner. Patrol cars filled Back Street, and yellow barricades formed a narrow exit from the parking lot, really just a large undeveloped lot between the business district and the riverbank.

I wound between the barricades to my sage green Subaru and pressed the clicker. My flashing headlights picked out a white paper bag from Jewel Bay Drug, snagged on a twig. I pulled it off, crumpled it up, and tossed it in my backseat.

Only then did I notice the car next to mine: swathed in yellow crime scene tape, Claudette's ancient black Saab.

The woods are lovely, dark, and deep. Happily, I did not have miles to go before sleep. It was nearly midnight when I pulled up alongside the cabin. This close to summer solstice, the skies stay light late, and on a clear night, you can practically read outside.

I stood in the clearing and searched for the North Star. There it was, standing out despite the light of a million other stars.

It is not in the stars to hold our destiny, but in ourselves.

What is with the quotes tonight, Erin? Murder making you maudlin? I shook it off. The quote had prompted my tattoo, and my cat was named for a poetry god, but he had come that way. Poetry and theater hadn't been part of my life for a long time.

Inside the front door, the alarm system touch pad blinked. My mother had made me promise to set it. "That's what it's for," she'd said.

As if Claudette's death put us all in danger.

Security systems irritate me. Everyone in Seattle had them, but I didn't want to live like that. Still, I'd promised. I punched in the code, then headed for my bedroom and changed into cotton drawstring shorts and a cami, my feet bare.

Back in the kitchen, I poured Sandburg a few cat treats,

which he pounced upon, and poured myself some sauvignon blanc. I hadn't finished a glass of wine yet all night. I'd snared leftovers from the caterers, so I tossed some lasagna in the microwave and took a bite of a cold stuffed mushroom.

And fumed. Someone had ruined the Festa. He, she, it—they—had shattered the peace and quiet of a rare town that still had peace and quiet. And they'd killed a good woman.

My red boots lay by the front door, where I'd pulled them off. My magic red boots.

I wanted that feeling back. I stalked to the door and punched off the alarm.

The microwave dinged. Food. Nurture and nourishment. I needed both.

Sandburg settled in next to me on the oversized chocolate brown leather sofa, sniffing at my plate. "Paws off, buddy. My turn for treats."

Before leaving the Merc, Kim had told me she'd reached the Seattle police, who would break the news to Claudette's ex-husband. Their son was taking a year off after high school to work and travel with his father, who imported Asian art and antiques.

Ian was just a year older than I'd been when my father died. I washed down the lump in my throat with a swig of wine.

At least they weren't suspects. So who was?

Not my problem. Kim Caldwell had charge of this one. And watching her tonight, it had been clear she still saw life as a competition, and she hated to lose.

"Movie time," I told the cat. I swung aside the hinged cover of the flat screen TV—a vibrant watercolor my sister had painted of a giant sunflower—on the stone fireplace chimney, and flicked on the screen. Brought up Netflix and contemplated my favorite comfort movies. *Sound of*

Music—too sappy. *Blade Runner*—no way. *Big Night*—too close to home.

Ratatouille. Just right. I warmed up another chunk of lasagna. As Chef Gusteau says, the secret to life is a good sauce.

· *Five* ·

Next morning, the sun rose like it always did and the lake sparkled so brilliantly that I almost didn't remember what had happened the night before.

Then it hit me, as the "if only" train sped through my mind. If only I hadn't gone scouting for more candles. If only I hadn't invited Claudette.

If only someone hadn't killed her.

"So what?" I said out loud. "So you brought them face-to-face. You didn't turn an innocent person into a killer."

But I still felt rotten. So many people had worked so hard. When business advisors say "expect the unexpected," they aren't thinking murder.

For the first time since coming back to Jewel Bay, I wanted to be somewhere else. I adored the Merc—always had, in all its incarnations, and never more than in the last few months.

But today, even with the deputies gone, the crime scene tape and barricades down, even with Claudette's black Saab towed to county impound and the Merc back to business, everything would remind me of her.

If only I could play hooky.

My mother always says throw yourself into the things you don't want to do; that once you get absorbed, you forget your fears, and before you know it, the project is finished.

If only it were that easy.

A cloud of yeasty sweetness perfumed the air outside Le Panier's screen door. Wendy Taylor Fontaine had adored all things French even before meeting Max in cooking school. After they married and he started the bistro, the menu inspired by his native Provence, she'd focused on his dreams. Finally, this past spring, she'd opened the bakery she'd hungered for. Good to support the neighbors, though Wendy and I don't always sing out of the same hymnal.

This morning, my mission was simple: sugar and caffeine.

"Hi, Wendy. Hey, Max. Nonfat latte, double shot, and a *pain au chocolat*."

Wendy's dark ponytail bobbed as she tamped espresso into the sieve, rammed it into place, and poured milk into a stainless steel pitcher. She wore her usual double-breasted white chef's jacket over loose cotton pants so colorful they'd make a clown jealous, and cherry red clogs. Her long working hours kept her from getting out much, but I thought she looked even ghostlier today, the red rims around her eyes the only color on her face.

The machine hissed and the aroma of fresh espresso nearly made me swoon. She poured hot milk into the coffee, using the handle of a wooden spoon to get just the right amount of foam. I love watching experts work. She set the white paper cup on the counter, next to the pastry Max had already bagged.

I thrust out a five. *"Non, non,"* Max said, waving his

hands wildly, his accent thick as the foam on my latte. "On the house. The least we can do, after last night."

"Thanks. You guys did a great job."

A short, enthusiastic man with salt-and-pepper hair, Max beamed. Wendy's thin lips hinted at a smile.

"Hey, Erin, how you holding up?" I hadn't noticed Sam come in. "Jen and I had our noses buried in the music. We're so sorry about Claudette."

"Oh, that gal who got killed?" This from a man I didn't recognize, drooling on the pastry case. "We heard it had to do with losing her job, some old friend stabbing her in the back."

My fingers twitched. Wendy's knives were so close.

Max saved me. "*Non, non.* It was not like that." More hand waving.

"Well, that's what I heard." The tourist bent over to ogle the tartelettes, ignoring us.

"Thanks, Max!" I grabbed my breakfast and left, not wanting to insult my neighbors' customer, even if he had unwittingly suggested my mother was a killer.

No doubt there would be plenty of talk like that today. But at least I'd be fortified.

Inside the Merc, all seemed kosher. Other than the wineglass I'd left on the kitchen counter, there were few signs that we'd thrown a party out back, let alone one disrupted by murder.

Six chrome stools with red vinyl seats flanked the stainless steel counter that divided kitchen from selling floor. Fresca—I was still retraining myself to call her that, at least during business hours—had scrounged them from an old diner in Pondera, thirty miles away, and re-covered them. They looked as though they'd always been here. I perched on one and sipped my latte. Hot, smooth, and dee-lectable. Then I broke into my croissant, its flaky pastry melting on my tongue. And the bittersweet chocolate inside—mmm. Dee-vine.

I heard a key in the front door. Footsteps echoed on the oak floor, then paused. "Who's there?"

"It's me, Mom." I swiveled on my stool.

"Why are you sitting with the lights off?" She flicked the switch and the kitchen lit up. I hadn't minded the shadows. They suited my mood.

Her olive skin looked ashen, but her dark eyes missed nothing as she gave me a slow once-over. "You couldn't sleep, either."

I'd fallen asleep about the time Remy the rat and Linguini the kitchen boy hatched their plot for culinary domination, and woken up at 3 a.m. Despite my brain fog, it had taken only a moment to remember why I was asleep in the living room and why I was so upset.

I'd tossed and turned on the bed till seven. Acting "as if" I felt festive, I'd pulled on a turquoise tiered block print dress with a pearl button placket. Stacked bright bangles on my left wrist. Tucked the red boots back in my closet, and strapped on my brown leather Mary Jane clogs. With the right clothes, you can fool the world.

But not my mother. In the bright light of morning at the Merc, she brushed an imaginary stray hair off my face, then frowned at my food. "I hope that's nonfat milk. With all the temptations around here, you're going to have to watch yourself."

"Oh, for Pete's sake. Claudette was killed last night, practically on our doorstep, probably because of me, and you're worried about my weight?"

"Just be careful, darling. You do tend to seek comfort in food. And what do you mean, because of you?"

"I invited her." Not logical, I knew, but the feeling wouldn't go away. I ripped into the last bit of pastry.

"We may not know what happened, but neither of us is to blame," she said.

"Why would you feel guilty? You didn't know she was coming to the party. You didn't know she was back in town until Ted told us about the rumors." I could hear the anxiety in my rising voice.

"She didn't deserve to die that way. No one does. But it's not your fault." She sank onto the stool next to me. "I've been racking my brain, trying to imagine who could have done this, or why."

We sat in silence far longer than typical for two Italian girls, even two named Murphy. (My brother-in-law likes to say that in our family, Murphy's Law means no silence can last longer than two seconds.)

"About the Festa, Mom." I needed to share my doubts. "It's too late to cancel this weekend. But maybe it shouldn't be an annual thing. Maybe—"

"Don't you dare." She held up a graceful hand in the universal stop sign. "Don't even think about quitting. Murphy girls don't quit."

"You weren't crazy about the idea in the first place—"

"Not true, darling. It just seemed like a lot to take on so soon. But you've done a beautiful job. We needed a summer opener. Both the Chamber and the Village Merchants Association got behind you, and that says a lot."

It said I would probably be recruited to lead one or the other before long. "I just don't want the Festa to be a constant reminder of Claudette's murder." I drained my latte and stood. "We'll come up with something new if we need to."

The front door chimed. If clothes make the man, they reveal the woman, and Tracy loved a bargain, the brighter the better. But today, she had not bothered trying to dress up her mood. In all my years at SavClub, I had never sent an employee home to change clothes. But Tracy's faded denim crops, tight across the thighs, and ancient navy sweatshirt might make today the first.

"Tracy McCann," my mother said, in a voice no

daughter could ever misread. "Are you dressed for work or the cleanup crew?"

Kinda nice to have a bad cop in-house.

"It doesn't matter, Fresca. Nobody's coming in today. Haven't you heard what they're saying?"

She gripped a Diet Coke can and a waxed paper bag that likely held her morning maple bar. If she'd stopped at the convenience store, as usual, she'd heard pure trash. When I'd approached the owner about the Festa, she'd rebuffed me soundly. "More village hoopla," she'd said, underscoring the animosity some highway business people carried for the downtown merchants. As if drawing more people to town for the weekend meant she'd sell less burned coffee and stale doughnuts—and less gas.

"Like what?" No doubt the same rumors I'd heard in Le Panier.

"That Fresca threw Claudette out on her ear. That she came back with a vengeance and came here last night to confront the two of you, to show you up in front of the high muckety-mucks." Tracy's voice shook. Had I ever seen her without earrings?

"That's ridiculous." Fresca's back stiffened.

"It's what Ted said yesterday. And my neighbor this morning. We'll be lucky to make a sale all day."

Fresca and I exchanged looks. The Murphy girls were on the same page.

"We've got extra fives and ones in the safe," I said. "Tracy, you're dressed perfectly to pack up the decorations from last night. Get one of the guys at Red's to help you haul the boxes down to the basement. You can change at noon when you run home to check on your dog."

"I'll check the stock," Fresca said. "With the tourists returning, the pastas and sauces are really moving."

"Don't forget the jams and jellies."

Tracy looked baffled. "You mean, gossip is a good thing?"

"Yes. I mean, it's awful. But if people are talking about us—well, you know what they say. No such thing as bad publicity." I didn't want the Festa associated with murder, but if it was, shame on us for not making the most of it.

Tracy looked like she might puke, and not from the Diet Coke and maple bar. "What about showing respect for the dead?"

"Trace, we loved her, too. But closing or acting glum won't honor her. Let's show this town how strong we are, and why Claudette loved the Merc and Jewel Bay." I had an idea. "When you're done out back, help Fresca restock. I've got a project of my own."

Upstairs in my office, I clicked on my laptop and scrolled through our photographs. Didn't take long to find a great shot. I cropped, cut and pasted, added text, and hit Print. While the printer whirred, I dashed out back, my clogs clattering on the courtyard's pavers, and scooped up one of last night's flower arrangements. Inside, I placed the pot on the front counter next to a small display easel and added my spur-of-the-moment poster:

The Merc remembers Claudette Randall.
A bright flower.
We love you. We miss you.

And across the bottom:

Fifteen percent of today's sales donated to the Jewel Bay Food Bank in Claudette's memory.

"It's perfect." Tracy burst into tears.

My mother blinked back tears of her own and kissed my cheek.

At ten, I flipped the hand-painted sign from CLOSED to OPEN, and customers began streaming in. And they weren't just browsing. They bought. We sold more huckleberry taffy before noon than in the last two weeks combined. Jams and jellies danced out the door and wild chokecherry syrup sold like hotcakes.

And every customer, without exception, spotted the picture of Claudette, dressed like an elf for last year's Village Christmas walk, next to the antique cash register and expressed sympathy.

Late morning, another idea struck. I sprinted next door for a few baguettes. (The summer I was thirteen, my parents took the family to France and Italy. My father's joke: How to disguise yourself as a Frenchman in Paris: Walk down the street carrying a baguette. How to disguise yourself as an American in Paris: Walk down the street eating a baguette.) We slathered olive tapenade on some slices and goat cheese on others, and set platters of spur-of-the moment snacks next to piles of red-and-white-checked cocktail napkins.

And promptly sold out of tapenade, goat cheese, and the handmade serving dishes.

Though the thought turned my stomach and made my heart ache, apparently murder can be good for business.

· *Six* ·

A few minutes before one, we reached the usual lull. The eat-late-and-miss-the-rush shoppers had gone in search of lunch, while the eat-at-noon crowd hadn't yet returned to shopping. Tracy had gone home to walk Bozo, a Harlequin Great Dane rescue dog, and change clothes. The morning sales spree had brightened all our moods.

Fresca roved the shop, picking up after our less tidy customers. "People," she muttered as she plucked a napkin out of the wine rack. "Were they raised in a barn?"

"Top of the cooler." I pointed to a stray paper coffee cup.

We were just filling our plates with leftover salad and reheated rigatoni Bolognese when the door chimed. I strode out to the sales floor, ready to greet our afternoon clientele with a smile.

But this visitor wasn't here to shop.

"Hello, Kim." Navy blazer and pants today, with a butterscotch silk T-shirt that matched her low-heeled ankle boots. She cleaned up good. I kept that thought to myself—not the best time for smart-assery.

She scanned the shop quickly and efficiently, then picked up my poster. "Nice touch."

I listened for a hint of sarcasm, but heard none. That was one of my faults, not Kim's. Still the no-nonsense ranch girl, even with a gun on her hip.

"Quiet in here today," she said.

"It hasn't been. You caught us during the lunchtime slow-down. Mom—Fresca—and I are just diving into last night's leftovers. Join us?"

"No, thanks. But you go ahead." She followed me back to the kitchen, and I noticed her eagle eyes as Fresca sliced bread. Was she hiding her hunger—or counting our knives, checking our inventory?

Didn't take us long to eat. Mom and I were used to grabbing a bite between customers. Still, it's irritating to be watched while you feed your face.

"Fresca, if you don't mind"—Kim's tone suggested it wouldn't matter if she did—"I'd like to speak with Erin first, alone."

The front door opened and the laughter of well-fed women ready to fork over their plastic tickled my ears. "Say no more," Fresca replied and called out a greeting.

"Let's go outside." I snatched two small bottles of San Pellegrino from the cooler. "More privacy."

Out back, Old Ned's crew had closed the wooden gate between our courtyard and his. The borrowed tables and chairs, lights and lanterns, and other party regalia had vanished, along with the festive mood. The space wasn't much larger than a double garage, and this morning, about as grungy.

"The shabby look," I said, "without the chic." Now that I'd seen the yard in party mode, I itched to transform it permanently. Later.

At the corner table where we'd talked last night, Kim slipped out her notebook and recorder. "I'd like to take your formal statement now, then we'll type it up for signature."

Anything you say can and will be used against you . . . With a glance at the recorder, I wiped a hand across the back of my neck. My hair felt damp. No reason to be nervous. We all needed to do everything possible to help. "Sure."

"Let's go over the incident in front of Dr. Vincent's office."

"Dr.—oh, Dean." After thinking of him as Elvis for so long, his real name jarred me. I described again how Claudette had dashed in front of me and I'd called out to her.

"How did you conclude that she'd been in Dr. Vincent's office?"

I tilted my head. "Circumstantial, I guess. She was near his front door. She told me—well, she didn't *say* they'd just had a fight, but she was furious. With him. And he came out looking for her."

"Tell me exactly what she said." Kim's voice was firm.

I repeated it the best I could. "She was convinced he'd lied to her about starting over together in Las Vegas."

"And when you asked whether she'd been telling people your mother stole her recipes and forced her out to create a job opening for you?"

"She adamantly denied it." I could still picture her shaking her head, her lively features distressed at the suggestion.

"What was her reaction to the question?"

"Shock. Which was why I believed her. She always seemed honest to me. And loyal."

"Did Dr. Vincent appear angry?"

"Not angry. Concerned." Although he'd been incensed later, when I blocked him from Claudette's body. Did he have a volcanic temper? I didn't know, but it was hard to hide that kind of thing in a small town.

Kim checked her notes. "So, who knew you'd invited her to the Festa?"

"No one, until I got back here an hour later and told Fresca." I reimagined the scene, the two of us sitting on the drugstore bench, my back to the door. I just wanted

Claudette to calm down. I hadn't a clue who might have walked by. Except Angelo, but he disappeared quickly.

"Who might she have told?"

"No idea."

"So when did Fresca first suggest that you replace Claudette as manager?"

"Late winter maybe? She knew I was ready for a change, and she thought Claudette would be happier working sales and demos." Nothing nefarious in it. Perfectly natural for a parent to want her child to join the family business, especially a child with useful skills and experience. A child at a crossroads.

"But Claudette got wind of it and left instead."

"Not according to her note." Kim gave me a questioning look. "She said she was moving to Las Vegas with Dean. She apologized for leaving the shop in the lurch, but said she knew Fresca would understand. Neither of us saw her again, until yesterday."

"I'll need that note."

"Sure. It's in her personnel file. Look, they had disagreements. I won't pretend otherwise. Fresca had a hard time giving up control. Claudette screwed up with inventory, and irritated a couple of vendors. Nothing unusual—just growing pains for a new business." Nothing to kill for. "They worked it out. You know how Fresca is."

"Tell me about the vendors. You mean suppliers?"

"Not a big deal. Claudette and Jennifer Krauss, the winemaker, disagreed over what varieties would sell best, and whether their label worked. The potter demanded a better percentage. Some problems with quantity and late payments. It's all resolved." Several vendors had actually threatened to pull their wares until I'd stepped in.

Kim studied me, eyes unblinking. "What happened in Seattle, Erin?"

I sat back and took a swig of warm, flat bubbles. Did they teach that look in cop school? The steady gaze that says, *I can wait a long time, so you might as well talk.*

"Nothing. I've heard the gossip, but I didn't get fired. I left on my own. Not an easy decision. Big pay cut." No joke. I'd gone from house-hunting condos that started at a quarter million to appreciating that rent-free cabin. "I loved Sav-Club, but my job wasn't going anywhere. Logjam ahead of me in the promotion line. If I'd wanted to move up the corporate ladder, I'd have had to leave."

"So you left anyway, and moved down the ladder."

Oddly, it felt like a step up. Even if I'd stayed, what would I have been? Vice-president of prunes? But all that was too hard to explain.

Something had happened, not in Seattle, but here, between us. It was time I knew what. "Kim, senior year, when my father—"

The alley gate opened and Tracy burst in, breathless. "Oh, sorry. The yellow tape was gone, so I thought—"

"Not a problem. We've finished the alley search and released the crime scene."

At the word "crime," Tracy blanched and wobbled. I gave her a reassuring look. "Why don't you give Fresca a hand? I'll be in shortly."

She glanced at Kim, her physical near-opposite, then fled inside. In her blue linen tunic, white crops, and woven blue ballet flats—Tracy favored solid colors and bargains from the designer consignment store—the queen of cheap chic was back on duty.

The moment had passed. Kim asked more questions about the Festa, the scene in the alley, Claudette's friends and family. I couldn't answer them all. "Ask Fresca."

"Oh, I will."

I pictured the two of us as teenagers after a trail ride, Kim taking hours to groom her horse, rubbing every muscle, checking each joint, hoof, and shoe. I'd be in the Lodge, drinking lemonade mixed with iced tea, eating freshly baked cookies and chatting up the kitchen staff, and she'd still be in the corral, teasing burrs from mane and tail.

Like she was doing now, metaphorically.

"Would you send your mother out, please?"

Sent packing in my own domain, and I didn't even mind.

Inside, I found Fresca ringing up a sizable purchase of pasta and sauces, mouthwatering fresh mozzarella, basil, and salad greens. "Kim's waiting for you," I said softly. Her face took on a determined look, chin set, eyes unreadable.

"My daughter will help you," she said to the customer, with a smile, and I took over, suggesting wine and strawberries picked that morning. Really wished for good chocolate to go along. We'd printed recipe cards for the Caprese salad, and while the customer debated between Viognier and Chardonnay, I tucked one into her bag.

"Don't forget a baguette next door," I called as she left, a smile on her face.

"How do you do that?" Tracy said when we were alone. "They end up buying stuff they didn't want and don't even mind."

"If they end up with stuff they didn't want," I said, "they mind. Show them what they don't know they want. Help them figure out how to make a simple meal memorable, without spending hours in the kitchen or tossing extra ingredients when vacation ends."

For the next half hour, Tracy and I waited on customers and assembled take-out picnic baskets. Each included a screw-top bottle of wine, compostable glasses, plates, and utensils, and napkins sporting lakeside scenes. We added crackers and a jar of basil pesto to some, and a bag of Le Panier breadsticks and roasted eggplant spread to others. In each went a list of pick-and-choose ingredients, all conveniently located in the cooler: creamy local goat cheese, an herbed goat cheese *croton*, a cow's milk Jack, mozzarella, or my personal favorite, herbed cheese curds. All certified organic, all from happy goats and cows I'd visited myself. (The Creamery had been full-scale only a few months, with aged cheddars and blues in the works. I'd had a taste, and could hardly wait to expand our offerings.)

The customer could then choose beef or venison salami, plain or peppered, or beef, venison, or buffalo jerky. Wild game doesn't suit every palate, so we also offer imported prosciutto and salami in resealable packages. (The hunt for a local source, and a butcher willing to cut to spec, was still on.)

And because everyone deserves something sweet, a bag of amaretto cookies. I dreamed of the day we could offer hand-dipped dark chocolate truffles.

"I'm next, right?" Tracy twisted blue and yellow ribbon into a bow for the handle of the last basket.

"No worries. Kim doesn't bite." At least, I hoped not. Fresca had been gone a long time.

"I don't know anything about the murder." Tracy twisted her finger in her thick hair. "I was helping take Food Bank donations when you found her."

"Answer her questions truthfully and you'll be fine." I set a pair of baskets in the front window, next to a sign reading LAKESIDE PICNICS READY TO GO—JUST ADD WATER. The window reflected back the blue-green of my dress, as if we were on the water. "Thanks for getting the decorations put away."

"Ted helped. You know, that basement's a rathole." She wrinkled her nose.

I hated the place. As did everyone in my family—we'd ignored it for years, while the dust and cobwebs and piles of half-forgotten boxes multiplied. A fall cleanup project, after tourist season.

Fresca came in, and Tracy, still nervous, went out. "How'd it go?"

She made a noise I couldn't interpret. She was prone to grunts and groans, sprinkled with Italian, though she was born and raised in Northern California and hadn't set foot in Italy until she dropped out of college to travel. That's where she met my father, Tom Murphy, an American college student in Florence. After he graduated, they married and moved here, his hometown, where he taught high school history and coached basketball, and she cooked and raised the three of us. He died in a car accident on his way home from practice fourteen years ago last winter, and I missed him every day.

The phone rang and the front door bell chimed. By the time I'd dealt with the caller and greeted the new arrivals, my mother had disappeared. I sold a picnic basket, three bottles of cherry wine, and half a dozen jars of honey and huckleberry jam, along with festive napkins, a fused glass serving platter, and a good supply of pasta and sauce.

I twisted open another Pellegrino and perched on a stool behind the front counter to catch my breath. Although several morning customers had mentioned the murder, there'd been scarcely a whisper of foul play this afternoon. But I'd overheard plenty of chatter about the Festa, the decorating theme carried throughout the village, and tonight's events. This might be one of our best days ever.

And I loved it.

Footsteps on the office stairs confirmed my suspicion that Fresca had snuck away for a few minutes' respite. She entered the shop area now, eyes a touch puffy despite fresh liner and mascara, her skin pale in contrast with her coral lipstick.

The back door creaked open and Tracy returned, a shaky smile on her plump cheeks. Kim walked in behind her, looking cool and efficient.

"Mom, did you find Claudette's note?"

Fresca plucked at her necklace, one of Chiara's creations, frosted pink and green glass beads reminiscent of sea glass strung on a silver cord. "It wasn't in her file. I'll look at home."

"Kim, we've told you everything we know," I said. "Time for you to return the favor."

"I'm sorry, Erin. Everything's confidential at this point."

All business. She would not let our friendship—or what was left of it—change that. Smart maybe, but it stung.

"Kim, you'll take some fresh pasta and sauce for dinner?" Fresca said. "Only a few minutes to prepare."

"Or more leftovers? Besides the lasagna, we've got grilled veggies and stuffed mushrooms—thirty seconds in the microwave." In the kitchen, I pulled out the goldfish boxes we'd stocked for the upcoming classes.

"I can't accept food from you," Kim said.

"Oh, for heaven's sake," Fresca said. "It's not a bribe. I've known you since you were twelve. You said yourself you don't eat enough when you've got a major case."

Before Kim could protest further, I handed her a bag of food. "And some palmiers. Everyone deserves a treat."

She took it. Clearly, all was not sweetness and light in Jewel Bay. I only hoped that whatever evil walked among us didn't hurt us any more.

· *Seven* ·

Four o'clock is the witching hour in retail. Every afternoon about then, serious buyers and window-shoppers alike run out of steam. Some retreat to a lakeside bar for a cold one, while others head home to put their feet up before a night out. After my restless sleep, and with the Festa continuing in full swing that evening—although I wasn't in charge, thank goodness—I ached to do the same.

And if Tracy actually understood that a good day wasn't a betrayal of Claudette, the Merc would be fine.

I slipped out the back door. Pitiful as the courtyard looked, it had potential. Ha. I'd learned some real estate code in my brief Seattle house hunt, before doing a one-eighty and coming back here instead. "Potential" meant cramped and in major need of cash and sweat.

Truth. Sweat, we could muster. Cash, not so much. Anyway, Fresca made all decisions about the building.

I sighed and opened our back gate. I'd walked to work this morning, wanting to avoid the alley, but the sooner I faced it, the better.

As Tracy had said, the crime scene tape was gone and, with it, all signs of tragedy. Only the faintest impression in the dirt and gravel suggested a body—none of the gruesome chalk outlines they use on TV. I knelt beside the trash barrel, where I'd knelt less than twenty-four hours ago. "I'm so sorry. You didn't deserve this. I promise—"

What could I promise? To find her killer? That was Kim's job. To never forget her?

My inner Catholic girl made the sign of the cross. Strange to think of an alley as sacred space, but death will do that.

I hadn't checked my phone since Friday. SavClub had a no-cell policy, both in-store and at headquarters, and I'd adopted it for the Merc. Business hours, business line only. On my own time, my phone was usually close at hand. But in the last twenty-four hours, routine had flown the coop.

I strolled and scrolled, scanning till I got to a pair of calls late Friday afternoon. First message: "Hey, Erin. Adam Zimmerman here. Still hoping to catch up, and to talk about the fund-raiser for wilderness education at the Club. Summer program for kids, outdoor recreation—we'd love to have the Merc's support. Give me a ring."

Give him points for persistence. He'd hung out with my roommate at UM and started calling me a couple of weeks ago. Part of the hiking boot crowd. Geeky-cute, if I remembered right. Which I wasn't sure I did. What did we have to "catch up" on?

Second message, 5:17 p.m. Friday—while I'd been on my way to the shower. A breathless voice: "Erin, it's Claudette. I don't think—I'm not sure—well, maybe I should just come to the Merc tonight after all. We'll talk?"

Gad. Had those been her last words? Didn't we all imagine we'd have something profound to say in our final moments?

More likely, something profane.

"Auntie Erin!" Outside the library slash community center, on the south end of the village, I scooped up a five-year-old tornado.

"Landon!" I swung him in a circle, his bare legs whirling like a windmill. "My favorite nephew."

"Your only nephew," Chiara said, a hint of exhaustion in her wry voice and dark eyes. She'd made clear one perfect child was enough, and Nick—well, my brother was busy dancing with wolves. Or whatever.

"How's it going, buddy?"

"We got two Hank the Cowdog books." Landon pointed at the basket his mother carried, crammed with the weekly library haul.

"Aren't they for older kids?"

He gave me a withering look. "I am an older kid, Auntie. I'm five now. You came to my party."

"So I did." I grinned at him, and the memory. My first weekend back in Jewel Bay, we'd celebrated his birthday and my homecoming.

"Mom?" Chiara's single worried word crushed the air between us.

I shrugged. "She's not talking."

My sister would never say, "This is all your fault," but I felt it anyway. Like the bumbling baby of the family whose ideas are either brilliant or whacko, and who can't always tell the difference.

"See you tonight?" I asked. She nodded and kissed me. Landon stopped pretending to be the famous cow dog—head of ranch security—long enough for a hug. They sauntered up Front Street, and I stepped onto the one-lane steel truss bridge spanning the Jewel River. Upstream raced the infamous Wild Mile, a stretch of whitewater that drew kayakers from all over the country. Below the bridge, river met bay and they flowed together to Eagle Lake, the largest freshwater lake west of the Mississippi. The rushing water danced a jig beneath my feet.

Was it possible to feel both deep sadness and overwhelming joy at the same time? Apparently so. Claudette's murder was tragic, and the rumors about my mother and me upsetting. And yet, Jewel Bay made me so happy. I'd had good times in Seattle—friends, a great job, a terrific city to explore. When the sun shines and the mountains come out of hiding, the Pacific Northwest purely sparkles.

But *here*—this was where I belonged.

With a spring in my step, I headed home.

The short walk left me hot and sweaty. I pulled a loose blue-and-white sundress over my bathing suit, packed up crackers, a goat cheese *croton*, and sweet green grapes, and trekked down to the lake. On the dock, I dropped my bag, slipped out of my dress and flip-flops, and jumped in.

The icy shock crystallized my blood. I shook the water out of my eyes and paddled around a few minutes, then swam to the dock ladder. Halfway up, Liz greeted me with a cackle and a sun-warmed towel.

"How can you stand it? I can't even stick my feet in till August." You can take the girl out of New Jersey, but her accent will never change.

"That water's positively glacial," Bob said. It flowed straight out of Glacier National Park—called simply "the Park"—not pausing for breath.

"Chicken." Teeth chattering, I sank onto a chaise and let the sun kiss me.

The Pinskys, both small, dark, and intense, had migrated to the Southwest decades ago, made a fortune in stone coasters, and retired young to become blissful snowbirds. Intrepid travelers and faithful friends.

"To think," Liz said, brow furrowed, "that all the while you were planning a summer celebration, someone was planning a murder." Her voice trembled.

"I don't think it was planned. The killer couldn't have expected Claudette to be in the alley. She didn't buy a ticket—she didn't know about the dinner until I told her." Where had she gone in between? Who had she seen? Why had she almost changed her mind, when she called me? "It has to have been spur-of-the-moment."

Bob handed me a frosty bottle of Eagle Lake root beer, made in Montana. An outdoor kitchen, with refrigerator and gas grill, hugged the hillside above the dock. When Bob built a thing, he saw to every detail. "We told Fresca we didn't think hiring Claudette was a good idea, but we never imagined this."

"They'd been friends for so long," Liz said. She and Bob exchanged grim looks. Was she reminding him why Fresca went ahead anyway, or warning him to say no more?

"Such a lost soul," she added with a shake of her dark head. "Didn't have her feet on the ground. Not like you and your family."

I took a sip. The cold drink made my still-frozen core shiver.

"Deputy Caldwell will get to the bottom of it," she continued, her tone leaving no doubt she considered Kim well grounded, too.

Nothing like a little relaxation to make you realize how tired you are. Everything from my eyelids to my little fingers to the balls of my feet felt overused. I stretched out on the chaise, listening to waves hit the shoreline. In the towering pines, an osprey screamed. Why yell before you kill? Didn't that warn the prey?

Had Claudette had any warning?

A few minutes later, I awoke with a start. "I've got to get to the Playhouse."

"Plenty of time." Liz laughed kindly. "Besides, you're just another guest tonight, remember?"

I wiggled my toes into my sandals. My sun-dried skin

felt clean and refreshed, though my head was a little sleep-drunk. "Sure hope it flies. A shame to waste a good idea."

"The Gala will be a hit—you'll see. The whole town's behind the Festa."

That reminded me. "Liz, the courtyard behind the Merc looks like a haunted house the day after Halloween. Any suggestions?"

"I'll stop by Monday and take a peek."

"You know what that means." Bob winked. "You've got yourself a project and a partner."

"Great. If I'm going to take on another project, I need a partner."

The hill had gotten steeper during my lakeside sojourn. I wanted to share the Pinskys' conviction that the killer would be found, and I didn't doubt Kim's abilities. But I could not forget—as no one in my family did—that some deaths were never explained. The mystery of my father's fatal accident—officially a hit-and-run—remained unsolved, even after nearly fifteen years.

One cold case was plenty. I vowed to do whatever Kim needed.

To be her best friend again, if that's what it took.

The back of my neck prickled, with the sense of being stared at. When I first moved into the cabin, more than one person told me to be careful in the woods and keep an eye on Sandburg, that a mountain lion had been spotted. But a wild cat wouldn't be out in broad daylight, would it? I peered around. Nothing.

Probably just a chill from the icy water. June in the mountains is deceptive—it only looks like high summer.

Or a shadow overhead. I glanced up at the cloudless sky.

I picked up the pace and hurried home.

· *Eight* ·

The warm fuzzy glow I got from watching people stream to the Playhouse was eclipsed only by my relief at knowing that tonight I was carefree. Wendy Fontaine and Linda Vincent cochaired the Festa's Saturday Night Gala, a musical evening seasoned with local flavor and a slight Italian accent.

Linda would not have been my first choice, but she'd made herself a mainstay in the community, and every event required volunteers. Just because I disliked her and her candy didn't mean she couldn't organize a Gala. Besides, Wendy had charge of the food.

Dozens of folks mingled in the lobby and outside on pavers stamped with donors' names. Jewel Bay had boasted live theater since the 1960s. Days after graduating from the University of Montana drama school, Wendy's parents started a summer program here to give college students a place to work. Their three kids practically grew up in the original building—an old movie house called the Bijou. I remembered tagging along after Wendy and Chiara, exploring nooks and crannies, tottering on the catwalk, sneaking into the costume room. The Jewel Bay Repertory Theater drew thousands of visitors every summer and auditioned actors from across the country.

As a teenager, I spent hours onstage, in high school plays and drama competitions. I had been here the night my dad died.

Eventually, the Rep outgrew the space, and through a massive fund drive, the community built the current theater. Another fund drive paid for a recent refurbishing, with new seats, an expanded lobby, and most important, more restrooms.

Tonight, the Playhouse sparkled.

"Wendy!" I spotted her white toque and jacket behind the serving tables that lined the lobby's long back wall. We'd been able to snare an open Saturday for the Festa, before the Rep swung into full production, because her parents and younger brother ran the place.

"Looks great." I snatched a chicken satay skewer and took a bite. "Tastes great."

"Thanks." She surveyed the offerings and I followed her gaze. Platters of chicken skewers and vegetables anchored each table. Metal racks held plates of kabobs made with tortellini, marinated mushrooms, and grape tomatoes, puff pastry cheese straws, brie *en croute* oozing with cranberry filling, and wild mushrooms on polenta rounds. And everywhere, bruschetta beckoned.

I grabbed a cocktail napkin reading JEWEL BAY FESTA DI PASTA: TASTE THE SPIRIT!—where had these been last night?—and chose a bruschetta with honey, Gorgonzola, and prosciutto. Wendy watched. Waiting for my reaction as I bit in. "Mmm. Love the contrasts—salt and sweet, the smooth texture of the honey and cheese with the toasted bread. Have you served this before?"

Her ponytail swung as she shook her head. "Our baguettes and ciabatta, Chef Angelo's toppings."

The last swallow stuck in my throat and my cheeks warmed. Chef James Angelo—he preferred to be called Chef, not James, and never Jim—had offered his services for opening night, but we'd decided to feature the restaurants instead. He'd taken it as a deliberate slight, since he'd begun marketing a line of prepared foods to compete with my mother's. This evening provided a perfect opportunity to showcase caterers and private chefs, like him. I was glad he got the chance to participate, but his nasty response when I turned him down had left a bad taste.

"It's really good." To prove I meant it, I took another—a more traditional combination of anchovies with fresh parsley and mint.

The ticket office had been converted to a wine bar for the evening. I chose Prosecco and let the bubbles tickle my nose before taking a sip. Heavenly.

"Erin, another marvelous evening." Heidi Hunter air-kissed me. Her sleek black sheath with its jet beaded neckline made me feel underdressed in my wide-legged white linen pants and floral print peasant blouse. And my leather wristband could not compete with her diamond and silver tennis bracelet. "Where's Fresca? How's she holding up?"

"She must be here somewhere." We scanned the crowd, but no sign. "It's hard. She and Claudette were friends a long time."

"Claudette was a dear," Heidi said, "and a pain in the ass." She touched my arm, the bracelet sparkling. "No one knows better than I do what a great friend Fresca is."

The lively notes of a jazz guitar duet began, and I craned my neck for a glimpse of the musicians. Sam and Jennifer again. The local music scene had exploded since the Jewel Bay Jazz Workshop and Festival began a few years ago. Instructors and students from around the world gathered the week before Memorial Day at Eagle Lake Lodge. Another idea that ruffled some feathers—"Why do we need something new?"—then wowed everyone with its success. Sam and Jen came to town as workshop students, then moved here to buy a decrepit orchard and revive it as Monte Verde Winery.

The lobby swung with laughter, music, and the chatter of old and new friends. Dean Vincent again sported full Elvis garb, this time a white jacket and pants with gold spangles and epaulets. He had an arm around Linda, who'd tried to outshine him in a shimmery sapphire sequined dress that was both a touch too elegant and a touch too short. The Prosecco eased the irritation she invariably provoked in me.

A table displayed CDs from tonight's musicians, a trade-off for asking them to volunteer their time and talents. I chose one from Jody Fisher and another from the Krausses, then mingled until the lights dimmed, beckoning us into the house. I snared a strawberry dipped in dark chocolate and found my seat next to Chiara and Heidi. But our fourth seat was empty. My sister gave me a wide-eyed, questioning look, puzzled by Mom's absence.

"She must be sitting with someone else." An otherwise full house. I smiled, more than satisfied.

Linda Vincent took center stage to welcome us. A tremble in her voice and a fluttering hand betrayed her nerves. After describing the musical program, she reminded us that tonight's event was a fund-raiser for the Food Bank. "Finally," she said, glancing at her notes, "be sure to thank our donors and volunteers," and rattled off a list of names, including Red's Bar, Le Panier and Chez Max, the Playhouse and Taylor family, and Chef James Angelo.

But not my mother or me.

Chiara raised her eyebrows and whispered, "What's up with that?"

"No idea." Surely Linda hadn't forgotten the Merc. But even she wouldn't be so petty on purpose—would she?

The first act, a trio with Sam Krauss on piano, Jen on bass, and Dave the Barber on drums, started us off. Then came the headliner, Jody Fisher, a small energetic man with an engaging grin who loved his reception at the Jazz Festival so much that he came back to Jewel Bay for the weekend. He opened with a lovely, smooth tune called "Spring Can Really Hang You Up the Most" on his curious headless guitar, his right leg bouncing in time. After another solo, the bass and drums joined him to rev things up a bit. By halftime, we were all grooving.

In the lobby, Wendy's crew had refreshed the appetizers and arranged desserts on tall round tables. I piled marinated asparagus and mushrooms, cheese straws, and more bruschetta on a small plate, snared another glass of Prosecco, and leaned against a square column adorned with tiny iridescent tiles in colors evoking the water and mountains surrounding town. Our little gem of a town. Juggling glass and plate, I bit into a bruschetta topped with tomato and herbed chèvre. He might be a jerk, but Angelo had created some terrific flavor combinations.

I heard the spit and fire before recognizing the voices.

"The trays are empty. Obviously everyone loves the food. Even your snob of a sister."

"I grant the man can cook. That's not the point." Chiara spoke slowly and deliberately, as if to a misbehaving child.

"So what is the point?" Ten feet away, Linda stood pointy-toe to painted clog with Chiara, the fair skin on Linda's throat red and splotchy.

"None of this"—Chiara waved her fingers with their paint-stained cuticles—"would have happened without my snob of a sister, but you thanked half the town and didn't mention her or Glacier Mercantile. And you kept Fresca off the menu tonight on purpose."

"At least Angelo creates his own recipes," Linda said, her full red lips curling in a snarl. "He's worked hard for what he has. No one's handed him anything."

"And your husband. His girlfriend's body isn't cold yet, and he's back with you dancing till dawn. Does that make you feel good?"

Linda's temples bulged, and she looked like she might slap Chiara.

I snapped to life and pushed my way forward. I had to stop them before something terrible happened. Half the crowd had fallen silent, stunned by the spectacle. Including one unexpected witness. At the Merc this afternoon, she hadn't known about the Gala, and hadn't hinted that she might come.

But the look on her face made clear that Deputy Caldwell had heard every word.

· *Nine* ·

"Chill," I said in a low tone, my fingers digging into my sister's arm. "Linda, thank you for a lovely evening. You and Wendy did a fabulous job."

Linda turned to Dean, blubbering. "Did you hear what that witch said to me? About you?"

What did I say? Oh, my sister. The other witch.

"I wasn't finished," Chiara said through closed teeth as I led her out the front doors.

"Oh, I think you said enough." I tightened my grip.

"That woman. First she has the nerve to suggest they didn't invite Mom to participate because her food isn't up to snuff. Then she said with all your talk about honoring Claudette, she was surprised you and Mom didn't propose a toast to Claudette's death."

I stopped so fast she practically tripped. "What? She's devastated."

"There you are." Outside on the paved walkway, Heidi pulled a white linen hanky out of her knock-off Prada bag, and handed it to Chiara.

While Chiara explained what happened, I tried my mother's landline, then her cell. Voice mail on both. Finally, I thumbed a text: *Where RU? Trouble!!*

Heidi stiffened her spine. "Do not let vicious gossip get to you."

"But where's Mom?" Chiara and I said in unison.

"After that little scene," Heidi said, "I'm glad she's not here."

Agreed, but still, it wasn't like Fresca to let gossip influence her actions. "Act as if you don't give a fig," and all that. So where was she?

Time to act as if I wasn't worried. In all the fuss, I'd abandoned a half-full plate and an untouched glass of wine. Suddenly parched and ravenous, I looped my arms through theirs. "Who needs a drink, besides me?"

We waltzed back in, three musketeers.

Minus Fresca, our usually fearless leader.

My driveway beckoned, but I skipped the turn and continued south on the narrow, winding highway above the lake. Where it veered lakeward at the next bay, I turned east and headed uphill on an even more familiar road: the road home.

Casa da Murphy had been an ideal place to grow up. Tonight, a week before solstice, the homestead basked in the last rays of pink and gold sunlight reflected off the lake. In the east, the waxing moon rose over Trumpeter Mountain, painting the sky a clear cerulean blue. I spotted my mother's ancient brown Volvo in the carport, and a soft glow in the living room. Relief washed over me.

I inhaled the scent of orchard in late spring, still my favorite perfume. An unexpected deep freeze had wiped out many of the famous lakeside cherry orchards one April years ago, but my parents had replanted, and my childhood saplings now produced tons of fruit each summer. My father had tended the cherries, apricots, and heirloom apples himself, with help from us, but like the Pinskys and many others, my mother contracted with a manager. My sister and her family lived one place over, on the original Murphy farmstead. And my brother, Nick, used a haphazard cabin at the top of the orchard as home base. Me, I was partial to the main house, and at the far edge of the orchard, where a lilac hedge grew fifteen feet tall, I felt closer to heaven than anywhere else.

"If you come in peace, come on in." My mother's clear voice pierced my reverie. She leaned against the doorframe, clad in one of her many vintage silk kimono-style robes. Mom's Scottie dog, Pepé—Italian for pepper—wagged her tongue and stubby black tail. "But if you've come to read me the riot act, go away. I just couldn't face all those people."

"You couldn't let us know?"

"You'd have argued and insisted I come."

Probably true. Inside, I slipped off my sandals and relaxed in a bentwood maple chair, reupholstered in a black-and-green jungle print with a splash of scarlet flowers. My mother loved to play up the house's 1950s modern style. I stretched my legs and put my feet on the matching ottoman, noticing that my toenail polish needed a redo. Pepé jumped in my lap and let me rub the magic spot between her eyes. "Since when do you care what people say?"

"Since my friend was murdered and people are staring at me just a little too hard."

Pepé whined in protest at my sudden move. "They're saying you copied her recipes and forced her to quit. They're not saying you killed her."

"They're too polite—or cowardly—for that. But I see it on their faces." She settled on the couch, slender legs folded beneath her. On the coffee table, a hand-blown martini glass held a lush coral red liquid garnished with a sprig of fresh mint. "And it's all a little too much."

They say women respond to fear with tears and men with

anger. They're wrong—I was furious. I set Pepé on the floor—gently, since my crankiness wasn't her fault—and paced, phone in hand. Texted Chiara: *At Mom's. OK. Tell HH.*

When I could speak, I said, "Mom, did it occur to you that maybe . . ."

"Maybe what?"

Blurt it out. "That when you didn't show up, or answer your phone, we pictured you dead in an alley somewhere. Like Claudette."

"Oh, honey." She stood and wrapped her arms around me. My heart beat slowed to normal.

A few minutes later, she asked the 64,000-dollar question. "Why would anyone want to kill me?"

And my equally weighty reply: "Why would anyone want to kill Claudette?"

She'd hear about the fight at the Gala sooner or later, so I gave her all the gory details. Her hand flew to her mouth in horror.

"Thank goodness her girls didn't witness that. Hard enough to have a harpy for a mother, without watching her in action in public."

My phone buzzed. Chiara, no doubt. I stepped outside to answer. Even in full leaf, the orchard looked ghostly in the moonlight.

"Hey, Erin. Kim Caldwell here."

Uh-oh. "You're working late."

"Just routine follow-up. I couldn't help overhearing that little disagreement tonight." So why call me, instead of the women directly involved? The perks of old friendship? "What can you tell me about the history between your mother and Linda Vincent?"

I sat on the low front step. "Nothing, really. Linda fancies herself a candy maker and she'd like to sell through the Merc, but that hasn't worked out."

"Why not?"

"Her samples aren't up to snuff."

"She angry with Fresca for that?"

"No reason she should be." Pepé poked my free hand with her nose. "It was my decision, though Claudette had already turned her down last fall." The connection dawned on me. "You don't think—that couldn't have anything to do with Claudette's death, could it? It was months ago." But whether Claudette had already started seeing Dean, I didn't know. Or whether he and Linda had separated first.

Kim made a noncommittal sound. "Everything's on the table at this point. Thanks again. We'll talk soon."

A promise or a threat?

"She'll get to the bottom of things," my mother said from the doorway. "She always does."

I wanted to believe her. The Kim I knew never cared about rumors and gossip. Besides, she would hardly expect me to rat on my mother and spill the details of some imaginary catfight with Linda. But a detective had to listen to everything, and use her judgment.

"I'm glad you two are friends again, honey. You need more friends." She handed me a drink twin to hers and sat.

"Don't worry about my social life, Mom. I don't." I took a sip. "This is great."

"Rum punch. I'm experimenting with the hibiscus coconut rum from the new distillery."

"We should host a tasting."

We sat in silence, enjoying our drinks and watching Pepé chase moths.

"Makes you think, doesn't it?" my mother said a few minutes later. "People say 'I could have killed her' all the time, but they don't mean it. Claudette could be aggravating, but I can't imagine . . ." Fresca shuddered and her voice trailed off. "Go home, darling. Get some rest." She rose and kissed the top of my head. "Things will look brighter tomorrow."

I watched the moonlight dancing through the cherry

trees. What did it take to do what the rest of us could never imagine?

And what did doing the unimaginable do to you?

I woke early, with an urge to bake. Cinnamon whole wheat scones with Creamery butter and apricot preserves. The jam maker bought fruit from Fresca, and I like eating food I've watched grow.

One thing I miss about city life is a fat, inky Sunday paper. On the other hand, sitting on my deck overlooking woods and lake with a plate of hot scones, a mug of Italian roast, and a book feels sinfully decadent. I've been working my way through the essays in last year's *Best Food Writing*. Hard to say which is more delish—the food or the writing.

The phone rang. I slid Mr. Sandburg off my lap and padded inside to answer.

My mother had promised today would be brighter, and watching the world awaken from my own back door, I'd believed her.

We'd been wrong.

· *Ten* ·

I threw on jeans and a T-shirt and zipped into town. Parked on Front Street, right behind the patrol car idling in front of the Merc.

My shop. My building. That gorgeous, maddening, demanding mausoleum.

The plate glass windows where Tracy and I had spent hours arranging the perfect display.

Smashed.

I gaped at the wreckage, unable to take it in. Who would do this? Why? Why not break the glass door instead? Less visible to a passerby, and easier access. An intruder would have had to climb through a window two feet above the ground, maneuver past the shards—most of which hadn't fallen out—and risk skin and blood.

For what? A case of huckleberry creamed honey?

But on closer look, I saw no sign that anyone had entered at all.

Which really ticked me off. If you're going to mess with

my shop—a piece of my family's history—you better have a darn good reason.

The uniformed deputy finished taking photos just as Kim rounded the corner, on full alert in the still-sleepy town. She wore boots and jeans—Sunday was probably her day off—with the ever-present jacket hiding the ever-present gun.

"Erin, what a mess. I'm so sorry. Nothing out back, thank goodness."

As if on cue, we stared at the ruined facade. They'd broken only one window. Even so, it felt like a violation. "Why?" I turned my anger on her. "Why?"

Her expression mixed sympathy with determination. In short, totally professional. She gestured toward the door, inset to protect it from the weather, and when my hands trembled with the key, she reached around me to work the lock. It opened with a soft snick.

Inside, shattered glass covered everything within ten feet of the window. A broken wine bottle gave off a heady odor, while busted jelly jars oozed red and purple goo on the plank floor.

"Don't," Kim said sharply as I reached to pick up a pebbled gray block, a stonelike brick. She poked it with a gloved finger and gave me a questioning look.

I shook my head. "Seems familiar, but I couldn't say why."

For the next half hour, I trailed Kim and her deputy as they searched for anything unusual. My grandfather's brass cash register sat untouched, as was the small wall vault in the office where I locked up the cash drawer and iPad we actually used for sales. All the damage had been done by the brick and the cascade of crashing displays it had triggered. "They might have tried the door," the deputy said and printed the handle, leaving a sift of fine black powder. Good luck with that. This is retail. When I asked about the brick, his face said, "You've got to be kidding," but at Kim's nod, he dusted, tagged, and bagged it. Humoring me, but I didn't care, if there was a chance it might help catch the culprit and spare someone else this ordeal.

Why? kept bouncing through my head. Someone had wanted to wreak havoc, not gain entry. *Why?*

"If he—whoever he is—wasn't after cash or products, then this is just vandalism, right? I mean, vandalism happens. But—two days after murder?"

Kim wasn't any more revealing about this incident than she had been about the murder. Infuriating. Still, coincidence makes me uneasy. And I suspected she agreed.

I called Fresca and Tracy for cleanup duty, then took pictures with my phone for the insurance claim and vendors. Readying the Merc for the day would be a challenge, but closing was out of the question. Festa volunteers were already setting up for today's events: sidewalk tasting booths, a kids' carnival, and live music outside the Jewel Inn. A rollicking Sunday.

"Good luck getting cleaned up," Kim said, extending her hand.

I took it, though the gesture felt oddly formal, like we were casual acquaintances, not childhood confidantes. "Thanks. We'll need it."

But you don't need luck in a small town. When you need help, others know it. The moment Kim left, brooms appeared. Someone found leather gloves so we could handle the glass safely. Burly Ted rolled a big trash barrel through the bar and muscled it into place on the sidewalk. Sweet, though the memory of finding Claudette near one like it made me cringe.

My brother-in-law, Jason, pulled up in his big white truck, Fresca riding shotgun. She hopped out and burst into tears. "Erin, why? Who? What's missing?"

In reverse order, I answered: "Nothing, as far as I can tell. Vandals. And I have no idea."

"We can't get glass today," Jason said, adjusting his specs as he scanned the damage. "I'll call Greg Taylor for plywood." Wendy's brother, who'd expanded his in-laws' lumberyard into a full-service building supply.

And here came Max and Wendy, in chef dress, bearing trays of coffee and croissants. My mother started bawling again. If I didn't get busy, I'd morph into a blubbering wreck myself, so I grabbed a croissant and a roll of trash bags.

"What a shame, girlie." Old Ned wielded broom and dust pan like the experienced barkeeper he was. "Don't you worry none. We'll have you cleaned up in no time, by jingo."

"Where would we be without our neighbors?" I said.

Tracy came in the back way. "Holy cow."

"Help me separate the damaged inventory from the good stuff, and put what's salvageable back on the shelves." I handed her gloves and fired up the iPad. "We need to account for every torn package, every broken jar."

"Holy cow," she repeated, eyes wide.

Minutes before noon, our Sunday opening time, the building supply truck rolled up, and Greg Taylor and Jason nailed plywood to the window frame. "I'll call that glass order in first thing Monday," Greg assured me. "We'll fix your panes."

"Here—thanks." I handed him one of the picnic baskets we'd assembled the day before, with pepperjack cheese and buffalo Thuringer. "Just watch for shards."

One window intact and the other boarded up, the Merc looked like it was winking.

If all this was some sort of cosmic joke, I wasn't laughing.

As I wrestled the trash barrel away from the door, Kim emerged from Puddle Jumpers, the children's clothing and toy shop, and strode toward the Bayside Grille. Trolling for lunch or information? Vandalism hardly warranted footwork by a detective on Sunday, did it? Not a high priority, unless there were a string of related incidents, which there hadn't been.

Probably just taking advantage of being downtown to ask if anyone had seen anything out of the ordinary—this morning or Friday night. I'd forgotten to tell her about Claudette's phone message. Later.

Chiara came in just as Tracy and I finished cleaning up the jam display. She handed me a knapsack. "A change of clothes."

I was forgiven for butting in last night.

We did a brisk business over the next several hours. Strains of live music wafted in the open door. Nearly every customer commented on the window, and several noted my makeshift memorial to Claudette. The shop reeked of spilled fruit, and we found a few more damaged items, but all in all, the afternoon went smoothly.

About three thirty, I snuck out to see the party for myself and catch a bit of gypsy jazz. A quintet called The Hot Club of Montana had driven up from Missoula to give a concert outside, and entertain diners at the Inn later.

My progress was slowed by shopkeepers calling out to me. To a person, they raved about booming sales, and thanked me for dreaming up this crazy idea of a new festival to kick off summer. And they expressed amazement at how quickly we'd reopened.

"Couldn't miss out on all the fun," I said. The weekend's success wasn't all due to me, of course—dozens of volunteers had played a part, along with the shopkeepers themselves. But the praise sure hit the spot.

The Inn's front deck and lawn overflowed with jazz fans. I perched on a low rock wall outside Dragonfly Dry Goods, the quilt and yarn shop next to the Inn, mesmerized by the guitarist's percussive strum and the bopping tenor sax. Dragonfly's owner, Kathy Jensen, raked a hand through her thick ash-blond hair and dropped down next to me. A sympathetic look filled her quick gray eyes. A silver-and-gold dragonfly pendant nestled in the hollow of her throat. A few couples danced in the Inn's circular driveway, and three tiny girls in pink sundresses bounced and twirled on the lawn. I had little doubt that the village merchants, when we met on Friday, would clamor for a repeat performance next year.

But it would be hard for me to agree until Claudette's killer was found.

When the musicians took a break, I gave Kathy a hug and moved on. At Le Panier, I thanked Max for the coffee and pastries.

"Stupid keeds," Max said. "Why do they think breaking things and making work for other people ees fun?"

No answer for that. Luckily, no one had been hurt.

In a booth outside, Wendy and her crew served Italian sodas, gelato, and other treats. With a vanilla soda and a chocolate hazelnut biscotti in hand, I strolled down to the bay, where a greenbelt separated shop-lined Front Street from the water. From a wrought-iron bench, I watched the waves sparkle and ripple gently in the late-afternoon breeze. Perfect. I glanced at my lucky stars. My first big splash back in town had gone just about perfectly.

Except for murder and mayhem. My eyes grew hot and the tears brimmed over.

A few minutes later, I dried my eyes and scouted for a place to toss my empty cup. Seeing a trash can behind the Playhouse, I headed up the gentle slope. As I neared the building, something caught my eye.

I took a closer look at the foot-high stacks of pavers, just like the stamped ones on the walkway out front but blank.

Just like the one some creep had hurled through my shop window.

Throughout my childhood, Sunday afternoon and evening had been sacred. My mother insisted every good Italian family gathered then for food, games, and togetherness. What, my father would tease, like only Italians eat, drink, and argue? They tossed the debate back and forth playfully. My grandparents always joined us, along with my father's brothers and their families, and a smattering of friends and neighbors—proving that some good Italian families are Irish.

But my father was gone, and so were his parents. My uncles had developed traditions of their own. And now my sister and I ran retail shops and, during tourist season, worked Sundays. So by the time Chiara and I made it to the homestead, a bright cloth covered the picnic table at the edge of the orchard, anchored by a heavy glass vase of home-grown Dutch iris.

Liz and Heidi relaxed in the shade in a pair of vintage metal lawn chairs.

"There you are," my mother called as she emerged from the house with a bottle of Prosecco and a handful of flutes. She seemed to have recovered from the morning shock, looking casually elegant in white crops and a teal linen tunic with a Nehru collar.

"Good show, little sis." Chiara raised a toast. "You pulled it off."

"Cheers!" Liz and Heidi chorused.

"Salute!" Fresca called out.

"I'll drink to that," I said, "but I couldn't have done it without a lot of help."

"Speaking of," Fresca said, her tone puzzled. "What got into Linda Vincent?"

"Let's not spoil the afternoon," Chiara said.

"And what's up with her and Dean?" Heidi asked. "My head's spinning, trying to keep track."

"Don't bother," Fresca said. "You know what dating after forty is like in this town. Musical chairs." The shallow pool of eligible males in a small town had been one point I'd raised against coming home. "But you're doing fine."

"You, too," Heidi said with a Mona Lisa smile. Before I could probe that remark, I sneezed.

"Seven point two on the Richter scale." My sister's old joke. "No more for you. You're obviously allergic to champagne."

"Bubbles in my nose." I sneezed again.

"Do you think he killed her?" Fresca asked.

"He's a no-good, lying, son of a—whatever," Heidi said. "I never understood what Claudette saw in him. I mean, jumpsuits and bell bottoms?"

I pictured the headline: ELVIS LIVES—AND KILLS—IN PICTURESQUE MONTANA VILLAGE. Not good for business.

Fresca's brow furrowed. "He flattered her when she was vulnerable, and that's all it took."

Landon zoomed through the trees into the picnic area, then dropped to all fours, barking. Jason stopped behind him, obviously unsure what his son was up to. "Daddy, you have to use four legs around humans. They don't know we can walk on two legs."

"Right." Jason obeyed.

"I'm Hank the Cowdog, head of ranch security," Landon told us. "This is my trusty deputy, Drover. What seems to be the trouble, ladies?"

How did he know? I glanced at my sister.

She rolled her eyes. "He's just playing. We've been reading the books together every night."

"Drover needs a break." Jason got up and reached for a beer from the ice-filled washtub.

"Hey, Landon. Let's go visit my special place. On two legs." He ran ahead of me into the orchard. In the far back, an old McIntosh had escaped pruning for a few years and grown too tall to be reclaimed. It wasn't sturdy enough to support a tree house, so my father had erected stilts under a platform built around the trunk. A roof of silver-gray cedar shakes covered the structure, and leafy branches provided a living curtain. We scaled the old orchard ladder and scrambled inside.

From here, we could survey our domain: Murphy Orchards below us, acres of forest on two sides, and to the west, Eagle Lake.

"Auntie, this is my favorite place in the whole world."

"Mine, too." I'd spent countless hours here, with my dolls or a book, or hiding from Nick's teasing. Even as teenagers, Kim and I had snuck up here when we craved the comforts of childhood. "And sharing it with you is the best."

The groans of an engine accelerating up the hill invaded our little kingdom. Nick back from the field? My wildlife biologist brother rarely gave much notice of his comings and goings.

Not Nick. A black-and-white Explorer with a county shield.

"Gotta go, buddy." Landon protested—I didn't blame him—but he followed me down the ladder and back to the house.

"I see tradition continues." Still in her jeans and jacket, Kim surveyed our small gathering—Mom, me, Chiara and her family, Liz and Bob, Heidi. If I hadn't known Kim so well, I might have missed the wistful look before she switched it off. She'd often spent Sunday afternoon and evening here when we were kids, except in high summer when the Caldwell clan joined Lodge guests for the weekly barbecue and sing-along. "Sorry to disturb you. May I have a word, Fresca? In private?"

"Certainly." My mother set her glass on the table and led Kim inside.

I tugged my sister toward the corner of the house and the open living room window. If we stood in the right spot, we'd be out of sight but not out of earshot.

"What's going on?" Chiara whispered. I held a finger to my lips.

"You can't honestly believe that," we heard Fresca say, her voice rising. "You know I would never hurt anyone."

"I'm not accusing you, Fresca. But the evidence strongly suggests—"

"Evidence, pevidence. Kimberly Caldwell, you know better."

Chiara's eyes widened. We knew that tone. But what evidence?

"I've studied the statements. I've matched the timelines. You were in the courtyard earlier, but you left, and no one saw you again until after Erin found the victim."

I scanned my mental image of the crowd for my mother in her distinctive coral dress. Was Kim right? Had she disappeared? For how long?

"And that means I snuck out back and stabbed Claudette?"

How could she have known Claudette would come through the back? Unless Claudette had called my mother, too . . .

"You had motive, means, and opportunity. I watched you in the kitchen, Fresca. You know your way around a knife, and I saw your knife drawer. Are you missing any?"

My jaw cramped and I felt my sister spasm beside me. What was she talking about?

"I don't count them," my mother said. "But none are missing."

"How do you know if you don't know how many you have?"

"Because a trained chef always knows where her tools are, and never loses track of a knife. And kitchen knife skills don't mean I stabbed anyone. Seriously, Kim, do you think I could kill anyone, let alone Claudette?" My mother's disbelief turned to impatience.

If Kim replied, I didn't hear her over the pounding in my heart and the buzz in my ears.

"They're leaving. Go!" Chiara shoved me away from the window and we scrambled to join the others and act normal.

Out front, Kim stood on the rockway looking back at my mother on the porch. "I'm so sorry, Fresca. But please understand. If the evidence bears out our suspicions, you'll be arrested and charged with deliberate homicide."

· *Eleven* ·

Once again, I slept badly, and once again, I stood at the Merc's front door well before business hours. This time, though, I wasn't so sure the village would rally around us.

Normally I love the shop early in the day, especially on Mondays. Clean and quiet, the shelves full of tasty Montana treats waiting for customers to discover them. Morning speaks of possibilities.

I did not like the possibilities running through my mind today.

Both Chiara and I had insisted Fresca needed to hire a lawyer first thing. Liz and Bob agreed. But Fresca refused. "I didn't do anything wrong," she'd said, "and I won't act like I did."

I'd never considered my mother naive, until now. Or maybe I was jaded, by city life and too much late-night TV.

Only a couple of Jewel Bay lawyers still had active practices, and both declined to represent her. They'd known Claudette, and one had been at the Festa Friday night, which they termed a conflict of interest. So I phoned a criminal lawyer in Pondera who'd been in the store a few times. She sounded sympathetic and interested, so I made an afternoon appointment.

Then I called a man my father had known—not a close friend, but he'd always seemed smart, and I'd read newspaper accounts of his victories. Yes, he could see Fresca this afternoon as well.

That taken care of, I sipped coffee from my travel mug and nibbled on one of Sunday's abandoned scones. Time to review our accounts. We were nearly making a profit, sooner than I'd projected—and that made the weekly book work a lot more fun.

Give Claudette credit for trying to systematize the Merc's records, but she hadn't been able to break down Fresca's resistance. I had a daughter's leverage. We'd computerized inventory and sales, using software designed for startups, plus the iPad credit card reader. I also insisted that everyone who rented our certified kitchen keep production records, with a copy to me, so we could track usage and keep the Health Department happy. The younger vendors used a spreadsheet program, but Fresca disliked the computer, so for her, I'd created paper charts she filled in by hand, recording every batch of every product. I made her count how many jars she gave away and how many she took home. Before, she'd whip up a batch of red pepper and garlic tomato sauce and shelve it without knowing how many cases she'd made or what it cost. I'd shown her how recordkeeping would help her watch expenses and trace which products turned a profit.

"I track that in my head," she'd said.

"How's that working out?" I'd replied. She'd rolled her eyes, but gone along.

Last week's sales had been good. Very good. Best weekend ever. Most customers bought several items, always a good sign. Added incentive to get cracking on plans for the

Jam Club, a rewards program. I made a list of suppliers to call for more product. Posted a Facebook status update thanking folks for the Festa's success, with a reminder about Food Underfoot, the wild food and herb walk and demo coming up. Retweeted Festa updates from Dragonfly and the Bayside Grille.

Except for the plywood window, the dead ex-employee, and the deputy sheriff's threats to arrest my mother, life was good.

My coffee had gone cold, so I ran next door for a double latte. Returned with two, plus a *pain au chocolat* for me and a plain croissant for Fresca. She sat at the counter, recipe binder open and a note pad in front of her. She cooks on Monday and Tuesday, and her first step is always making a list of ingredients. But the pad was blank, and she stared into space. I gave her breakfast and a printout showing our inventory of her sauces and pastas, and pointed out where we were low.

"Exactly what I thought, without your fancy programs and ana—what do you call it?"

"Analytics." Pretty basic, actually, but who could blame her for being in a sour mood? I didn't think Kim's evidence amounted to much, but Fresca didn't know Chiara and I had eavesdropped on a private conversation, and she hadn't revealed the particulars, so I kept my lips zipped.

But when I told her about the appointments with the lawyers, she was firm. "No."

"Mom, don't you think you should be prepared?"

Clearly, she did not.

I tried again. "Is there somebody you'd rather call? Someone in Pondera?" Pronounced "Pon-duh-ray" by locals. "Or Missoula—that guy from Chiara's class is a big-shot lawyer down there."

"I don't need a lawyer. You may be manager of the Merc, but I am still your mother, and it is my life, and I said no."

Why so stunningly vehement? Simple denial? Was she hiding something? Protecting someone?

None of that made any sense.

"Gotcha, loud and clear." I couldn't say more without admitting we'd spied on her. Still, we had time. If Kim turned up the heat, we could call the lawyers then.

When I told my boss at SavClub why I was leaving, she'd given me her blessing, along with a warning about going into business with family. "All your buttons will get pushed, regularly. You'll need to set firm boundaries."

That goes both ways. But when someone you love won't do what you're certain is right—well, sometimes you have to push back.

Tracy arrived, dressed appropriately today in a long navy skirt and a cream loose-weave sweater that suited her stocky build. First task: restocking shelves. We had gaps from goods sold and gaps from goods damaged. We were low on several kinds of jam, gnocchi, and pumpkin ravioli. The fresh mozzarella was gone and, of course, the olive tapenade.

Goody, goody.

Fresca hadn't gotten very far on her list of supplies. My heart ached, seeing her dejection. But if an angel with a platinum American Express card came hunting locally sourced groceries for the clan's family reunion, I was not going to let her walk out thinking we couldn't deliver the goods.

"I'm off to the bank," I called, waving the zippered vinyl deposit bag. "Don't burn the place down while I'm gone." After the last few days, a little humor seemed in order. Alas, no one else thought so.

I strolled up Front Street past Le Panier and Chez Max. Past the Playhouse, which reminded me of the paver. At the corner, I waved at Kathy, out sweeping the Dragonfly's sidewalk, and headed up Hill Street.

So great to be part of this little town, despite its unimaginative street names. At SavClub—like any corporate conglomerate—I rarely got to see my plans come to life. You line them out and hand them off to other people, and go on to the next project, hoping someone tells you what worked and what didn't. Here, you're idea person and trash picker—I scooped up a stray plastic water bottle—rolled into one. And as the Festa demonstrated, the risks might be higher, but so were the rewards.

Jewel Bay Bank and Trust had opened in 1910, the same year as Murphy's Mercantile. It had long outgrown the original sandstone structure, but managed to keep functioning with a tasteful addition and a branch up on the highway.

While the teller checked my deposit, I checked my phone. I hadn't told Kim about Claudette's message, and I hadn't returned Adam Zimmerman's call. Both made me feel a little guilty. Before I could decide who to call first, I felt someone watching me, and turned.

Linda Vincent. If looks could kill . . . No crime lab could detect that.

She stalked past me to the next teller, the spiky heels of her black pumps clattering on the slate floor. I admired her ability to walk in them. But her heel caught in a gap between tiles and she nearly went down, catching hold of the counter to steady herself. She turned and glared, as if her fall were my fault.

"Here you go, Erin." The teller handed me my deposit bag. "What a great weekend. Loved the jazz, and all the kids' stuff. We're seeing lots of happy merchants this morning, too."

"Thanks." I gestured toward the other woman, who stood

on one foot, clutching her twisted ankle. "Thank Linda, too. She organized the concerts and recruited the volunteers."

Linda's burning stare followed me out the heavy doors. No doubt she thought I was being facetious, after her spat with Chiara on Saturday night. Or did her aggravation stem from something else?

In a small town, it seems like everything has something to do with everything else.

I was on the phone with Jen at the vineyard, cadging for more Viognier, when the front door chimed. Not many men shop alone at the Merc, and never on Monday mornings. Early thirties, blond, clean-shaven, about six-two. Built like he might have played college football. The Grizzlies won back-to-back national titles while I was at UM, and I'd never gone to a game. Maybe I should have. Our eyes met, and though I was sure I had never seen him before, a flash of recognition shot through me. He stepped forward, a question on his face, then spotted the phone in my hand. I gestured to Tracy, who offered him help. On the other end of the line, Jen dithered over whether she could make a delivery or maybe she could spare two cases if I could pick them up and didn't I want more Chardonnay and what about cherry, wasn't that always a hit with the tourists?

Maybe the inventory issues had stemmed from Jen's indecision, not Claudette's mistakes. While I listened to Jen, Tracy showed our visitor the shop and answered questions I couldn't hear. Her animated gestures and expression made her appreciation for him clear.

"So, that's a case of dry cherry, one of Chardonnay, and two Viognier. And a case of elderberry, to replace the bottles that got broken. I'll pay you full retail for the broken bottles."

"Oh, no, you don't have to do that." Her tone said she really hoped I would, despite her protests.

"It's only fair," I said. "I'll run down later in the week."

"Looks like you had some trouble." The visitor gestured at the plywood.

"Expect the unexpected. My new mantra." I held out my hand. "Erin Murphy. How can I help you?"

He held my gaze as we shook hands. Nice gaze he had, and I felt it take me in—with interest, not intrusion. "Rick Bergstrom, Montana Gold Grain. Sorry to hear about your loss. That must have been a shock." We both glanced at the countertop memorial. The flowers needed water. "This may be a bad time for a sales call, but you requested information through our website, and I was in the area."

"Thanks. And the timing's fine. We're always looking for new products, and we'd love to carry organic, Montana-grown flours and grains. My mother, Francesca Conti Murphy, makes our pastas, and she's interested in your semolina. Maybe the spelt and amaranth flours, too."

"Semolina straight or blended?"

"On the rocks," I said with a laugh. "You're gonna have to have that conversation with her."

A blue button-down may be favored by salesmen to project sincerity, but it also complemented his Big Sky blue eyes.

"I brought samples," he said, indicating a sturdy carton labeled MONTANA GOLD. "We've also got baking and cereal mixes, and we just launched a line of ready-made breads and crackers. All grown and milled in Montana, mostly in the Golden Triangle."

The north-central part of the state, fine farming country. No wonder he looked so—well, wholesome, though that is not a word I often use to describe an attractive man.

"Let's finish that tour." I showed him some of my favorite products, described our philosophy, and explained the certified kitchen. He paid attention, asked questions, watched me closely.

Tracy interrupted with a customer's question about

sulfites in the wine. While I talked to them, Rick continued scanning our shelves, reading labels.

"It's the only place like it in the state," I told him a few minutes later. "We're giving small producers a chance to break into the market, without breaking the bank. At the same time, we're helping customers find the real Montana food they want."

"It's got potential."

That word again. I felt my guard go up, unsure of his meaning.

"So here's a sample of what we've got," he said, unpacking on the kitchen counter bags and boxes that bore the company's simple but uninspired logo.

I looked it over. "I'll have to say no to the bread, with a bakery next door. And flour won't be a big seller, with so many of our customers tourists, but I'd like to give it a try. The mixes will be popular."

"They do well at the gift shops around Yellowstone."

"We're more than a gift shop." I gestured at the meat and dairy case, feeling a little defensive. "You saw that luscious produce cart outside. Our focus is local and regional, sustainable, farm-to-market. It may not be possible to eat an all-Montana diet—not if you consider chocolate an essential food group, like I do—but we aim to show that even in this climate, a community can do a lot to feed itself."

He met my gaze, his tone more businesslike than it had been. "If that's your goal, Erin—and it's a good one—then you need to go beyond the specialty items you've got right now. Fewer treats, more staples. You've got some produce and meat, but no eggs, milk, or butter. And there's a world of wild game and ranch-raised beef, pork, and poultry out there." This time his smile felt a touch patronizing. "We'd love to do business with you, though I suspect your sales volume will be fairly low."

I felt my Jell-O rising. I had worked groceries for years. High-end, but SavClub sold more apples and chicken than champagne and filet mignon. Yes, we needed to provide for the daily table, but we also needed to get the business in the black.

And we were just getting started. "There's some truth to that. Ordinarily, we do carry local eggs and poultry, and more of my mother's products. We had a terrifically busy weekend, hosting the village Summer Kickoff, and we're wiped out of a lot of things. In fact, our kitchen will be in full steam this afternoon." At least, I hoped so. No sign of Fresca since midmorning.

The back door creaked—I'd deliberately not oiled the hinges, so we could tell when it opened—and heavy footsteps pounded in. A short black-haired Asian man in faded fatigues stopped where the back hall met kitchen and shop, a five-gallon bucket brimming with morels in each work-worn hand.

"Miss Erin," Jimmy Vang said. "Bad time?"

"Always a good time, Jimmy. Be right with you." I extended my hand to Rick Bergstrom. "Glad you stopped in. If you'll excuse me, I've got to see a man about mushrooms."

He held on longer than I did. I hate that—makes me feel like I've misread the business code manual, at least the one men get.

"Enjoy the samples. I'll give you a call to see what you think."

"You bet." What had briefly seemed like it might have deeper potential was "just business" after all.

Ten gallons of mushrooms would go fast, and the season was ending. Like many of the Hmong refugees in western Montana, Jimmy made his living gardening and foraging, so I knew he'd be back with other offerings soon. I set some morels aside for Fresca and me, and hand-printed a sign for the produce cart: FRESH MORELS INSIDE. Typed up a recipe card to hand out. When I came downstairs with the cards, a customer was just leaving and the shop was empty.

"Farm boy's hot," Tracy said in a lilting voice.

Agreed, but our conversation had demonstrated the perils of mixing business with pleasure. Fine. I didn't come back to Jewel Bay to get involved anyway. "We don't pass muster. Not pure enough."

"Outsnobbed in your own shop? That bites." She plowed through the samples on the kitchen counter. "Organic oat bread, multigrain bagels, seed loaf. Honey buckwheat pancake mix. I see what you mean." She held up a heavy paper bag with a resealable folding top. "What on earth is Wheat Coffee?"

"Brew some up," I said. "Let's find out if Rick Bergstrom can stand a little hot water."

· *Twelve* ·

That afternoon, my mood swung like a 1940s big band on too many triple espressos. On the one hand, the Festa had lured a crowd to the village to eat, drink, and shop, and they'd done all three merrily. Merchants who'd questioned the need for another festival now eyed their empty shelves and full tills, and hummed a different tune. I had created A Good Thing.

On the flip side, a family friend and former employee had been murdered. My childhood BFF suspected my mother of involvement. And the only interesting guy I'd met in months had left the shop with "all business" written on his face.

He had a point. If I meant what I said about increasing awareness of local food sources, we had work to do. But I hate when people point out the obvious.

Chiara's poster for the wild food walk caught my eye. Maybe it had caught his, too, and showed him we meant business.

Unless he considered eating wild onions and nettles more frivolity.

Kathy from Dragonfly interrupted my pity party, toting a basket full of handmade placemats and napkins, and a small shelf-talker sign sporting her blue-green dragonfly logo. I'd suggested the Merc carry her products to complement our own—why compete by selling linens made in China when we could promote our friends and neighbors instead?

"Listen, Erin," she said in a confiding tone as we laid a place setting on the display table and tucked napkins into pottery mugs and goblets for a shot of color. "You need to know what people are saying in town."

I stopped, a square of cotton printed with rainbow trout in my hand. "Go on."

"They're saying your mother may be a prime suspect in the murder. They don't blame her for being angry with Claudette, not with the way she took off, but they—they think Fresca just snapped." Her pinched expression made clear she hated telling me this.

My worst fears confirmed. "Who's saying that? Linda Vincent? Why would anyone believe her? She must have hated Claudette."

Kathy looked miserable. "That's why they believe her."

"Didn't her behavior Saturday night show she hates Fresca, too?" A chill crept up my spine. "What if Linda's trying to deflect attention from Dean—or herself? Fresca had nothing to gain from Claudette's death. Dean might have been the one who snapped—he sure is quick to anger. And Linda could have wanted revenge—or to eliminate a potential rival. After all, what's to say he wouldn't have left her again?" I thought back to Friday night. They had both been in the courtyard before I went out to the alley and found Claudette's body. Had they come in that way, following a deadly encounter?

"One more thing," Kathy said. "But it's just more nasty gossip."

"Spill," I said, looking squarely at her. "It's not gossip to tell us—we need to defend ourselves."

"You broke your own window to get sympathy."

"What? Me? That window?" I pointed to the plywood, a blatant reminder of someone's malice. "I love this building. Do they have any idea what that costs, or that our insurance may not cover vandalism?"

"Apparently someone your height and size was spotted running away from here early Sunday morning. I'm sorry, Erin. I thought you should know." She hugged me, squeezed my hand. "It will all work out."

"Thank you. Thank you for telling me."

So this was what reached Kim as she worked her way through town. No wonder she suspected Fresca. How could I convince her otherwise? Especially if my mother wouldn't hire a lawyer to help her protect herself.

I was sitting on a stool nibbling a carrot when Tracy returned from her lunchtime dog walk. She looked as peeved as I felt.

"I love living here," she said. "I never considered moving when Mitch left me. But sometimes . . ." She shook her head and plopped onto the next stool.

"What?" More rumors, more nastiness?

"The sheriff's office hasn't released the cause of death, right?" Not as far as I knew. "So at the gas station, I heard she was stabbed. Or shot. Or beaten to death. Everybody has a pet theory."

Sounded like the guess station.

"And Rick? The grain guy? Somebody spotted an unknown man in a sport coat leaving the Merc, and before you know it, he's some hot-shot detective the sheriff's office brought in to help Kim. Or take over, because of her connection to your family, and because she hasn't made an arrest yet."

The first twenty-four hours are critical. Bring in the big guns to help the hicks. Sounded like I wasn't the only one who'd seen too many late-night cop shows.

I squeezed Tracy's shoulder.

No two ways about it: I would have to find the real murderer. Like Hank the Cowdog.

But with only two legs, and no trusted deputy, could I stay ahead of real trouble—and catch a killer?

· *Thirteen* ·

If I ran, it would have been a ten-mile day. But running is against my religion, so I called my sister to meet me for a planning session, aka a drink.

For a cowboy bar, Red's not only cleans up good—it pours unexpectedly tasty wine. Not the snooty stuff, but very drinkable. And generous, too—a healthy glass of a spritely sauvignon blanc set me back all of five bucks.

Chiara flopped her red leather handbag—shaped like a bowling bag, and not much smaller—into the booth and slid in, exhaling about ten pounds of carbon dioxide. "Criminy, what a day."

"Really? Light traffic on our side of the street."

"Ours, too, though we're still recovering from the weekend." She ran Snowberry, a co-op gallery, with five other artists. "The smart remarks and funny looks started to get to me."

"Like, 'Oh, it's your mother who—' and then they clam up like they shouldn't say anything but it's too late."

"Exactly. Worse for you, though, since you found the body." Sympathy mixed with horror on her face.

"Practically at your back door," I mimicked as Ted delivered her gin and tonic. The old-fashioned glass looked like a toy in his hand.

"At whose back door?" He'd obviously overheard our exchange.

"At least here, it's idle curiosity. Blood and guts go with the atmosphere."

"Heck, no. This is a classy joint." Hard to tell if he was teasing.

"Ted, be a dear," Chiara said, "and bring us a basket of waffle fries. With Dijon mustard, since you're upscale. Seriously," she said after he left, lowering her voice. Her loose hair swung as she leaned forward. "I'm worried about Mom."

"I called two lawyers, but she refuses to go. Monday's sauce-making day, but she came in for a while then left without doing a thing."

"I talked to her a little while ago. She wants to be alone. Doesn't even want to see Landon."

We sat back and stared at each other. That was a bad sign. My mother didn't get all gaga and googoo over babies, but she did adore her only grandchild, who often spent an afternoon or evening with her.

"Erin?"

I looked up into coffee brown eyes, a mess of dark, curly hair, and a face I couldn't quite place.

"Adam Zimmerman." He extended his hand—long, slender fingers, grip firm but not overbearing. "It's been ages." If he'd been this cute in college, I would have had no trouble remembering him. He'd outgrown the geeky stage. "Adam. I'm so sorry—I've been meaning to return your call. Do you know my sister, Chiara Phillips?"

"Adam Zimmerman," he said, shaking her hand. "I

followed Erin around like a puppy dog all through college, but she barely noticed me." He grinned. The bar wasn't dark enough to hide my blushing cheeks. To me, he said, "No worries. I spent the weekend at wilderness camp, helping the staff get settled before the kids come on Thursday."

Which explained both the three-day beard and the clothes that looked like he'd just crawled out of the woods. And the bottle of Moose Drool in his left hand.

"Join us," Chiara said, flashing me a wicked smile. "If you're alone."

"Don't mind if I do." He slid in next to me. I scooted over to make room, but not before his thigh touched mine. I nearly jumped.

"Hey, Z. What's up?" Ted set the basket of fries on our table and pulled a bottle of Dijon out of his apron pocket.

"Hey, Ted. Just enjoying the pleasures of civilization." He grinned at the two of us.

Ted hrrmmphed, then turned his attention to me. "Erin, you just gotta expect some gossip these days. Especially 'cuz of how Claudette left."

"Claudette?" Adam asked. "The fireball who burned your burgers?"

Ted glowered.

"She worked here? Did you know that?" I looked at Chiara.

"Before she started at the Merc. For six months, maybe?"

"You were away," I said to Adam. "You didn't hear." We filled him in on the murder and investigation. He asked all the right questions and made all the right sympathetic noises. "So, ever since Friday night, there's been a lot of guessing going on."

"Stick to the facts," he said at the same time as Chiara said, "Ignore it. We need to focus on Mom."

"We have to find out who the killer is."

"Leave it to the police," Ted interjected. "Stay out of Kim's way."

Why was he standing there? "Still carrying a torch?"

His face darkened to a purple that clashed with his red bandanna and made his nearly new biker leathers even more ridiculous. The damp bar towel in his beefy hand didn't improve the look. "You are a witch. You've even got a black cat."

"He's sable. And I am not."

Chiara burst out laughing and I joined her. Ted spun on a heavy heel and left. "Does he really have the hots for her?" she asked.

"I'm missing something here." Adam reached for a waffle fry and dipped it in the mustard, his arm brushing my shoulder.

My drink was empty. If I stayed and had another, I'd end up explaining all my fears and anxieties, and what suddenly seemed like a totally messed-up situation. I did not want to walk away from this guy. But I also did not want him to think I was totally messed up.

"I need to get going," Chiara said, laying down cash and gathering up her things.

"Me, too. Adam, it's been great to see you."

"So early?" he said. We slid out of the booth, then I stood there, not sure whether to shake hands, hug, or kiss his cheek.

He took my hand, leaning close for a half hug. "Let's get together again. Soon." I nodded.

Outside, Chiara and I watched him saunter up Front Street. Nice guy, nice view. "You got a live one, little sister."

On the phone, he'd wanted to ask me something. No doubt for a donation to the wilderness program, not a date. He hadn't asked for either one. I sighed. I did not remember feeling nervous around Adam Zimmerman ten years ago. What had changed?

Chiara and I both promised to check on Mom. But there had to be more we could do. More I could do. Like find out where Claudette had gone after I left the drugstore and before she turned up dead in Back Street. Or who she had talked to. But where to start?

And how, I wondered, did Ted Redaway know I have a cat?

Back at the Merc, Tracy had closed up and gone home, and the shop stood oddly quiet.

The box of Montana Gold samples still sat on the kitchen counter, though Tracy had snared the bagels—the pinnacle of her personal food pyramid. I dug out a box of cracked wheat crackers, added goat cheese and peppered antelope salami, and took my plate, a Pellegrino, and my personal iPad to the courtyard table.

I didn't know who Claudette hung out with in Jewel Bay, and we weren't Facebook friends. But my sister and I were online pals, so I checked Chiara's profile, found Claudette on her friends list, then guessed her password. (Landon08, and she'd be furious, but she'd never know.) Voilà! About eight seconds to climb on Claudette's wall.

She called herself an "aspiring restaurateur." Okay—as good a description as any for an unemployed retail manager whose last two jobs had involved food.

One hundred thirty-two friends. Her son, her sister, half a dozen local business folks, some other names I recognized. Several Elvi and a surprising number of Elvira, no doubt recent meets from Dean's impersonation—excuse me, *tribute*—program. Looked like she'd been the unofficial photographer at Elvis school—her photos included dozens of shots of various tribute artists doing their best to honor the King.

She wasn't friends with Dean or Linda Vincent. I'd scout them out next. FB threads weave an intricate web, and I wanted to make sure I stayed the spider, not the fly.

Why friend James Angelo? Nothing inherently sinister

about her online connection with my mother's professional rival. No reason they shouldn't be friends. Business gurus preach that competitors should be cooperative where possible, cordial at the least, and never take their contest personally. Especially true in small towns, as I'd said myself more than once.

Except that he's such a creep.

No FB activity since Friday morning. Claudette hadn't rushed home to post about her plans for the evening. In fact, it was so unlike her to wear the same dress for an afternoon of errands and an evening do that I wondered if she'd gone home at all.

So what had she been up to?

I smeared goat cheese on a cracker—tasty, they were—and scrolled through her updates and her friends' posts. All standard exchanges.

Whoa. I scrolled back to a message I'd nearly missed. Ted Redaway saying, *Welcome home, we missed you!!!* Last Wednesday—two days before he told us she was back and spreading rumors about Fresca and me. Rumors she denied any part of.

Why would she have confided in him? Had his name been on her friends list and I missed it? I double-checked. Not there. She must have unfriended him. My word of the week—*why?*

I scrolled slowly this time, searching for more messages from Ted. A post about his motorcycle ride around the lake, with a shot of him on his bike at a turnout. Another about a band that played at Red's two weeks ago. I bit into a hunk of salami and kept reading. In the last few weeks—even before her return—he'd sent her several links to sites giving advice about starting up a restaurant. She called herself aspiring, and she did have some experience. While I see Red's mainly as a bar, it serves burgers, wings, and a few salads and other snacks. And waffle fries.

Still, if I were opening a restaurant, Ted Redaway would not be my first choice in mentors. And his father ran the place, not him.

I jotted down names of other local friends—people she might have seen or talked with since her return. Or who ran into her Friday afternoon and might have known she was coming to the Festa.

That reminded me—Angelo spotted us on his way into the pharmacy. I clicked on his page, but the handful of posts were all business: Announcements of new products. A description of his contributions to last Saturday's Gala. Photos from catering jobs. Frustrated, I begged my friend Google for more. A few mentions in the weekly newspaper's coverage of charitable events, all for his food contributions, but nothing more. No YouTube videos, no Twitter feed, no blog. Nothing personal—not one hint of his hometown, family, past work, education, or a single hobby.

He claimed he lived to cook, and it appeared to be true. Odd for a forty-year-old man to leave such a slim cyber trail—especially a man in business. Ripe for Jason's web design and marketing services, though I didn't seriously think Angelo would want to do business with a man closely related to Fresca and me.

I prowled around online awhile longer. Nothing unexpected turned up about the Vincents. Their twin girls got their share of ink—on the tennis court, on the Honor Roll, onstage, and on the walls of the student art show. Striking blondes with bright eyes and innocent faces. For Claudette, I found little more than her death notice in the newspaper and a mention of her appearance in a musical review last fall, with a photo of her onstage, looking adoringly at the star—Dean as Elvis, natch. Maybe where they first hooked up.

Darned if I knew what any of this meant. I washed another of Rick Bergstrom's crackers down with mineral water and leaned back, soaking in the last bit of warmth before the courtyard fell into shadow. Even in mid-June, Monday nights in the village were dead.

I cringed. As the Bard said of Denmark, something was rotten in Jewel Bay, and not just my choice of words.

· *Fourteen* ·

"Love what you've done with the place," I told Deputy Caldwell, seated behind a gunmetal gray desk in a room maybe ten-by-ten and last painted in another century. The outer office had fared no better. In the dull-and-dingy design category, the sheriff's satellite office took first prize.

They'd hidden the entrance well, too, on the back side of Jewel Bay Fire Hall, marked only by a foot-high sheriff's department seal—and Kim's rig nearby.

She didn't offer me a chair, but I sat anyway. Her jacket, a tan number with a subtle weave, hung on a hook behind the door. Shadows under her eyes marred her otherwise clear complexion. On her desk, a three-ring binder lay open to photographs from the Festa. Another binder was labeled STATEMENTS. One wall held a bulletin board with pictures of Claudette—dead and alive—and the crime scene, a diagram of the alley and Red's courtyard, and a June calendar.

On the opposite wall, a whiteboard sported a timeline for last Friday, and a To Do list in blue marker: IV F&F, LAB,

ME—TOD, MOD/COD, WEAPON??? No decoding needed to get the gist.

But what gave me the willies was the outline of a body, a single large wound marked in red.

My first thought had been that it all looked like prep for a new product release—timelines and checklists for QC approval, pricing, final labels, catalog copy, and on and on.

My second thought: The wound was on the left side, just below the breast. Consistent with the blood flow I'd seen.

I looked back at the murder board. No scribbled notes about calibers, no photos of entrance and exit wounds. A knife, then, thrust upward into the heart.

"Those question marks mean you're waiting for information, and you haven't located the weapon yet?"

"Erin, I'm not going to discuss this case with you."

I met her gaze. "What case, Kim? The one where you're investigating Claudette's death, or the one where you've already decided my mother is a cold-blooded killer?"

"We have to investigate every possibility." Did her voice waver slightly?

"What other possibilities?" I gestured at the boards. "Don't they usually list the suspects and their motives? What's my mother's motive?"

"Don't get in my way, Erin."

"Don't tell me what to do." We glared at each other until I remembered the paper bag in my hand. "Brought you a snack." She withdrew each item—Montana Gold crackers, goat cheese, and a jar of roasted pepper spread—gingerly, as though expecting a bomb. Or a snake—she hates snakes.

"Rumor mill says you can't handle this investigation, that a new detective's been brought in, and was seen snooping around the Merc today. He's actually a sales rep for a grain company out of central Montana. I thought you'd want to know. Those are his crackers."

A smile tugged at the corners of her mouth. "What else does the rumor mill say?"

"Nothing you haven't heard, I'm sure. But we promised we'd cooperate, so I have two things to mention. Fact, not fiction. Friday when I was home getting ready for the Festa, my phone rang. I ignored it, and with everything that's happened since then . . ." I wasn't going to lie and tell her I'd just discovered it, but no reason to admit I'd withheld evidence—if it was evidence. "Claudette called me at five seventeen p.m., maybe half an hour after I ran into her." I played the message for her, and she noted the time.

"You said two things."

I told her about the pavers piled behind the Playhouse. "Doesn't tell us who threw it, or why, though. I hear tell that someone was seen running through the village on Sunday morning, after the window was smashed, and speculation says it was me. It wasn't." I gave her a wry smile. "You remember how I hate running."

"I remember." A poker voice to match her poker face. And I held no cards.

"But how is the broken window connected to the murder?" I asked. Were we at risk? Did someone out there want to hurt my family, my employee, my customers—or me?

"Erin, I'm sorry." She stood, not looking the least bit apologetic. "We should both go home."

My mother had urged me to renew my friendship with Kim, even though I hadn't ended it all those years ago. Any doubts I'd nursed about the depth or permanence of the rift vanished. My father's death had changed something between us, and Kim's face made crystal-clear that my family's connection to another mysterious death would not change it back.

I pushed myself out of the chair and left without another word. No plan, but when did that stop a Murphy girl?

Maybe a drive would substitute for a plan—or spark one. I left the Fire Hall by the back road. In Seattle, even in the suburbs, driving had not been relaxing, so when I'd needed to think, I walked. But the old habit had returned and I thought—or worried—best behind the wheel.

A few minutes later, I drove down Old Stage Road, near the cozy garden cottage where Claudette had lived since her divorce. Had she rented it out, or left it empty when she followed Dean to Las Vegas? The same shiny red rocker and white wicker table I remembered from past visits sat on the porch, and the same white lace café curtains hung in the kitchen window. No car, no lights, no petunias cascading from the planter boxes, but otherwise, unchanged.

Like she'd just dashed out to meet a friend.

Stiff upper lip, Erin. Channel the Cowdog. I strode up the cracked concrete sidewalk to the front door, painted the same beckoning red as the chair. Knocked and waited. Knocked again.

"Hello!"

No reply. Through the window, I saw only shadow. Did it move? I couldn't tell. I wished my vision were as sharp as Hank the Cowdog's. I marched around back. Claudette had sunk herself into the garden, creating perennial borders and an herb bed that even Martha Stewart's gardener would appreciate. Anywhere else, these flowers would have long gone to seed, but gardens—and gardeners—follow a delayed schedule on the northern Rockies. Her spirit animated the place, dancing among the peonies and bleeding hearts, the daisies, foxglove, and iris.

A dark blue VW with a kayak on top pulled into the rear driveway of the house next door. James Angelo stepped out, wearing his customary black-and-red pants and white chef's jacket, and glared at me.

"You're trespassing, Erin." A bass voice in a small man is always startling.

"Paying my respects." I held up a small bouquet of yellow-gold coreopsis and scarlet monarda. "Claudette let my mother harvest herbs for her sauces. She wouldn't begrudge me a few flowers."

He gave me a long, silent glare.

"I didn't know you lived next door. Did you see her again, after you saw us talking outside the drugstore?"

His head tilted. "What are you getting at?"

Whoever killed her either knew she was going to the Festa, or ran into her there. "Just trying to figure out where she went and who she talked to."

"You think I followed her to the Festa and stabbed her in the alley? It wasn't enough to exclude me from dinner—now you're trying to shift the blame from your family to me?" He shouted across the fence and garden. "It won't work. I wasn't anywhere near your precious dinner. I was out on the river, where a man can be left alone. Maybe you ought to look closer to home." He stalked toward his house, loose cotton pants billowing. The back door slammed behind him.

"Closer to home." Meaning maybe my mother really had killed Claudette? Holy cow. What set him off? I had never imagined he'd been anywhere near the courtyard Friday night. Did the gentleman protest too much?

But if he had wanted to kill Claudette—for some unknown reason—why do it there?

Unless he wanted to make it look like Fresca had done it. Or that I had.

Alone on the river wasn't much of an alibi. And as a chef and an outdoorsman, he'd know how to use a knife.

Was I clutching at cheese straws?

Behind the Chef Boyardee facade, James Angelo was hiding something. But if it wasn't connected to Claudette's murder, did I even care?

I left town with the images from Kim's bulletin board still in my mind. They twined and tangled with images of Claudette's garden, the bright, untamed splashes that captured her so perfectly. I passed the old bowling alley, half-dismantled, a redevelopment project stalled by the economy and not yet resuscitated. Burgundy iris bloomed against the concrete block foundation. Beyond lay the lake, the cloud-filtered sunlight casting shadows on the waves. It was the light that usually caught my eye, its bright sparkle. How had I never noticed that the shadow side overtook the light as the wave rocked and roiled?

What had Claudette been up to, with her talk of opening a restaurant? Why had she wanted to talk to me before the dinner? Had she decided to come after all to see me—or someone else?

And why was Angelo such a creep?

Oh, Erin, I heard nearly everyone I knew say to me. *Stay out of it.*

Stay out of it.

Clearly many people trusted Kim—the sheriff, townspeople—and they might be right. But she had given me no reason to put my trust in her again.

I passed my turnoff and kept going. Past the old elk farm, past the cliffs and trails where my brother had once tracked mountain lions until my father found out. Past a tall sign on peeled log poles. In my years away, Ten Commandments billboards had sprung up across the valley, but I could swear this one had sprouted in the last twenty-four hours.

Thou shalt not commit adultery.
Thou shalt not kill.

Almost before I knew it, I'd reached the road to the orchard and turned in.

Thou shalt not butt in and try to solve other people's problems.

Thou shalt not stand idly by when someone accuses your mother of murder.

* * *

I knew my mother was in trouble when I smelled the prosciutto frying.

When I first left home, I'd been surprised that my idea of comfort food horrified my friends. To them, comfort food was pale and undemanding: mashed potatoes with butter or gravy, macaroni and cheese, scrambled eggs. Foods that slide down the gullet easily, barely touching the taste buds. Not that I don't love those dishes, with fresh herbs and a special touch or two. To me, comfort tastes like spaghetti Bolognese, with thick chunks of tomato and bell pepper, ground beef, pork sausage, and salty pancetta. Or a garlicky-green pesto, the aroma of crushed basil mixed with fruity olive oil chasing away whatever ails me.

Or my mother's personal choice, fettuccine carbonara, made with crumbled pork sausage and crisp prosciutto, butter, and fresh parsley, mixed—at the table is best—with beaten eggs and freshly grated Parmesan. As kids, we'd thought it our special treat. Only later, in those months alone with her after my father died, did I realize that when my mother made carbonara, she needed mothering herself.

One look at her face as she drained pasta in her battered enamel colander confirmed my diagnosis.

I brought the salad to the table and she filled our bowls with steaming pasta and sauce. She wore no makeup, and her eyes were tinged with red.

"Why is Kim wasting time investigating me when there's a killer on the loose? She must know I had nothing to do with it." Fresca rapped the end of her spoon on the table edge, the equivalent to my ears of fingernails on a chalkboard or the mindless click of a ballpoint pen. I grabbed her wrist.

"It's got to have been Dean," she continued. "They ran into each other in the alley and argued, and he got angry. He wanted to put his marriage back together, and her presence threatened that. Or maybe it was Linda. She can be pretty nasty."

As half the town had seen. "They both had motive. Mmm. This salad is terrific." Wedges of romaine, Belgian endive, and radicchio, with a country mustard vinaigrette, croutons, and shaved Parmesan. "Basil in the dressing?" She nodded.

"I went out to Claudette's," I said, trying for nonchalance. "The place looked the same, and not the same."

"I know. I went out there, too."

I stared at her, my fork in midair. "Mom, if anybody saw you—anyone who thinks you killed Claudette—that could look really bad. This is why you need a lawyer."

"Darling, don't be such a worrywart. No one was there. And Kim's not going to arrest me. She didn't tell me not to leave town, like they do on TV."

"That's TV. This is real life." Funny, since what little I knew about police investigation came from TV. "I went to talk to Kim tonight, Mom. I think—"

She held up a finger and disappeared into the kitchen. How could I tell her what I thought? That Kim had targeted her. There was no list of suspects, with photos, on the murder board. There didn't need to be. She was only waiting—

For what? For the one piece of evidence that would convince the prosecutor to file charges. The knife, the eyewitness who put them both together, or who swore he or she had seen my mother sneaking around back to meet Claudette.

She returned with a bottle of Chianti in hand and refilled our glasses. This ordeal was getting to her, I could see by her pale skin and deer-in-headlights expression.

"Mom, Friday afternoon, did you talk to Claudette?"

She played with her pasta, a slow warmth creeping up her neck. What wasn't she telling me?

"Your sister stopped by to check on me," she said. "I hear

that fellow from the Athletic Club has his eye on you. What's his name? She says he's cute."

Too bad I'd never been able to will myself from blushing. "Adam Zimmerman, and yes, he's cute, and don't change the subject. I heard a rumor that Claudette was planning to open a restaurant."

My mother's hand froze, the glass partway to her lips. "That's ridiculous. Where did you hear that?" I ignored the question—she didn't need to know I'd hacked my sister's Facebook account. "As if this town needs another restaurant," she continued. "Besides, Claudette couldn't do it alone—she'd need a chef. And where would she get the money?"

Questions swirled in my head like the pasta in my bowl. "Her divorce settlement?" I asked.

Fresca shook her head. "She needed that to live on."

How to phrase this? Turns out it's not easy to question your own family without letting them know you're snooping. "Was she after you for money?"

"Blackmail? Heavens, no."

Back to the unanswered question. "Did you talk to her Friday, Mom?"

"I called her. I was hurt, but I wanted to see her, and I told her so. She said—she said she needed to talk to me but she didn't want to be seen at the Festa. So . . ." She took a swig of wine. Her glass hit the tip of her knife and wobbled before I caught it. "So she asked me to meet her in the back alley."

Holy cow. "Why?"

"She said she couldn't come to the dinner without telling me something first. As if I wouldn't want her there if I knew."

"Did you tell Kim?" Her face said she hadn't. But Kim must have taken Claudette's phone. Which was why she hadn't been surprised to see that Claudette had also called me. She knew what calls Claudette had made, and she knew Fresca was withholding information.

"I never got there, Erin. I got occupied with the caterers and early arrivals. And, well, there was someone else I needed to see. The next thing I knew, everyone was rushing out back and she was—gone."

I believed her. But how on earth would we convince the rest of the world?

· *Fifteen* ·

I really ought to open an espresso bar. Tuesday morning, and here I was on Le Panier's doorstep again. I'd recoup the investment in no time, just from the savings on my own daily double. But I'd miss Wendy's croissants and éclairs too much.

Besides, as my mother said last night about restaurants, Jewel Bay hardly needed another coffee shop, especially off-season.

Ah, last night. I'd pushed my mother to tell Kim about the phone call—the irony after my own snooping not escaping me—and she'd finally agreed to think about it. If Kim had discovered it already, Fresca's silence would have raised more suspicions. But who else had she seen?

"That's my own business," my mother had insisted, "and no one else's."

But when murder's involved, the rules change.

I consider myself a creature of good habits when it comes to food, but variety is the spice and all that—and a change in habit might shift my perspective. So I chose a *pain au raisin* instead of my usual. Just as I started to push the door with my elbow, it swung open and I stopped before dousing Jeff Randall, Claudette's ex-husband, with hot coffee.

"Sorry." We spoke at the same time.

"It's so awful," I said. "We're so sorry." Behind him, Ian radiated pain and loneliness.

He nodded. "Must have been hard on you, finding her. We've heard the gossip, and we don't for a moment think Fresca had anything to do with it. She would never hurt anyone. They were friends, and friendship matters."

As his father spoke, a shadow crossed Ian's face, so like his mother's. His jaw clenched, and below his close-cropped hairline, his neck pulsed. Oh, the mix of emotions: shock, anger, grief, betrayal. I well remembered.

"The memorial service is scheduled now. Thursday afternoon," Jeff said. "I hope you both will come."

"Of course. Thank you for not believing the rumors." If Claudette's own family refused to suspect my mother, surely Kim would look elsewhere.

They ordered, and we chatted about life in Seattle, traveling in Asia—small nothings to fill the gap Claudette's death left. I asked Ian about school—still thinking drama at UM, or in Seattle? I'd left my own theatric ambitions behind, but was genuinely curious about his. Had he seen any Kabuki theater or Chinese opera in their travels? Though we were about the same size—Jeff was not a big man, and Claudette had been tiny—Ian seemed to stare past me, arms crossed, uninterested in chitchat. At nineteen, he was barely older than I'd been when my father died. A hit-and-run was traumatic, but it wasn't murder. No comparison, really.

Or was there? I wasn't an only child like Ian, but my brother and sister had already flown the coop. The family—both Murphys and Contis—had rallied around us, but when they went back home, whether to California or five miles down the lake, it had been my mother and me, alone together, in the house that suddenly seemed far too big. That seemed empty without my father's steadiness.

The fresh grief in Ian's eyes made my heart ache, though whether for his loss or mine, I couldn't say.

"Here you go," Wendy called, and Ian stepped to the counter. I started to tell Jeff what a great kid he had, but the exhaustion on his face silenced me. Too much sympathy can be as difficult as too little.

Ian handed Jeff a cup and paper bag. "Do either of you know what Claudette was planning to do next? When she came back from Vegas?"

"No idea." Jeff sounded baffled. But Ian looked like there'd been a goldfish in his cappuccino and he wasn't sure whether to swallow or spit it out.

It isn't squealing if someone guesses. "Was she planning to start a restaurant?"

He looked like he didn't want to respond, but saw that his father was waiting for the answer, too.

"Not start. Take over." He stared at his feet.

"Which place?" Nothing in the village was publicly for sale, but I didn't know about the rest of town. And the right offer could always be persuasive.

But he didn't know. "Where are you staying?" I asked.

Jeff answered. "At Claudette's house. It's Ian's now, until we figure out what to do with it."

Of course. "Good, good. I'm sure it's nice to be home. I bet the neighbors are glad it isn't sitting empty."

"Mrs. Taylor is nice, but her other neighbor's a creep," Ian said. Wendy's grandmother—I'd forgotten. And James Angelo. "He gave Mom a hard time."

"About what?" But Ian's tongue had loosened all it would. He shrugged, and said no more.

"We'll see you Thursday. I'm sure Fresca would be glad to help with lunch after the service."

"We'd like that," Jeff said. "Claudette would like that."

I blinked back a tear.

* * *

What restaurant had Claudette been eyeing? I carried my coffee and bun up to the office and mentally ticked them off. In the village, Chez Max, the Inn, Applause!, and the Bayside Grille were all chef-owned and set for the long haul. The others all appeared to be in safe hands. None of the cafés and casinos on the highway were a likely option, either.

I sipped my latte. What about that shuttered place north of town? It had undergone half a dozen incarnations, none successful. Bad feng shui, Liz said. Bad food, Fresca said.

Tracy arrived a few minutes later, Diet Coke and white grocery store bakery bag in hand. Time for me to go a-snooping.

First stop, kitchen shop. Heidi kept her bejeweled fingers on the hidden pulse of the village.

"Heidi, can you get real estate info from your hunky pal?" She answered with a slow, sly smile. "Say a person wanted to buy a restaurant in town. What's available?"

"You are not buying a restaurant." A statement, not a question.

"Not me. Claudette. When she was alive."

"No way. No money. Unless she had a partner. Who would have to be crazy," she said. "Claudette Randall was a delightful woman and as flaky as a box of Wheaties."

"And you told my mother so."

"Francesca makes her own decisions. I take no pleasure in having been right."

So why had Fresca been blind to Claudette's faults? Or hired her despite them?

On the sidewalk outside, I debated my next move. I needed to know Claudette's plans, her movements Friday afternoon, and who'd been repeating the stories about Claudette, Fresca, and me.

A restaurant owner might know who was buying and

selling. Much as I love Max, it wouldn't be fair to pepper him with questions given Wendy's reticence. But Ray Ramirez at the Bayside Grille—like half the town, I thought of it as "the Grillie"—was a straight shooter, and friendly.

The Grille mixed modern with Western decor for a look both warm and breezy: birch tables, driftwood hanging from the ceiling, abstracts and landscapes in bold colors on the walls. It felt handcrafted, and so did the food.

The breakfast rush had ended, though the dawdlers still nursed their coffee. Ray's *huevos rancheros* are killer, but I couldn't let food deter me from my mission. A pass-through separated the kitchen from the front counter, where I took a seat and caught Ray's attention.

"Rock and roll all weekend," he said, snapping his fingers. "Breakfast, lunch, and dinner. We don't usually do so well this early in summer—thanks."

"Great. Quick question. A chef friend from Seattle's thinking about a move, opening his own restaurant. Any possibilities around here?"

"That place north of town is empty again." He squinted, thinking. "I bet the guy at the golf course would sublease in a heartbeat—great room, tough location. Oh, and the old marina, but that kitchen needs a serious overhaul."

"Heard talk of anyone interested? My friend might like a partner." If my friend existed.

He shook his head. Behind him, in the kitchen, my eye lit on someone I totally did not expect to see. "Angelo's working for you?"

"Yeah. You know, the guy's not a half-bad cook. I needed help, and he's still got evenings free for catering."

"Did he help you Friday night?"

"Don't think so." His brow creased as he thought. "Yeah, yeah, he did, but prep only. He was gone by four, four thirty."

And stopped at the drugstore on his way—where? The swing gate opened and Angelo zipped out. "Ray, got a moment? I was thinking . . ." And then he spotted me. "What are you doing here? Tailing me all over town?"

"Just checking in after the weekend," I said. "Finding out what worked about the Festa, what didn't." Other than murder. "Congrats on the new job."

Angelo glowered, turned, and flew back into the kitchen. Ray shrugged, brown eyes placid. "Temperamental. Goes with the territory sometimes."

I murmured agreement. Did that signal a violent streak?

Next stop, Puddle Jumpers. Every town has an owner like Sally. Or two, if the karma's bad. Nothing's ever right. No one listens to her. A clique calls the shots and plays favorites. When the Merchants Association hangs flower baskets on the lampposts, she complains that the one by her shop is ugly. Blah, blah, blah.

But if I remembered right, Claudette had worked there once. What better launching pad for rumors?

"Oh, how cute." I fingered a hot pink sundress with white straps and green-and-white polka dots. "Makes me wish I were five again."

"It hung there all weekend and I only sold three."

Leaving one on the rack. Ohhh-kay. You can't please some people. "Hey, just wanted to check on you. I know you were friends with Claudette, and it's all so sad."

Sally was carefully dressed and made up, the oversized diamonds in her ears complementing her short, moussed, and frosted curls. But her features and her eyes had turned bitter long ago. "Well, it's convenient for you."

I frowned. "What do you mean?"

Sally was defiant, her glare hard as steel. "With her gone, no one can prove what your mother did to her."

One wheel in the rumor mill identified. "Which was what, exactly?"

"You know. Took advantage of her talent, her ideas, her hard work. Ran her off with no warning."

"Claudette left on her own, to chase Elvis dreams with Dean."

Her eyes darkened and she pursed her lips before speaking. "And you don't think your mother encouraged her?"

First I'd heard of that. "Fat chance. Fresca trusted Dean about as far as she could throw him."

A trio of well-heeled grandmothers entered, chattering over the cute clothes and toys. Sally's bread-and-butter, and I didn't dare stand between her and a sale. But her parting look as I walked out said I'd learn no more from her, no matter how many questions I asked.

A sign of the temperature in the village, or Sally's usual malcontent?

I sighed and pushed open the florist's door. The oversized worktable in the back screamed bad idea. It was deep with gladioluses in white, coral, and deep red. Funeral flowers. The very sight of them sent me back to the high school gym where my father's memorial service had been held. The death of a popular teacher in a hit-and-run was a tragedy for the town, not just my own family. He'd belonged to every kid who'd ever been in his classroom or on one of his sports teams, to their parents, to our friends and their parents, to every one who'd grown up going into Murphy's Mercantile for groceries or to buy a quarter's worth of double-chocolate malted milk balls from the glass canister on the front counter. But the very public grief had seemed to rob my family of our own time to mourn.

Shake it off, Erin. It's not like no one else is ever going to die in your life.

I'd handled my father's death well for years. But now, back in my hometown, with my mother and my former best friend caught up in another death, my defenses slipped.

At the sight of the box filled with birds of paradise, I fled.

· *Sixteen* ·

The knit and sew bug has never bitten me. But who doesn't love wandering through quilt and yarn shops, filling your eyes with color, twining your way through magic? And though Jewel Bay calls itself The Food Lovers' Village, Dragonfly Dry Goods is a key ingredient in the town's appeal.

For me, it was respite after my confrontations with Angelo and Sally. As always, I drooled mentally over the quilt hanging behind the cutting table: a kaleidoscopic dragonfly hovering above garden green foliage, all made more vibrant by the black background and red-and-gold fabric frame. While Kathy cut yardage and chatted with her customer about a quilt project, I stroked lustrous mohair from Angora goats raised at the foot of Jewel Basin, in the mountains east of town, and touched a skein of kid mohair to my cheek. Softer than Sandburg, though I wouldn't tell him.

Her customer left, and her gray eyes turned sympathetic. "That bad, huh?"

"I need to solve this crime before the whole town turns against Fresca."

She rewrapped and pinned the bolts she'd just cut. "Strong women aren't always popular."

"Claudette worked here before she went to Red's, right? What happened?"

"Too many mistakes. Measuring fabric was like rocket science to her."

I smiled. "I mean, at Red's."

She cocked her head. "My impression was she wanted to work more closely with your mother and Tracy. And restaurant work is hard."

"She said that? So why would she want to go back to it?" I told her what I knew.

"Sounds crazy to me. I never heard Claudette express any entrepreneurial ambition." Neither had anyone else. But there were those Facebook posts. "Wish I could help you more, Erin. But I don't listen to talk. Rumor doesn't sell yarn."

If the killer were local, and not random—as Kim seemed convinced—maybe the key question was not who would benefit from killing Claudette, but who would benefit from casting suspicion on my mother.

At that thought, a firecracker exploded in my chest.

A pair of full-figured middle-aged women entered and beelined for a yummy display of yarn. Hand-spun, hand-painted colorways inspired by the West, according to the sign.

"Thanks, Kath." I left Dragonfly and trudged back to the Merc, mulling over the various threads and threats. My mother hired Claudette to manage the Merc against the advice of her friends, all successful business owners. Claudette was gathering info on restaurant management and told her son she planned to take over an existing operation, but she had minimal experience and no cash—and no local joints were for sale. With Ian out of high school, she had few ties to Jewel Bay—but I'd uncovered nothing to suggest she had her eyes on another town.

The aroma of fresh bread brought me back to the present. Despite her closed mouth—or because of it—Wendy did hear a lot about the goings-on in town. Getting her to talk could crack things open. I popped in, but the young woman at the counter—a member of the summer Playhouse stage crew at night—said she was elbow-deep in dough. Later.

In deference to her grief, I hadn't quizzed Tracy about the rumors or Claudette's plans. Might be time. Buttonhole her now, or query Old Ned?

Before I could decide, a white truck outfitted with racks and huge sheets of glass pulled up in front of the Merc.

"This would be the place," the driver said, eyeing my plywood window.

"This would be the place," I agreed.

The crew had obviously done this before, but it was all new to me, so I watched the painstaking—or panes-taking—process from a safe distance. First, they carefully removed the plywood and broken glass. The sight of those sharp edges pricked my skin. They fitted the replacement window onto a roller, glided it across the sidewalk, then lifted it into place using powerful suction cups. Two men kept their grip on the bottom, and I held my breath while the third tipped the glass up against the back frame, using heavy tape to hold it secure. Next, he reinstalled the wooden stops. I couldn't help noticing that the old wooden trim needed a touch-up. One more project for the list.

One man cleaned the glass while the others packed their gear. Finally, they popped open frosty water bottles and leaned against their truck to catch their breath and admire their work.

I fetched them each a jar of jam as thanks. Nobody ever refuses.

Talk about an instant mood lift. Light poured in and the gloom that had clung to the Merc the last few days vanished.

So, unfortunately, had my opportunity to chat up Old Ned before his lunch rush. He'd be flipping burgers and boiling waffle-cut potatoes in oil for at least another hour. And I couldn't talk to Tracy, either. With no one else to watch the shop, any probing conversation would have to wait.

Tuesdays aren't hot for tourist traffic. Last week's visitors are on the road to elsewhere, and the new crop hasn't arrived yet. But inside the Merc, Tracy held a picnic basket for a woman in white crops and a royal purple sweatshirt. Their conversation mirrored our talk about helping customers create a meal with our products—not pick out odd ingredients they didn't have a use for. She might not be committed yet to the Mission, but I sensed progress.

And maybe she was getting over her resentment of me.

In the kitchen, I found Fresca organizing for a sauce-making stint. "Erin, darling, where have you been? Go out to Rainbow Lake Garden for me and pick up tomatoes and basil. And eggs. I've already called Johanna and told her you're on your way."

We'd agreed she would let me make the orders, but I didn't have the heart to chide her. Better to see the Fresca we all knew and loved back—at least for a while.

"And no one would even know we carry cheese—we're wiped out," she continued, deep into command mode. "Swing by the Creamery on your way back."

Summertime, and the living is busy. I slid Jody Fisher's CD into the player and cranked up the volume. Good stuff. On the dirt road that led to Rainbow Lake—not much more than a swimming hole—I closed my windows to keep out the dust, then turned at the rustic sign marking the farm lane. A movement on the right caught my eye and I braked. In the meadow, a tiny spotted fawn wobbled next to her mother. Behind her, a larger doe sized me up. Grandma, or an aunt, on guard duty.

The first fawn sighting. Summer had truly arrived.

Jo and Phyl—short for Phyllis—had Fresca's order boxed and ready by the garden gate.

"Three fawns," Phyl said in her Kiwi accent. "Twins in the far meadow."

"You heard about Claudette," I said. They didn't get into town much—town came to them—but they knew everyone.

"Shame," Jo said. "We liked her, though we had our trials."

I'd worked hard to clean up the problems other vendors had experienced with Claudette. "Not to gossip," I said, "but just to make sure we don't repeat her mistakes, can you be more specific?"

They traded one of those subtle couple-looks that spoke volumes to them and nothing to me. Danish Jo, blond and golden tan, six inches taller than ruddy Phyl, who wasn't stocky but looked it next to her partner. How they'd met and how they'd gotten here, I couldn't imagine.

"Big row last summer," Phyl said. "She ordered for both the Merc and your mother, and messed up quantities constantly. She'd call midaft for stuff we'd already picked and insist we pick again, despite the pain in the arse and the effect of the heat on the veg. Or she'd ask us to bring things in, then say she needed something else instead."

"That's why we don't deliver anymore." Jo fanned herself with her straw beach hat.

"None of that nonsense with you," Phyl said. "You value us and what we offer the community. Who needs Whole Foods or Trader Joe's?"

Not the time to confess I planned a trip to SavClub in Pondera later. "The climate's a challenge, but I believe we can develop a market."

She nodded. "Good on you. And your support's spurring us to work harder, too—try more early-and-late season varieties, more storage crops. Maybe build a winter greenhouse."

They were counting on me to make this work. My jaw tightened. Every decision I made had a ripple effect.

"You two supply quite a few restaurants, don't you? Any changing hands—new owner or manager?"

"A few seasonal changes in menus, but that's all," Jo said. "Why?"

I rubbed the back of my neck. "Just following a wild hare."

"Gotta watch those wild hares," Phyl said. "Or they'll bite you in the arse."

I laughed and slid the last box of produce into my car. Jo handed me a bouquet of Shasta daisies, pink and purple delphiniums, purple foxglove, and blushing pink peonies with ruffled white edges. "Keep an eye on your mother. She's a friend to us."

Back on Cutoff Road, I drove east half a mile to the Creamery. The owners, who'd built their kids' 4-H goats and dairy cows into a family business, exchanged the empty cooler I'd brought for one loaded with Fresca's shop order. I delivered the huckleberry honey they'd asked for and took off.

As I pulled onto Cutoff Road, a dark blue VW with a kayak on top whizzed past me, inches away and well over the 50 mph speed limit.

Innocent enough. Everybody in town drove this road from time to time—why not Angelo?

So why did I suddenly feel like those wild hares were getting way too close?

Back Street still made me shiver, but I took a deep breath and parked outside our gate. The hinge creaked, reminding me of my date with Liz to brainstorm a courtyard makeover.

To my surprise, the section of fence dividing our courtyard from Red's stood ajar. I kicked it shut.

A crate of tomatoes in my arms, I freed two fingers to open the Merc's back door, then wedged my foot and backside in and wriggled through. With my head down and the door slamming shut behind me, I didn't see or hear Ted Redaway before we smacked into each other.

"Criminy." I managed to keep my grip on the box, but the top layer of tomatoes went flying. "Watch out!"

Ted pushed past me, his face beefsteak red, as fruit splattered the walls and floor.

I carried the box into the kitchen and grabbed wet rags, muttering bad words. I was prying a tomato seed from between two planks with my thumbnail when Fresca descended from the office, a vegetable-print apron protecting her navy-and-cream-striped T-shirt and cropped khakis, her feet in the cherry red Keds she saved for sauce-making day.

"Ted," I said. "Blustering through without watching where he was going."

Only then did I notice her unusual pallor, followed by a rapid deep flush. Her eyes flared and her right hand rose sharply then fell, as if to lift a cleaver but deciding there was no point.

She sat on the bottom step, her face in her hands.

"Mom, it's okay. Six tomatoes, eight max. There's dozens left, not even bruised. And more boxes in the car."

She raised her eyes, bright with rage, and shook her head.

"What is it? Did something happen?" Something else . . .

"It doesn't concern you, Erin." She pushed herself up and headed up front without another word.

What the heck? But no time to find out—not with a car full of perishables and a wet, sticky floor.

A few minutes later, I'd hauled all the produce inside. Only the cooler was left. It really needed two people, but Tracy had the shop and I didn't want to disturb my mother. She was disturbed enough.

A knight in black leather approached, hands up. "Erin, yell at me all you want. I deserve it."

Apologetic was not Ted's style. Sarcastic, rude, crude, and on occasion, mildly amusing. He'd gotten my Jell-O up, as he was prone to do, but grudges weren't my style. "Help me drag this cooler inside and you're forgiven."

He slid one end out of the hatchback while I maneuvered the other. "Geez, what you got in this thing?" It came out "whutchew." "Bricks?"

"Not geez—cheese." I grinned. "Cheese bricks."

He set his end down, forcing me to do the same. "Erin, I got to talk to you. Seriously. I been thinking."

He sounded so earnest that I stifled my smart-ass comment. "Shoot."

"I been thinking about your plans for the Merc—one-stop shopping, farm-to-table, all that stuff." He fingered the edge of his red bandanna sweat rag. "Wouldn't you be better off up on the highway?"

"Nope. The action's in the village."

"But downtown's always crowded. Never enough parking." He gestured at the dusty lot behind me, half full even on Tuesday. "More visibility out there."

"More walk-in customers down here. The highway's great for essentials, like gas, auto parts, the Laundromat. But people don't stop and browse out there—they come into the village for that." I reached for the cooler handle.

"I'm only thinking about you, Erin. Do you want to be reminded about murder every time you unload your car?"

Good question. But I would never give up this property, and I knew Fresca felt the same, even though it had come from my father's family, not hers. She viewed it as our legacy. You'd think Ted would understand that.

"Murphy's Mercantile is staying put," I said.

"Then you better hope your pal Kim gets that Elvis creep behind bars soon, so we can all put this tragedy behind us."

We dragged the load inside and Ted left, not saying another word about the mess. It was as much my fault as his, but heck—I run the joint. No reason to be on alert for blindsiding neighbors in my own back hall.

Yellow plums, red Romas, and Early Girls obscured the kitchen's stainless steel prep surfaces. Stainless steel bowls held garlic, peppers, and basil.

A large white cutting board lay next to the sink, where Fresca washed and sorted tomatoes. The sights and smells whisked me back to childhood—pots bubbling, steam on windows, all three kids with mouths watering crowding the kitchen doorway.

And she hadn't even started cooking yet.

I glanced at the knife block. All accounted for. I grabbed the whiteboard and marker, scribbled, FRESH GARDEN SAUCE—DEMO TODAY, and propped it on an easel. Demos are a great enticement. And a great appetite whetter. I popped a frosty Pellegrino Aruncíata—love that sweet-tart orange flavor—and headed next door to check out Wendy's lunch specials. The call of the wild quiche quickened my step.

No quiche today, and the spinach and three-cheese croissants had sold out. As Wendy readied my prosciutto Caprese panini—with fresh buffalo mozzarella—for the press, I considered my approach. You never know what will raise her hackles.

"Your grandmother lives—lived—near Claudette, doesn't she? I hope she's not too upset by the . . ." I hesitated over the ugly word.

"The murder?" Wendy wiped her bread knife clean. "Of her next-door neighbor, who watched out for her? Who was sweet and generous to everyone? She's terrified. Plus the sheriff's been crawling all over the place, and God knows who else."

Me, for one.

"She can hardly sleep." Wendy's voice cracked. "And to think—oh, never mind."

"Wendy, never mind what?"

The panini press buzzed and she whipped around, busying herself wrapping my sandwich. She thrust the bag at me.

"Wendy, if you know something about the murder, tell me. Or tell Kim."

"Butt out, Erin. You don't know what you're asking." She shot me daggers, then stalked away into the floury recesses of Le Panier.

No, I sure didn't. And it didn't seem like Wendy Taylor Fontaine was going to help me figure that out anytime soon.

Not until I was back inside the Merc did I realize I hadn't asked her about restaurants.

I grabbed the latest issue of *Entrepreneur* and took my lunch to the courtyard. I'd gotten halfway through—Wendy makes a wicked panini—and deep into an article on motivating your sales force when Liz called "Hello!" and stepped into my dusty oasis. In forest green knit pants and an orange, yellow, and green print top, she provided much-needed color to the dreary place.

Hands on her hips, she surveyed the landscape. "What's your budget?" I tried not to look freaked out. "Don't worry," she said in a reassuring tone. "We'll work the same kind of magic out here as you've created inside."

"I hadn't planned on a courtyard project this year, but after the Festa, the place is begging for a boost."

She nodded, her dark bob barely moving. "Let's start with a cleansing. Then we'll have a better sense of the energies we're facing."

Ideas that sound whacky off other tongues seem perfectly reasonable when Liz suggests them. When I moved into the cabin, she'd smudged it thoroughly, and oriented me to the feng shui quadrants in the space. Now she extracted a sage and sweetgrass braid from her bag and lit it. What a smell—sweet, pungent, and wild, like a prairie fire without the danger.

Slowly, we walked the perimeter, pausing at each corner to fan the smoke. At the gate between our place and Red's, she took an extra moment, muttering an incantation. I latched the gate. Why had Ted come into the Merc this way? Why had he been in the Merc at all?

When we reached our back gate, Liz's prayer grew longer and louder. "Hang something red here," she said. "To enhance the fire energy."

All I could offer was a leftover geranium, in a heavy wire hanger.

"This will do for now," she said, "but look for something else—a fire symbol, or a human or animal shape, in a shade of red. Until then, water it every day. Can't have dead things in your fame and reputation corner."

Certainly not.

I couldn't keep myself from glancing down the alley.

"Show me where you found her," Liz said. Chilled in the bright sunshine, hand trembling, I pointed. Liz waved her smudging stick in the four directions, then lifted it to the sky and lowered it toward the ground.

The sharp odor brought a sense of peace.

Peace and determination.

After Liz left, I checked on my mother. Rich tomatoey smells punctuated with garlic and fennel filled the place. As usual, when she was in "creative chef" mode, I had to call her name three times and rap a wooden spoon on the counter before she noticed me. Whatever had upset her earlier didn't seem to bc bothering her now.

What a relief. We talked briefly about dishes for the funeral lunch and I headed into the shop. As always, the sight made my heart pulse an extra beat.

The memorial sign for Claudette would stay up until

after the service. Meanwhile, I replaced the plant with a vase of Jo and Phyl's fresh flowers. Stimulate that feng shui.

I make a big deal of "buy local," and I do mean it. But you just can't get everything you need in Jewel Bay. Brain-tanned doeskin jackets, check. Montana sapphire earrings, check. Socks and underwear, get thee to Pondera. I see no reason to give my money to the chain grocery store in town when I can give less of it to a chain store in the next town for the same items. After all, a community like ours draws from the entire region, so I try to support the region. Plus I strolled into SavClub in Pondera with the Merc's shopping list in my pocket, so I told myself I was here on business.

Or maybe it was all an elaborate ruse to treat myself to a berry smoothie and stock up on imported cheese at a great price.

A visit to SavClub is a bit like old home week. As a buyer, I'd been headquarters staff, but I'd also worked two shifts a month in a store in the Seattle area. These days, a trip can take hours as I study new products and spy out changes. Helps me stay current, too—nobody spots the trends, knows its customers, or solves problems like SavClub.

No time for that today. I loaded up on supplies for home and shop, and picked out a few new wines to try. En route to the paper products, I paused to marvel at a Father's Day display of gourmet cookies and candy—a gaping hole in our product line. We really needed some primo chocolates—truffles, toffee, bark.

A runaway cart crashed into mine, scooting it sideways, followed by a string of loud curses. "Well, if it isn't Miss Buy Local, sneaking in a trip to the big city."

"Hello, Linda." I pointed to the case of tissue in my cart. "Nobody in Jewel Bay makes TP." I glanced at her cart—everyone does it—then stifled my surprise. Bags of powdered sugar and candy sprinkles, along with plastic buckets of chocolate clusters and chocolate-covered peppermints. Had she been trying to pass commercial chocolates off as handmade? Or dust them with sugar and cocoa powder and claim full credit?

Anyone willing to commit such a sin could easily be a killer.

She sniffed, grabbed her cart, and sashayed off, her plush fanny swinging like a pendulum. She must buy her clothes in the one-size-too-small shop, where pockets are outlawed. A straw hobo bag hung off one arm. I tried to picture her Friday night. She'd carried a bag—one of those teensy beaded things just big enough for a lipstick and a tissue.

Nowhere to hide a knife. I piled cases of San Pellegrino in my cart and conjured up an image of Dean in his Elvis suit. No extra room there, either.

It was a serious question. Kim had considered the Merc's kitchen knives, but the weapon could have been much smaller. How long a blade would be lethal? Would it depend on the victim's size—tiny Claudette, or paunchy Ted?

I scooped up a jar of mixed nuts with extra cashews—an occasional indulgence—then remembered 9 volt batteries for the smoke alarms. And there on the end cap was a display of folding knives. Some had three-inch blades, some four, sealed inside clear plastic. A stainless steel clip could slide over a waistband or a pants pocket.

"If you want to try one," a male customer said to me, "go to Sporty's. Heck, you can even find these in the drugstore, though the price is better here."

Dean's office was next to Jewel Bay Drug. Everyone in town shopped there at one time or another—Angelo, Fresca, Tracy.

Even me.

· *Seventeen* ·

I walked into the Merc cautiously this time. The kitchen stood empty. I'd just deposited the last box on the counter when Fresca dashed in, clutching her phone.

"What do you think you're doing?"

Therapists say no one can make you feel bad without your permission, but they're obviously forgetting about mothers.

"You've been interrogating people," she continued. "Asking questions about me and Claudette and this—this tragedy."

"Well, you're not doing anything to defend yourself."

"I don't need to defend myself. I need you to stop interfering."

"Kim Caldwell's rattling her handcuffs in your ear, and you still think she's a harmless teenager who'll come to her senses any minute now. Smell the coffee, Mom. It's burning."

Something was burning, and it was the look in her eyes. No, it was the pan on the stove, smoking. I grabbed an oven mitt, tossed the pan into the sink, and turned off the flame.

My mother had disappeared.

This is why I hate small towns. Why I couldn't wait to leave when I graduated, why Nick preferred wolves. And why Chiara had lit out for San Francisco, though she and Jason had responded to Jewel Bay's siren call when Landon came along.

Another word for small is microscopic. As in, under the microscope. Under scrutiny. Underfoot and under eyes. They see all, they know all, they tell all.

And even when you're thirty-two, they can't wait to tell your mother.

Fresca had fled the building, leaving her phone on the kitchen counter. Her Volvo was not in its usual spot. Worry and anger warred in my brain, and in my gut.

The killer was still out there. How could she be so blind to danger?

Out front, Tracy sat behind the cash register, reading the weekly paper, Diet Coke at hand. I wanted to crush the can.

Watch out, Erin. You are not fit for human company. I retreated to the office, swiveling my secondhand Aeron chair like the rusty Tilt-A-Whirl at the county fair. I'd begged my dad to let me ride, then thrown up all over him. Which I felt like doing right now.

All that hard work, and everything was crashing down.

"You don't have to do this," I said out loud. "You didn't create the problem and you don't have to solve it. You don't have to rescue her, and you don't have to rescue this shop. You can go home, grab Mr. Sandburg, and ride off into the sunset."

My laptop sat on the desk and I punched it to life. Figures—the first icon I spotted was our mission statement, and next to it, the vendor list.

I'd wanted to be the center of the wheel, not just another cog. But the spokes depend on the center. It must hold. If I walked away, the Merc would fail. Maybe I couldn't keep my mother out of jail, but I had to try. And I had to keep the Merc up and running, and keep Tracy, Jo and Phyl, and all the other vendors in the game, too.

Dang. I could really use a pound of huckleberry truffles right now.

Lacking good chocolate, I needed a plan. First, find the real killer. I thought about *Law and Order*, and *Homicide*. Sure, they were made up, but TV writers understood what cops really did, didn't they? Kept paid consultants on staff, even. And the true crime shows, like *Dateline* and *48 Hours*—who hadn't seen a few reruns, on sleepless nights? Or *America's Most Wanted*.

Dean Vincent, local bone cracker and Elvis Impersonator, hardly seemed to fit the killer mold, although Ted seemed convinced of his guilt, too. But didn't those shows prove that you never knew the killer next door?

I created a spreadsheet with a list of names and columns for motive, opportunity, means. I saw what the initial letters spelled, and reversed the last two labels. Dean first, then Linda. Motive, easy. Means? Kim's questions made a knife most likely, though I couldn't rule out a shooting. Consider everyone and everything, then narrow it down—isn't that what Mark Harmon or Mariska Hargitay would do? If they were real and working homicide in Jewel Bay.

Dean didn't seem like the hunting type, but looks are deceiving. And plenty of men and women own guns for protection, especially if they live in the country or hike a lot. Though I still thought we'd have heard a bang if Claudette had been shot.

Who else had Claudette dated? Any killers lurking in those shadows? Who could I ask, besides my mother? Why was I coming up with more questions than answers?

Next column, opportunity. Which really meant: *Could they have been in Back Street at 6 p.m. last Friday night?*

I had provided the killer's opening, by bringing all these people together and inviting Claudette. But I hadn't pulled the trigger or thrust the hilt or whatever had happened. *Shake it off, Erin. Shake it off.*

I closed my eyes and tried to visualize all the people I'd seen come in the back gate. Gordy Springer, the pharmacist, who'd stayed with the body till the paramedics came. He'd come solo—his wife, an antiques dealer, had gone to a show in Missoula.

The musicians had been in and out for a good thirty minutes. What about Sam and Jennifer? Jen and Claudette had clashed big-time, and I'd had to work hard, offering business advice and my sister's design services, to calm Jen down. Murder, over that? Too ridiculous to contemplate. I input her name anyway. For all I knew, she could be an escaped serial killer hiding in plain sight.

Talk about ridiculous. But the real point stuck out: Perfectly pleasant people have secrets they'd rather not expose. Unexpected tensions buzz just beneath seemingly smooth surfaces.

And everyone gets their Jell-O up from time to time.

In all fairness, I had to add Fresca to the list. And myself. People thought I had motive, and the point of this exercise was as much to rule suspects out as to rule them in. Tracy. Ned. According to Kathy at the Dragonfly, Claudette had quit work at Red's abruptly and left Ned in the lurch. His kind heart aside, this was about opportunity. I couldn't believe anyone on my list had killed Claudette deliberately, with malice aforethought—whatever that was.

But in the heat of the moment, maybe.

A new theme emerged. Claudette had made a habit of quitting jobs abruptly. Who else nursed a grudge? I added a note. I love spreadsheets.

Speaking of notes, where was hers? I scribbled Fresca a reminder to look for it.

One by one, I worked my way through the names and columns. What about Jeff? He and Ian made the five-hundred-mile drive—or two-hour flight—from Seattle regularly. Any viable list of suspects should include the spouse. At least on TV. I added him.

The only other person whose whereabouts—now there's a criminal word for you—I felt reasonably sure of was Tracy, who'd been standing next to me before I went out to the alley. And just before that, she'd been scurrying around the courtyard, doing Fresca's bidding.

Where had Fresca been at the key moment? That blank cell on the spreadsheet dared me to find another explanation.

Ned had been right there, too. Or had he? Truth be told, I hadn't paid close attention. We'd each had our tasks, and I'd trusted everyone to get them done.

Finding a killer would be a lot easier if there'd been a stranger in our midst. Someone who didn't belong.

I rubbed my eyes and put the computer to bed. On TV, the killer lurks in the shadows the whole time, where the cops barely notice him, thumbing his nose at justice until all the pieces fall into place, three minutes before the hour.

In real life, no such script.

I knew I ought to run my mother's phone out to her house, but I was still too peeved. Later, after we'd cooled off.

Meanwhile, when in doubt, rule everyone out. If that wasn't an official investigator's motto, it ought to be. Maybe I'd suggest it to the Cowdog.

I left the village by the back road and swung by Claudette's house. Jeff sat in the front porch rocker, a beer bottle on Claudette's white wicker table.

"Hey, Jeff. Just wanted to say Fresca will bring a tortellini salad and fruit skewers on Thursday." Lame opening, but this unobtrusive probing was tricky.

"Thanks. Care for a cold one?"

I shook my head. "So you and Ian were in China? Buying and selling antiques? That must be fascinating."

"We'd just gotten back to Seattle Thursday night. Thank

God this didn't happen earlier. I handle some antiques, some reproductions, working with local craftsmen and small factories. I go over a few times a year. Been great to have Ian traveling with me."

"I know it isn't really any of my business"—though I'd been acting like it was—"but did Dean Vincent break up your marriage?"

Jeff looked surprised. "No. Claudette and I were never right for each other. The travel didn't help. She knew Dean, of course—our kids were friends, and it's a small town—but I'm sure they didn't get involved until we were through." His eyes filled and closed. I sensed another presence, and spotted Ian standing at the open window. Bowls and plates filled with food, no doubt brought by friends and neighbors, covered the kitchen counter. How much had Ian heard? Jeff rubbed his eye with his left hand, drawing his fingers down to his square jaw. He opened his eyes slowly, gaze still focused on the past. "Claudette was like a baby bird. No matter how infuriating she could be, you'd never hurt her."

His description of Claudette was right on, but his conclusion wrong. Someone had hurt her, and I was no closer to knowing who.

But violent crime has many victims. I glanced up. Ian was gone.

"Wise men say, only fools rush in . . ." Not a great soundtrack for an impromptu interview of a possible killer, but here I stood, on the sidewalk in front of Dean Vincent's condo. The uncurtained window gave the neighborhood a full frontal view of his living room rehearsal. No question, he had the look—the tucked chin and earnest eyes, and the moves—those famous swiveling hips.

Maybe the King had just needed a decent chiropractor.

"I was in the neighborhood." Thinking up excuses to drop in on people is tough. "Hope I'm not interrupting."

Dean smoothed his hands over his royal blue hip-hugger bell bottoms, the shirt open way too far. "Rehearsals go better in costume. It sets the mood."

"You must have loved Vegas." The living room looked like a designer's sketch for a casino hotel lobby, circa 1970: a sleek black leather banquette-style couch, a pair of chrome chairs upholstered in white leather, a zebra-patterned shag rug beneath a glass-topped table. The only things missing were neon lights and a lava lamp. "Bet it was hard to come back."

He raked a hand through his gelled hair, not quite as rakish as Elvis's. "We all need a break now and then. I'm lucky to have my work and my art."

Art. I supposed so, in a certain light. "So you didn't intend to leave Jewel Bay? To give up your practice?"

"Heck, no." He sank onto the couch and waved me toward a chair.

Surprisingly comfy. "Where'd you find this furniture?"

"Vintage, mostly. Linda and I collected it over the years." He reddened at the mention of his not-exactly-ex wife.

"From the looks of things, I'm guessing you'll be moving it all back to her house soon."

What was that line about building dreams on suspicious minds?

"Did we all misunderstand Claudette? We thought you two made a permanent escape."

His hands twitched reflexively. "Claudette believed what she wanted. Don't get me wrong—she was great." A bead of sweat dripped down his cheek, and not from exercise.

"But?"

He shrugged. "As I said, magical thinking. She blew it all out of proportion."

In other words, what happens in Vegas stays in Vegas.

"Did Claudette tell you I'd invited her to the Festa dinner?"

"That's why she was there? I thought maybe—" He interrupted himself, then stood. "You should leave now, Erin."

"What did you think?" He had the pout, without the sex appeal. "That she intended to harangue you in front of your wife, and the whole town? Does that sound like her?" The sound system—karaoke with costumes—started a new tune. *"Don't be cruel, to a heart that's true."*

He looked lower than an ant's belly, as my grandfather Murphy would have said. Maybe Dean and Claudette had a real connection after all. "No. She could be a drama queen, and she was angry enough that she wouldn't have minded embarrassing me. But she would never deliberately humiliate herself in public."

True enough. "You and Linda arrived together?" He nodded. "Which way did you come in?"

"Which way did we come in? Through Red's front door. We got lucky and found a parking spot out front. I told the detective all this." He shut the door firmly behind me. The music stopped and started up again. *"Love me tender."* Yeah, right.

Of course, no reason they couldn't have been using each other. He for a break from his marriage, and she for adventure, in a life lacking direction. Still, I did not believe she had meant to hurt anyone—least of all my mother,—with her abrupt departure, or the supposed rumors.

And you, Dean Vincent. You ain't nothing but a hound dog. I'd love to see you make that jailhouse rock.

The Pinskys' covered deck is as near to paradise as you can get with a roof overhead. I leaned on the rail and gazed over the landscape below, lush with native shrubs. Across the lake, the Salish hills formed a pattern against the sky, each ridge a layer of slightly deeper blue, though up close, they were a mosaic in green. Light and distance change everything.

The crisp, citrus-y wine tasted like sailing. When all this was over—whatever this was—I'd cajole Bob into taking me out for a day on the water. I had a hunch Adam Zimmerman would be up for any outdoor adventure. And a lot more fun than that hunky-but-snooty Rick Bergstrom. Liz patted the spot next to her on the love seat, its burnished aluminum frame vaguely old-world, the loose cushions perfect for my modern derriere.

"Best to treat the courtyard as an extension of the building. The space has good bones. Perfect proportions. But you need a focal point." She touched a sunset orange nail to a drawing of the cement block wall between the Merc and Le Panier, and a fountain surrounded by rocks and ferns. "A water feature will add ambience, without protruding into the usable space."

Ambience. Just the ticket.

"We'll soften those hard surfaces with greenery. Grape vines, I think—they turn such a vibrant red in the fall." She rattled on about tables and chairs, colors and elements and enhancing the feng shui, especially in the wealth and prosperity quadrant. "You'll feel the change instantly."

In the bottom line. No magical thinking here. "It looks fabulous. Let me show the drawings to my mother." If she would talk to me. I might be the manager, but she did own the place.

Dinner started with a salad of mesclun greens, baby carrots, and thinly sliced cucumber, all from Rainbow Lake Garden, and a light sesame-ginger dressing. Bob had skinned the salmon fillets, marinated them in rosemary, olive oil, garlic, and cayenne, added a squeeze of fresh lemon and seasoning, then grilled them on skewers with onion wedges and chunks of red and green bell pepper. I hardly needed any more carbs today, but couldn't refuse a hunk of country bread. If Le Panier didn't have a successful summer, Wendy couldn't blame it on me.

Stomach content, mind churning, I drained my glass. I couldn't relax. I needed answers.

"My head is spinning. Not from the wine. Turns out

that everything I thought I knew about Claudette was wrong."

"Like what?" Liz said, swatting a mosquito. Bob lit a citronella lantern—red glass, strategically located in the fame and reputation spot.

"I thought she was a great friend of Fresca's, but she accused my mother of stealing her recipes. I thought she was a trusted, reliable employee—now I hear she worked in half the shops in town and quit on a dime for the next great thing. And instead of moving to Las Vegas for good, she planned to come back here and start a restaurant—"

"You're joking."

"—but the biggest mystery of all is how my mother, whom everyone agrees has great people sense, how she could know all that and still hire her."

They exchanged looks and I could almost hear them trying to decide, over the air waves, what to say and what to keep to themselves.

"You know something, don't you? Don't tell me to ask my mother—she won't talk. But if I'm going to keep the Merc afloat and hang on to the Murphy legacy, then I deserve to know."

Liz sighed and extended a hand, nails flashing in the last rays of sunlight. "Fresca will be furious with me for talking, but I'll take my lumps. Bob, would you bring out the lemon tart? And more wine?

"Erin, honey," she said, her tone low and serious. "Your mother had a really rough time after your father died. More than you know. More than we knew—we were strictly summer people then. I called to check on her regularly, but I couldn't see how lost she was. Adrift."

My mother likes to say that Italians let everything hang out. But she'd hidden her feelings from me. Or I'd been too self-absorbed to notice.

"Don't blame yourself, Erin," Liz continued. "You were young. You could not have understood what she was going through. Claudette was new in town, with a young son and a traveling husband. She became the friend Fresca needed. They spent hours together, talking, listening, cooking—comforting each other."

My eyeballs felt like they were stretching their lids. A million images flashed through my mind—Power Point Brain. My dad alive, then dead. My image of his smashed car—I'd never actually seen it. Why hadn't she let me see it? Or see him? Why did I never insist?

Why was everyone always trying to protect me?

"Fresca held it together through the summer, until you left for college. She was terrified that if you saw her struggle, you'd quit school and come home."

The mental slide show sped on: Fresca taking me to the university that fall. Watching from my room in Turner Hall as she came out, alone, then turned and looked up to search for my window.

I tried to remember her at Thanksgiving and Christmas breaks. Nothing. A blank. Which said a lot. "Nick and Chiara?"

"Already caught up in their own lives. They didn't worry her so much. Realize, Erin, she kept it from you because she loved you. The last thing she wanted to do was add to your pain."

"But why Claudette?"

"The right friend at the right time. She understood how to help Fresca cope. And you know your mother. When Claudette got divorced just as her son was leaving home, she felt unmoored. Fresca became her anchor. Fresca never forgets a friend."

The lantern flickered. I closed my eyes, not sure how much more I wanted to hear. "You said they cooked together. What about the recipes? Fresca says they were hers, from Noni and Papa."

Liz spoke. "Launching a business alone is tough. Fresca

needed a sounding board and a dog's body. No reason to think Claudette played any other role."

To the west, the hills had become shadows, the ridges merging into one another. "If she didn't want me to come back home then, why ask me this time?"

"This time," Bob said, "coming home was your choice, not a reflex. An opportunity, not a retreat."

I picked up my dessert fork. No retreat.

· Eighteen ·

Sandburg sat in front of the open closet, yowling. It looked like fun, but I needed to get to the Merc. There were threads to follow, questions to ask.

He reached out and pawed my red boots. My power boots. Perfect for the back gate, if I didn't love them so much. I slid into a navy skirt and my cute new button-back tank—red, blue, and yellow swirls on white—and the boots.

Bob and Liz's revelations about the depth of my mother's despair and her loyalty to Claudette had surprised me—but also explained what I had glimpsed and never understood. Ask anyone to describe Fresca, and even if they don't like her, they'd say "smart, energetic, and loyal."

Which makes her sound like Sparky the Border collie, my childhood dog.

Hadn't Sparky been one of Dad's nicknames for Mom? One of half a million.

My parents had adored each other. Half the town had adored them. Mr. Murphy, beloved history teacher, respected coach, trusted friend. But when he came home, he was just Dad—half of Mom-and-Dad.

As a kid, of course, I knew that they had a bond separate from their relationships with each of us. But still, they always made me feel like part of their team.

Had I never understood what losing him meant to her? Or did I simply see it in a different way, now that I'm older, and she and I are in business together? Now that we stand on adult ground.

Working with, or for, your mother requires more flexibility than I had anticipated. More than learning to call her Fresca instead of Mom. More than holding my own in discussions, expecting her to listen and respect my decisions, not turning to her for a rescue in sticky moments.

It also means seeing her vulnerabilities. Recognizing when she's off center, and giving her enough space—but not too much. I had assumed she'd be fine, that she'd be Mom, always sure of herself, never too far off-key. Bouncing back. Sparky.

But Claudette's murder had reopened the wounds of my father's death, touched that same pain. How could I be the daughter-friend she needed now?

I parked behind the Merc and walked around front to admire our shiny new window. Wednesdays are delivery days in the village, with vans and trucks of all sizes jamming the street. Men with dollies carted boxes of products and supplies into shops and restaurants for the busy days ahead.

"Buy you a cup of coffee?" A hint of his Minnesota upbringing clung to Adam Zimmerman's resonant voice.

I hid my go-cup behind my skirt, then snuck it surreptitiously into my carry-all. "Sure."

We sat at an outside table in front of Chez Max and Le Panier, with other morning coffee customers. "What brings you downtown? You're a highway business guy."

He shook his head. "That village-highway rivalry makes

no difference to the Athletic Club. We serve the whole community."

"Tell me more about what you do there. And what you've been up to all these years." He'd been a Parks and Rec major, with an emphasis on Wilderness Management. That might sound like basket weaving for the outdoorsy set, but in the Rocky Mountain West, all things related to forestry and land management are serious business. Adam had bounced around the state a bit, working in the Park, then for a nonprofit that negotiated a major land swap with a timber company. Then he'd landed in Jewel Bay, running the outdoor programs for kids at the Athletic Club.

"Best job ever," he said. "And I'm so glad you came back to Jewel Bay."

We caught up on my doings, and on a few old friends. He was surprisingly easy to talk to, with a ready smile and a gentle laugh. A guy who'd found his niche. I felt his warm brown eyes focus on me. The attention made me a little nervous. "And you're looking for a donation to the kids' wilderness program." Merchants are always being hit up for contributions. Food, maybe, instead of our scarce cash?

"Yes and no. I did come down to solicit a few business owners, but . . ." He uncrossed his legs and recrossed them. Long, tanned, shapely legs. Hiking legs. "What I really wanted was a chance to talk with you. And—I'd like to see you again. Maybe this weekend?"

As a woman, I sometimes forget that it's not always easy for a man to say that. But as soon as the words were out, I realized I'd wanted to hear them.

"Dinner?" I said just as he said, "A hike?" We laughed. "Let me see if Tracy will work alone Sunday so I can sneak out."

"Great. Up in the Basin? Birch Lake?"

"Perfect." Which meant skipping the family Sunday dinner. Which might require explanation. His smile was as warm as his touch on my arm as we said good-bye. I'd worry about tradition later.

Inside, Tracy was already counting out the till. She raised her eyebrows in a "Who was that?" look. My cheeks pinked.

"What are these doing here?" The huckleberry chocolates sat next to Claudette's memorial flowers.

"People ask for them, so I moved them. You always say, give people what they want."

I picked up the box. "I know you love the Merc. And we couldn't function without you. But if we're going to keep working together, we need to be on the same page." Her expression turned to stone. "You know half the town. Our customers love you. You could be a terrific ambassador for the Merc's new direction."

"If I drank fancy water instead of Diet Coke? If I ate croissants instead of jelly doughnuts?" Her voice shook. "You can't tell everyone what to do."

Yes, I can. I run the joint. But no, I couldn't. And if that's how snooty I sounded . . . The phone rang and Tracy turned her back to me, a little more deliberately than necessary, to answer. I put the chocolates back where they belonged and headed upstairs.

I updated the Facebook page and sent some Tweets, then remembered the coffee mug I'd stashed in my bag. In the bottom of the bag lay Fresca's phone. I set it on the desk.

My eyes kept drifting to it. Who had she been talking to yesterday afternoon? Who'd told her I'd been snooping and set her off? Heck, as long as I was snooping . . .

Her phone was easy to use—I'd set it up myself. Two calls in the key time frame. One from Chiara—who wouldn't have revealed anything to Mom without talking to me first. The second number looked unfamiliar. I pushed Call.

Got voice mail. "You've reached Chef James Angelo. If you'd like to book an event, or order some of the Chef's outstanding Italian products, leave a message and . . ."

Holy cow. I glanced at the little arrows in front of the numbers. He'd called her.

He hated her. What was up?

Two new voice mail messages. Why not? I pushed Listen.

Yesterday, after she'd split. "Fresca, it's Ted. Sorry things got heated earlier. I hope that doesn't stop you from considering my offer. It would be best for everyone in the long run."

What on earth? Yesterday afternoon he'd come barreling down the back hallway into me and the tomatoes, and she'd been visibly upset but insisted it had nothing to do with me. Which meant she hadn't been referring to my snooping—if he'd ratted on me, she'd have lit into me then.

So what had they discussed that had gotten so tense?

He'd left a second message just past seven last night. "I've got the appraisal and sales info for the frame shop and gallery that sold last year. I'll match that, plus ten percent. Two days. Call me."

If blood could freeze, I'd be a human ice cube. Ted Redaway wanted my mother to sell him Murphy's Mercantile.

Where would he get the money? Far as I knew, he had wages from Red's, and no ownership interest. He lived rent-free in a cabin behind Old Ned's place, and had blown his wad on the Harley. No question, he'd need Ned's money.

But the idea was so ridiculous, why had Fresca let it upset her? Unless she took it seriously.

Which meant I had some planning to do, and some careful stepping.

The kitchen smelled like an olive harvest, accented with the pungent smell of homegrown Rocambole garlic. It sounded like a helicopter landing pad, as Fresca whirled Kalamata olives, oil, the garlic, and fresh parsley in her industrial-strength food processor. I changed the demo sign, and got out bowls, platters, toothpicks, and napkins for samples, then sat on a stool to wait.

When the whirring stopped, she looked up warily.

"You left your phone yesterday. It's upstairs. Can we talk?"

She wiped her hands on her apron, poured coffee, and slid a cup across the counter toward me.

"Erin, you're not a kid anymore. There are things I need to tell you."

No, you can't sell. I know, the Merc hasn't turned a profit yet, but we're just getting started. There's so much more we can do—

The front door chimed and Kim Caldwell entered before I could say any of the things I'd been thinking. Her boot heels hammered on the wood floor as she strode toward us. My mother's face said her thoughts were echoing mine: *What now?*

"Ian Randall's in the hospital, since last night. Food poisoning. He'll recover, but it's been a scare."

My heart stopped, started, revved. My mother went ghostlike, and I zipped into the kitchen to support her. "And Jeff?"

"Anxious, upset, of course, but not sick."

"I ran into them Tuesday morning in Le Panier, but I don't remember what they ordered." Did it matter? I'd eaten there and hadn't gotten sick.

"The docs say it's probably something he ate Tuesday evening. The Health Department's checking into it, of course, but without other reported cases, they'll rule out restaurants. The symptoms were pretty severe. Cramping and vomiting, blurred vision, an irregular pulse—weak, slow. Anyone else who'd been affected would have gone to the ER, too."

"Casseroles. Fruit salads," I said. "Their kitchen was filled with food when I dropped by yesterday."

Kim nodded. "It's all been taken for testing." She turned her bullet eyes on Fresca. "The only thing he ate that Jeff didn't was your artichoke pesto."

The butler at Downton Abbey would have called for brandy, and Sam Spade would have dowsed my mother with whiskey. No such options at the moment, but I did get her safely seated.

According to Kim, the jar was open in the fridge, but no one knew how long it had been there. Neither Jeff nor Ian remembered opening it, but who remembered such a mundane thing?

"You only sell that variety here, right?" I asked. Fresca nodded. "And Claudette didn't stop in when she came back to town, so she must have taken that jar months ago."

"It was her favorite," Fresca said, her voice thin and strained. "Ian's, too."

"We've sold dozens of jars of that pesto with no complaints," I said. "Even if Claudette had left a jar open in the fridge, it wouldn't have gone bad, not with all the acid in it. So someone tampered with it, on purpose." Kim nodded. Now I felt sick. No doubt dozens of friends and relatives had been in and out of Claudette's house since Saturday. Had someone targeted Jeff or Ian?

Did one of them know something about Claudette's murder—that the killer wanted to keep quiet? But they hadn't even been in town when she was killed.

"I need—to go to the hospital. Jeff shouldn't be alone." When I started to protest, Fresca continued, "Stop worrying. I'm fine. You've got a store to run."

Ouch. Meaning, don't go out investigating. "Don't forget your phone."

"Wait a moment, Fresca," Kim said. "There's another way Ian could have gotten that pesto, isn't there?"

I interrupted. "Did you check her pantry? She's bound to have kept some jars." Except that Claudette thought she was leaving town for good. She'd have cleaned out her cupboards, maybe taken her favorites along.

"You took a basket out to Jeff and Ian, didn't you? Monday afternoon?" Kim said, eyes trained on Fresca.

So that's why Kim was here. I knew from my years at SavClub that a case of suspected food poisoning would not normally involve a detective. But when the victim was the son of a murder victim, the rules changed.

And Fresca's failure to volunteer her little offering wouldn't help.

Kim insisted Fresca write out an inventory of what had been in the basket, even though they'd no doubt confiscated all the contents. Testing her memory—or her honesty?

Before leaving, Kim slipped an envelope out of her jacket pocket. "Your statement, Erin. Review and sign."

I resisted the urge to salute. "You'll let us know the lab results? Can we visit Ian?"

"Oh, you'll know, all right. And yes—if Jeff will let you."

Criminy. He hadn't believed the rumors before, but what would he think now?

The moment the door swung shut behind her, I turned on my mother. "Why didn't you say you'd dropped off a basket?"

"Because I knew how it would look."

"It looks worse now. Didn't you think she'd find out? And you did take them artichoke pesto, didn't you?"

Her eyes watered and she nodded. "They all loved it. But I don't know what to think anymore."

Neither did I. I'd been thinking Kim had come as a friend. I'd been thinking my mother was a sensible woman just about to reveal whatever she was hiding.

I'd have to uncover it myself.

Tracy burst into tears at the news, and she and Fresca dashed off to the hospital in Pondera. The shop was blessedly quiet, letting me gather my thoughts.

Kim and I had talked for two hours, but my formal statement ran only two pages. Deflating to realize that most of what I'd said wasn't relevant. But maybe that was a good sign—for me, at least: Kim had explained that the written statement was intended to present the key points of my trial testimony, if charges were brought. I didn't think I'd seen or heard anything critical Friday night, and the statement seemed to confirm that, focusing instead on Claudette's history with the Merc and our drugstore meet-up.

I scoured it for anything that might hurt my mother. Nothing, to my eyes. Why wouldn't she talk to a lawyer? I signed the statement and slid it back in the envelope.

My retail training kicked in and I decided to take the artichoke pesto off the shelves for now. I piled the jars on the kitchen counter. I was a thousand percent certain it was fine—even opened a jar and helped myself to a few bites just to prove it—but no amount of profit was worth any risk to our customers. The back door squeaked open, and I tossed the spoon into the sink and wiped my mouth.

When I reached the shop floor, Jimmy Vang was trying to explain something to a couple in their mid-fifties, obviously tourists, in his gesture-laden English. "Oh, here, here. Miss Erin." He waved at them, then at his buckets by the back door. "More mushroom? Last of season."

"Thanks, Jimmy. I'll be right with you." I helped the customers choose a few items, then made the deal with Jimmy. As he stuffed my receipt and check into his worn brown Carhartts, I noticed a small steel clip, almost like a barrette, folded over the edge of the pocket.

As ubiquitous as cell phones.

"Jimmy, may I see your knife?"

With a nod that involved his whole body, he pulled out the knife and extended it to me. I picked it out of his palm and examined it. Your standard jackknife I understood—still carry my green Girl Scout model in the Subaru—but how to open this one?

Jimmy took it in his nimble fingers. "Like this, Miss Erin." The three-inch blade flicked out with an almost imperceptible snap. "You try."

I tried. Easy to do, but I did not like it. Three inches of sharpened steel looked plenty long, and plenty deadly. "Thank you, Jimmy." He nodded, the knife disappearing back into his pocket. We traded full buckets for empties and he left.

Now that I'd seen a folding blade up close, I knew Claudette had been knifed. I rustled up a sweater, poured a fresh cup of coffee, and drank it half down.

The door opened and I put on my happy face. A walking confectionary wafted in. In cotton candy pink Roman sandals, tight black capris, a form-fitting pale pink top, and a black-and-pink polka dot scarf around her waist, hot pink sunglasses tucked into her fuchsia-streaked black hair, she carried a woven basket big enough to hold baby Moses with room to spare. And all of it exuded an overpowering scent of sugar. Pink sugar.

"I'm Candy Divine? Heidi called you about me?"

Good thing I'd already swallowed the coffee. When Heidi had said she was sending over a woman making the rounds with samples, she hadn't mentioned her name. Or her voice.

But good things can come in unusual packages, so I invited Ms. Divine to give me her spiel. "I've got Frufalla—it's like Turkish delight, only fruity? Made with real rose water?" Wasn't fruit the essence of Turkish delight? The Northwest version, Aplets and Cotlets, does well at SavClub and I admit a weakness. Hers fed that powdered-sugar craving nicely.

"And nougat? In seven flavors? Oh, you'll love them." Tasty, but they glued my tongue to my teeth.

Then it turned out she wasn't real sweet on chocolate. "It's kind of bland, don't you think?"

Chocolate—my personal Vitamin C—bland? What was she smoking? I wiggled my jaw and worked my lips to free my nougaty tongue. "What brought you here?" Clearly not a Montana girl, not even a newcomer. We have no pink-only shops.

A decidedly unperky look crossed her face. "I'm—in transit? And this seems like a great little town."

But if I took her on, would I need a new supplier next month?

"What I'm looking for," I said, sounding like a bass to my own ears after hearing her piccolo, "is the Montana flavor. High quality, nicely packaged—and you've got all that." In pink paper candy cups wrapped in pink cello, tied with pink ribbons. "Something tourists can take home for themselves or their friends, and at the same time, a treat locals will pop in for."

"Oh, you mean like chocolate river rocks and chocolate bear paws with raw cashews for claws?" Exactly like that. I nodded, hopeful. "Cherry bark." She made it sound like something the dog threw up.

"Not your thing, I take it."

"No-ooo." With sad eyes and a flat voice, she repacked her basket, leaving me a few samples. "Call me if you change your mind?"

The moment she left, I called Heidi. "Her name."

"What's wrong with it? Candace DeVernero. Good Italian name."

I howled. Poor, sweet Candy Divine.

· *Nineteen* ·

When I emerged from the bathroom, after washing away tears of laughter, Rick Bergstrom stood by the front counter, holding a small carton. He looked as much like a sunny day on a farm as he had on Monday, but wore a sheepish expression.

"Pasta flour. Two strains of semolina, and a bag of our semolina-durum blend. Plus a sample of our new spinach flour. Love to have your mother test it."

I took the box. "Thanks. She'll be delighted."

"Hey, uh." He glanced at the floor, then back at me. "I stepped in it the other day. Rode in on my high horse, and came off like a self-righteous pig." Three farm animal metaphors in five seconds—impressive, even for a Montanan.

"Yeah. You kinda did." I smiled.

"Can I buy you lunch and start over? I'd like to have your business, and well, maybe your friendship, too. If that's possible." The tip of his nose turned pink.

Talk about unexpected. "I was a little prickly myself. Lunch would be great, but I'm alone in the shop."

Saved by the back door. Fresca and Tracy, looking relieved, reported visiting with both Jeff and Ian, who'd turned the corner toward full recovery. I introduced Fresca to Rick, and he gave her the rundown on the Montana Gold samples.

"Bayside Grille?" Rick said as we headed out, leaving Tracy in charge. "They make their own bread and buns, and I promised Ray I'd drop in for a chat."

A few minutes later, we were sitting on the deck drinking minted iced tea, waiting for a Reuben and a sesame-seared ahi tuna salad with wasabi vinaigrette. Another gorgeous day, with three months of gorgeous days ahead. I could almost forget the cloud of trouble hovering over my family.

Like me, Rick had angled his chair toward the bay and the stunning views beyond. No eligible men in sight since I had come home, and now two? *Hold on, Erin. This is a business lunch, not a date.* We talked flour and grains, and I gave him my thoughts on the samples. "Tracy loved the bagels—not too soft, but not too chewy. What's the secret?"

"In New York and L.A., the bagel shops and delis boil their bagels before baking. Traditional method, love it, but it creates a chewier texture than some people like. But if you steam them . . ." He grinned and spread his hands in a "voilà!" gesture.

Lunch came, both my salad and Rick's sandwich picture-perfect.

"I couldn't see myself living in California forever. The family business had grown to the point of needing an outside sales rep, so here I am."

"Did you go to college there?"

"Bozeman," he said around a bite of juicy-crisp pickle.

"You're a Bobcat?" I said in mock horror. "But you seemed like such a nice guy."

He grinned. "I take it you went to Missoula."

I drizzled tangy-sweet dressing over my salad, then

speared a chunk of avocado. "Yes, but I left Montana after college, too. It's a different world out there."

"Sure is. Terrific sauerkraut on this sandwich."

"They soak it in beer."

"No wonder I like it. They should bottle and sell it." Our eyes met. Obviously, neither of our minds strayed very far from food or business.

On our way out, Rick told Ray he'd be back in a few minutes with flour samples.

"Hey, Jay. How you doing?" Rick called to someone in the kitchen. I turned reflexively, but all I saw was Angelo. I still needed to figure out why he'd called my mother. Later—I needed a plan first.

"Wasn't that Jay Walker?" Rick said on our way out.

"What? That's James Angelo. Or Chef Angelo, as he prefers."

"No way. He was in my sister's class." In a Hi-Line farm town a couple hundred miles away, not some urban Italian restaurant community, as he'd implied. "I'd swear it was him."

"Jay Walker? Really?" I suppressed a giggle.

Rick shrugged. "Seven boys, one girl, he's the youngest. I guess they ran out of names. Actually, his dad was the town drunk—probably his idea of a joke. The whole family seemed to pick on Jay. So did the kids at school."

"Takes the right personality to carry a goofy name." Like a girl I grew up with, Polly Easter.

"The name was the least of it. Some kids seem to invite bullying."

There's one in every class. "Jay cooked in the Prairie Winds Café for a while, after high school, but what he did or where he went after that, I have no idea."

Knowing his real name, though, might give my research a boost.

Outside Le Panier, Max and Wendy stood on the sidewalk, gesturing at their windows, discussing the display. As we approached, Rick spoke in a low voice. "She's the baker, right? Can you introduce me?"

Max greeted Rick warmly, always happy to meet someone new. When Rick extended his hand to Wendy, she paused before holding out her own, barely touching his fingers.

"What's eating her?" Rick said a minute later at the door of the Merc.

I shrugged. "Who knows? Thanks for lunch. It's been great. Should I make my order online, or call it in?"

"You bet. Great. And I'll call you for the order." He took my right hand with his left and squeezed it slightly. Like a promise. But of what?

As he turned back to his truck, his sport coat parted slightly and a glint of steel caught my eye. Another man, another knife clip.

They were everywhere.

Rick's apology set a good example. I certainly owed Tracy one.

I fetched a Diet Coke from the private stash Tracy kept in our kitchen, and handed her the peace offering. "I come on a little strong sometimes. I apologize. But when you squeeze the can"—I cringed at the thought—"it's like nails on a chalkboard. Stupid, I know, but you know how some sounds just send you through the roof?"

Her stubborn expression turned to relief. "Is that all? I thought you were telling me not to drink it, and what a snob you are, and I was afraid I'd have to find a new job." She reddened.

"No! No, don't quit. Don't even think about it. We need you. But could you maybe buy your pop in plastic bottles instead?"

"Piece of cake," she said.

"And I owe you some time off, but that might have to wait—early next week?"

"I'll probably spend it here, baking dog biscuits. They're selling like crazy. And a new product I'm working on."

"Great." We hugged.

No sign of Fresca, which wasn't all bad. I wasn't sure I could take any more apologizing. Plus she owed me one for keeping secrets. But I did wonder where she'd gone to, and not just because we were almost out of egg pappardelle and spinach linguine, and the tapenade jars needed labeling.

Tracy had found Candy Divine's nougat and fruit jellies, washing them down with Diet Coke. I preferred a different treat and headed next door.

Wendy stood behind the bakery counter. Her nostrils flared and her eyes flashed. "I thought you of all people would be more loyal to local producers and shop owners."

"What do you mean? I'm in here every day. We send you customers by the dozens."

"Our bread and rolls are a darned sight better than anything shipped in from halfway across the state, even if they send a slick salesman to wine and dine you."

For Pete's sake. "Wendy, are you talking about Montana Gold? I'll carry some of his products, but I'm not buying his bread. Yours is better. I told him I wouldn't compete with you."

She raised her chin, jaws tight, eyes wary.

"Wendy, you know we all prosper when we support each other." I grinned. "So could I get a couple of hazelnut sablés?" I'd grown fond of a similar cookie at Pike Place Market in Seattle, and ate as many as my waistband allowed.

She tucked two into a small white bag.

"Thanks. Hey, you keep your ear on comings and goings, don't you?" I explained about Claudette's plans. "So if we knew what restaurant or building she had her sights on, and who her business partner was, that might give us some clues to who killed her, and why."

She crossed her arms and glowered. "I heard you talking to Jeff and Ian in here the other day. She fooled everyone. You all think Claudette was so sweet and innocent, duped by Dean."

I waited. As kids, of course, we'd called her Wendy the Witch—conveniently forgetting that cartoon Wendy was a Good Little Witch. But when had she actually become one?

"She runs off with my friend's husband, and everybody thinks it's funny."

Wendy and Linda had cochaired the Saturday Night Gala. I hadn't known they were friends, too.

"And she was screaming up a storm last Friday, disturbing my grandmother, who's ninety and not well. Well, you don't care."

"Claudette yelled at your grandmother?" I was shocked.

"No. At James, her other neighbor." She tilted her head slightly. "If she was scouting for a restaurant, he might know which ones are changing hands. He'd like to run his own kitchen."

"Is that what they were arguing about?"

She shook her head. "No idea. I just told them to shut up so Nana could rest."

I thanked her and took my cookies for a walk. Had Claudette and Angelo been planning to open a restaurant together? He as chef, she as manager? She knew the town well; he was fresh blood. They were neighbors—it would be natural for the subject to come up.

But then, something went wrong. A million things could go wrong starting a business, or taking one over, as I well knew. Probably two million with a restaurant. They fought. And Angelo followed Claudette to the Festa.

I'd reached the bridge at the south end of the village, and stood on the walking lane looking upstream at the Wild Mile. A kayaker in a red boat shot through the last rapid and raised his arms in victory before paddling to the takeout. Angelo—aka Jay Walker—had said he was on the river Friday night. What if he'd been right here and seen her drive into town? Then followed her—to talk, or to finish their argument—and they fought and he stabbed her.

And he fled.

It made perfect sense, except that I hadn't a shred of evidence.

Two things I still couldn't figure out: If Claudette had gone to Vegas with Dean thinking the move was permanent, why not rent out her house or put it on the market? If the move had been an impulse, as everyone seemed to think, she may not have had time. Planning ahead was not her strong suit. That puzzle I could put aside.

Everybody also thought she wouldn't have left town if she hadn't believed Dean was offering her a chance for a new life. Had she hatched the restaurant plan, getting business info from Ted, when she realized Dean was bailing on Elvis and coming home?

No place for a knife on a kayaker in his wetsuit. Not until he was back in street clothes. No way to find out if Angelo carried one without a close-up look—after hours, when he wasn't in chef garb.

What else could I dig up about Jay Walker? Poor guy—no wonder he'd shed the past and adopted a nom de frying pan.

Maybe I could ask Rick Bergstrom to tap into his own small-town roots and help me research.

And the most important question: Would Kim Caldwell believe any of it? I'd have to move fast, before she closed in on Fresca.

First, I needed to confirm my suspicion that Claudette had been stabbed. I sat on a bench overlooking the river and fired up my phone. Not my usual field of research, but surely my friend Google knew all. I typed in "Lethal wound knife."

The most promising option was a doctor's site with medical and forensic info for writers. Apparently most knife attacks came from behind, which made sense. But Claudette had been stabbed on the left side, which probably meant from the front. "A thrusting stab wound to the heart is lethal most of the time, and fairly quickly." I read on, shivering despite the eighty-degree temp. Not much blood, unless an artery was severed. Which would explain the small stain I'd seen, and the lack of splatter on her dress and the ground.

And on her killer.

To get from her car to Red's gate, Claudette would have either crossed the parking lot weaving between cars, or looped around the end of the lot, then come up the alley. I followed that route now. As I'd expected, it led directly past the garbage and recycling bins where I'd found her.

How would she have been standing, to fall and land as she had? I lay on the ground and positioned myself as she'd lain, then tried to reverse-choreograph her movements.

She'd been barely five feet tall. Even a small man towered over her. I pantomimed the possibilities, playing both victim and killer. I thrust an imaginary knife upward and got a chill. If anyone saw me, I'd pretend I was practicing Tai Chi. Wound on her left side meant a right-handed killer, which didn't exactly narrow it down. An underhand thrust would slide in between the ribs. Bingo.

I rose on my toes, imagining various height differences. A killer carrying a knife in his pocket, or on his belt, could slip it out, flick it open, and hit the target in seconds—whether he was practiced, or lucky.

Had he watched in horror while she fell? Had he tried to help, run like a coward, or vanished into the crowd?

Or she. Because my reenactment had proven that the killer could be almost anyone.

Which didn't help at all.

· *Twenty* ·

The red geranium on our back gate drooped pitifully. I brought it into the courtyard for a drink, and pictured Liz's ideas come to life. I still hadn't had a chance to show my mother the sketches. We had a lot to talk about.

A tour bus of visitors headed for Glacier Park for the annual opening of the Going-to-the-Sun Highway stopped in town, and we did a brisk business the rest of the afternoon.

As the last group was leaving, the door opened and Landon sashayed in, wearing shorts, a Superman T-shirt, and a straw cowboy hat and scuffed brown boots.

"Hey, bud," a balding elderly man said, "I didn't know Superman was a cowboy."

Landon gave him a withering look. "He wasn't. But all cowboys are supermen."

The customer was either an accomplished actor or an experienced grandfather, judging by the micromovements in his face as he kept from bursting out laughing. "Got a point there, pardner." The man tipped an imaginary hat at

Landon and winked at me. I handed his wife a bag with her considerable purchases and they left, sharing a smile.

"Do cowboys hug their aunties?" I said, crouching. "And where's your mom?"

He hugged me quickly, then remembered his errand. He pulled a green wad out of his pocket. "She needs ones."

I made the change, then walked outside with him. Chiara stepped out of her shop. I held Landon's hand until it was safe to cross—he knew our routine—and blew him a kiss when he reached the other side.

Tracy offered to stay late and help me finish restocking and rearranging, but I sent her home with the leftover candy samples and a bottle of cherry wine, and locked the doors.

The jars of pesto still sat on the kitchen counter. We tossed empty boxes in the basement, so I headed down to find one. Tracy was right—a first-class creep hole. Despite the low ceilings, hand-hewn rock walls, and lack of windows, it hadn't felt scary when I was a kid. I remembered coming down here with my dad many times. But then, his presence had always made me feel brave.

I brushed a giant cobweb out of my hair, then shook the sticky mess off my fingers. Maybe we had something red down here to hang on the back gate. I found a box for the pesto and set it on the landing, then plunged farther into cobweb world.

Our Friday school colors displays, now on summer vacation, were primarily pennants and pom-poms, and not weatherproof. The Christmas decorations seemed like a better bet. A bell, or a lantern? Liz said human or animal shapes were best—did reindeer count? Snowmen and angels? I hadn't worked Christmas at the Merc yet, so our organization scheme escaped me. No luck on the first two tries: silver and gold garland in one crate, ornaments and packages of holiday-themed napkins in the second. Decorations and store merchandise intermingled—what a mess.

In the third carton, I found a vaguely familiar wooden

box. Inside were four-by-six note cards covered with fading type. I flipped through them, pulling out a few. Recipe cards, mostly for sauces, pestos, and pastas much like the ones we sold upstairs. Others were for dishes based on those ingredients.

But Fresca had never typed. Even now, she e-mailed and texted reluctantly. Her recipes had always been scribbles and notes no one else could decipher. Out of impatience, not fear of plagiarism. She'd worked out complete recipes years ago when she began catering and needed to replicate results from one large batch to the next. Handwritten, but at least they listed all the amounts and ingredients and could be followed by anyone. The binders upstairs brimmed with them.

So what were these? Precursors, apparently, but who'd typed them?

A spark of fear flashed in my brain. Did these cards prove the rumors true? I held the box shut and flipped it over. Hard to make out the initials in the dusty light. No doubt shop students still turned out similar projects, but the carving looked a lot closer to NM than IR.

I carried the box upstairs and set it on the kitchen counter. Stared at it. Claudette had denied telling anyone Fresca had stolen her recipes when I'd confronted her, but would she have admitted it to me? But if they were hers, how had they gotten into Nick's box?

Oh, man, did my mother and I have a lot to talk about.

But first, finish my research.

I made a quick salad, grabbed a minibaguette and artichoke pesto, and carried my tray to the office. Fired up Google and began stalking Jay Walker. A surprising number of men bore that name, often a nickname. Adding "Jewel Bay" didn't help. Hadn't Angelo cooked for a fancy joint in Missoula before moving here? No luck. I repeated it all on Facebook, and again got zippo.

Our Jay Walker could not be found. Or didn't want to be.

Next stop, online archives. I slathered artichoke dip on bread and crossed my fingers. Not every small-town newspaper had survived in recent years, or digitized its older editions, but Rick and Jay's hometown paper had done both. I pegged Jay at around forty, and searched his likely high school years. Came up with one grainy photo of the graduating class, listing all twenty-seven seniors. I found his name, enlarged the shot, counted from the left, and landed my finger on a girl. Counted from the right—the kids weren't standing in straight lines—and got a boy. Average height, skinny, a full head of light brown hair, glasses. James Angelo at eighteen? Impossible to tell. The faces were too small, too distant and blurry.

I dug out Rick Bergstrom's card and e-mailed him the page, asking if this boy was the one he'd remembered. He'd seemed sure that the man he'd seen this afternoon was Jay, but Angelo had not responded to his greeting.

I plowed through the newspaper archives for another forty-five minutes. Walker was a common name, but in such a small town, the Walker boys on the high school sports pages were probably brothers or cousins. No references to Jay himself. The Law Log reported several arrests of men named Walker, mostly on minor counts. Again, no Jay. And David Walker, age fifty-six, charged with DUI third offense, twenty-plus years ago.

Five years ago, the paper reported a head-on collision on Highway 2, killing one woman and severely injuring two men, including the driver who crossed the center line, Dave Walker, no age given. Suspected factors: alcohol and speed. I checked the obituaries. Dave, aka David, Walker died days later from injuries sustained in a car crash. Survivors included wife Doreen (O'Keefe) of the family home, a daughter, seven sons—one named Jay—and other assorted relatives. No mention of where the kids lived. Memorials to the hospital cardiac care unit.

All very sad. But it didn't confirm that Jay Walker had become Chef James Angelo.

While I was here, might as well get the scoop on one Rick Bergstrom. Two years older than me, he was all over the sports pages. Football, basketball, and track, and a football scholarship to MSU. A triple threat wasn't uncommon in small towns, where a good athlete could stand out in several sports, and be voted homecoming king, too.

The kids the rest of us wished we could hate, if only we didn't like them so much.

Over the years, Bergstrom Farms had morphed into Montana Gold, and now dominated the local ag scene. Articles mentioned a mill expansion, new contracts with growers, supply agreements with some of the state's best-known restaurants, the new baking operation. A short piece dated a few weeks ago noted the addition of Rick to the family business, as outside sales rep.

I took a break to stretch and plot. If James Angelo was Jay Walker, so what? Montana has always been the last best refuge in the lower forty-eight. The perfect place to reinvent yourself, even if you only moved across the Continental Divide. Half the people on the west side had never been east, and vice versa. The privilege of starting over was hardly limited to trust fund babies or ex-cons. Though with a population a hair under a million—most folks are connected by two degrees, not the usual six—starting over inside state lines could be tricky. But Jay may have had good reasons for not moving farther away.

Nothing to be gained from unmasking him. At least, nothing I'd discovered so far.

All this computer time made me sleepy, but coffee didn't sound good. I snuck one of Tracy's Diet Cokes—it hit the spot.

Time to update my Spreadsheet of Suspicion. I added Angelo, but while he had means, so did almost everyone else, and his motive and opportunity were speculation. Still, filling in little boxes is always satisfying.

What about Dean? I paced the small room. He downplayed his role in Claudette's departure, calling it a vacation. But she'd told everyone it was a permanent move, a chance to start over without small-town scrutiny.

He'd referred to her "magical thinking," but despite her flighty, romantic nature, she wasn't naive. She wouldn't have left the town where she'd lived for nearly fifteen years and abandoned the cottage and garden she adored on a whim.

We needed that note. Doubtful that Fresca overlooked it, but better check anyway. I unlocked the drawer that held the personnel files—not much to them, but I'd been trained to safeguard employee privacy—and withdrew Claudette's file. Between the emergency contact info and tax forms was a narrow slip of paper, ripped off a pad labeled GROCERIES—the kind you get in the mail from charities looking for money. Wrinkled and smoothed out, blank on the back, bombshell on the front.

Dear Fresca:

After all our years of friendship, I hate to give my notice this way, but if I told you in person, we'd both cry. And you'd try to talk me into staying. Dean has an opportunity to go to Las Vegas, to perform, and he's asked me to go with him. It's a new beginning for us—I know you understand how rare and precious that is.

The Merc will prosper in your hands.

Love always, Claudette

She'd signed in red with a flourish. Had he lied? Told her he had a job that hadn't materialized? Or overstated his prospects, hoping for a coveted Elvis job that had not magically appeared—and a fling with a cute gal?

A faint sound like something breaking caught my attention. Tentatively, I crept downstairs to check on our beautiful new window.

Intact.

So was the front door, and I saw no problems outside. Must have been next door at Red's—a bar fight, or a dropped tray of glasses and bottles in the courtyard.

Back upstairs, I found the Nevada College of Impressionism's glittery website, with a soundtrack to match. I lowered the volume and scrolled through the pages. Offerings included a one-week Introduction to Elvis, a three-week Immersion, and a six-week program leading to a PhE—a Doctor of Elvisology. Glad I hadn't just swigged pop.

The Careers page boasted: "Our graduates are highly qualified and professional tribute artists. Many find full-time jobs in the entertainment field. Others find pleasure recreating beloved music and artists for audiences at corporate events, public festivals, and private parties, in their hometowns and beyond."

Meaning a handful make it big, but most go home to sing in their garages and living rooms, for long-suffering friends and relatives. "Personal enrichment," in HR terms.

Had Dean set his sights on the Strip, but flunked out and come home with his tail between his spandex-clad legs? Had he lashed out at Claudette when she threatened to expose him? Had she been that angry?

A woman not known for flying off the handle had been home two days and had two rip-roaring arguments. Too bad I hadn't heard more of her Friday afternoon clash with Dean. I needed to talk to Angelo. Who else had seen her and might be able to gauge her temperature?

I made a note in my phone calendar to call the school the next morning.

Before leaving the site, I watched several student performances. Incredible. Dean Martin risen from the grave, a swoon-worthy Tony Bennett, and a pseudo Lady Gaga who made my jaw drop. A long clip featured Elvis tributes from the recent classes, but no shots of Dean. Looked like he hadn't made the cut.

Off to YouTube. You can lose half your life there, gaping at the amazing things people get up to. The cat videos always make me itch to train Sandburg and see if he can buy his own cat treats, but while I don't doubt his talents, neither he nor I have the patience.

Dean had his own channel. Easy to tell the lip-synching from his own singing—his timing was off and his vocals lacked Elvis's richness. The recent clips showed a noticeable improvement over his preclass performances, but no one would see him and think Elvis lived.

Had he really managed to convince both himself and Claudette that he could make a career change?

One last thing. I hacked my sister's Facebook account—sorry, Chiara, I owe you a random act of kindness—and sent a message to Claudette's friends from Vegas. Sucky way to tell them she'd died, but I had no other option. And maybe they'd reply with useful details.

Computer off, the recipe box in my carry-all, I headed out at half past eight. I crossed Back Street and the mostly empty parking lot to the Subaru and hit the clicker. In the flash of my parking lights, I saw my windshield covered in red.

· Twenty-one ·

"At least they used a cheap brand." I pointed to the broken jar of spaghetti sauce lying next to my right front tire, contents splattered across my windshield. "Not my mother's good stuff."

"'Go back to Seattle.'" Kim read the note tucked under my front wiper.

"You know, this is beginning to feel personal. And it's starting to piss me off." When I'd first read the note, I'd crumpled it up instinctively, then realized it was evidence and smoothed it out.

"It's a warning of some kind."

"No shit, Sherlock." She ignored me. "Two random acts of vandalism is too much coincidence. The first attack was on the building, the second on me—or my car. So is the real target the Merc, my family, or me? And how is any of that related to Claudette's murder?"

"You know I'm not going to discuss my theories with you, Erin."

Which I chose to interpret as meaning she didn't have a

theory. But as with the Merc's busted window, she wouldn't be here if she didn't have the same questions I did.

"And another thing. Nobody saw this? Look how light it is." I told her about the crashing sound I'd dismissed as an accident in Red's courtyard. "Ask Ted." He stood at Red's back gate in his white apron. The patrol cars' lights had drawn attention the vandalism hadn't. Max Fontaine, also in a white apron, stood outside the bistro's back door.

When I looked back at Red's, Ted had gone back inside. If he or his customers had seen anything, Kim would find out. I crossed the lot and called out to Max. "Just spaghetti sauce. Nobody hurt. See or hear anything?"

He shook his head, waving one hand. "*Non, non.* I am focused on my stove. Who will be next? This must stop."

The deputies finished photographing the scene, and tagged and bagged the jar and note. They printed my wiper, door handles, the hood. The car wash was closed, but I didn't want the acid to damage the paint job, so as soon as Kim gave me the okay, I dumped a bucket of warm soapy water on the front end and washed off the tomatoey mess.

By the time I got home, I was spitting mad. Kim might not want to share her theories—fine. Then I wouldn't share mine. As soon as I had some. Okay, so she had research tools and investigative staff and other stuff I didn't have. Like arrest powers. And a murder board. But I had a killer spreadsheet.

And a killer cat, who usually greeted me. "Sandburg," I called from the front porch. "Saaaan-deee."

Dang. The one flaw in Bob's cabin remodel had been his decision to reuse the original hardware. The front latch had a tendency to pop open, leaving the door ajar an inch or two. Which wouldn't be a problem if I didn't have a mouse-loving cat who liked to bring his friends home.

Inside, I set my carry-all on the bench and lifted out the recipe box, dusty from its days in oblivion. Cleaning the basement would be a pain in the behind, but at least it wouldn't cost anything more than a bottle of ammonia and some scrub brushes, unlike the courtyard project.

I'm not superstitious, and while the spaghetti jar incident angered me, it hadn't made me nervous. But something didn't feel right. As if the air had been disturbed.

I glanced around. Was that book where I had left it? Had those bananas been moved? Was that a partial smudged footprint on the floor, or a spot where Sandburg had rolled on his back?

I shook my head. Nothing out of place. No signs of an intruder. Surely Sandburg's absence was just a coincidence.

No such thing. I snatched up my keys and phone and dashed outside. "Sandburg." Over and over, I called his name. I circled the cabin, crouching to peer under shrubs, stretching to spy into cubbyholes a young, limber cat could crawl into. I spiraled outward, into the woods, hunting, calling, wishing I'd fetched his treat tin to rattle, to summon him home. The forest seemed to have eyes, but none of them belonged to my cat.

I tramped and stomped, then leaned against a tree, the bark snagging my shirt and hair. How had ten pounds of fur wriggled so deeply under my skin?

In a flutter of wings, a robin landed on a branch near me. "*Hope is the thing with feathers,*" my teenage self recited. He cocked his head and flew off.

I checked my phone. What felt like hours of searching had been only fifteen minutes. I called Liz and Bob.

They hadn't seen him. "It's still light out. He's probably hot on the mouse trail. He'll come home—don't worry."

"Don't worry." Right. I wound my way back to the cabin, and sat on the front step, clenching my jaw. With so much going on—from good things like the success of the Festa and our growing sales, to annoyances like the broken shop window and my vandalized car, to real tragedies like Claudette's murder and Ian's poisoning—every nerve cell in my body felt fired up. Oversensitive.

A movement at the edge of the woods caught my eye, and a small, dark cat emerged from the brush. Sandburg trotted past me and hopped on the porch as if nothing had happened.

Nothing had.

I burst into tears.

Wednesday evening's stresses had one upside: They'd been the perfect pretext to put off confronting Fresca. But I had no excuse Thursday morning. Today. I had to talk to her today. I even made a list, so I wouldn't forget anything: The courtyard project. Cleaning out the basement. Rebuilding her inventory. Claudette's note.

And what about the recipe box?

On the chance that someone had overheard Dean and Claudette arguing, I swung by the drugstore on my way into the village. Polly Paulson—she'd always be Polly Easter to me—had started working in the drugstore in high school and, three kids later, still greeted every customer with a genuine smile and knew ninety percent by name.

"Hey, Polly. When you gonna stop slumming and come work for me?"

Her laugh jingled like charms on a bracelet. "I hope you didn't come in for more candles, Erin. You wiped us out."

"Polly, Friday afternoon, did you see Claudette Randall talking with anyone?"

"That poor girl." She closed her eyes a moment. "I saw her with you. And who's that fellow—half bald, wears those silly pants like pajama bottoms all the time?"

Black cotton, covered with red peppers. "James Angelo. Caterer, cooks at the Bayside Grille."

"Yep. Him. Can't believe I blanked it. After you left, they talked outside for a long time. Looked serious. But that's all I remember. The usual after-work rush to pick up prescriptions and whatnot had me chained to my cash register."

The continuation or the start of the argument Wendy had witnessed? I hadn't asked what time she'd seen them raising Cain across Claudette's backyard fence. But Wendy had been futzing around Red's courtyard with steam trays when I arrived, so she must have gone to her grandmother's earlier in the afternoon, knowing she'd be working the Festa dinner that night.

I snuck a surreptitious peek at the display of huckleberry products on my way out. Nice enough, but nothing we needed to carry. And no chocolates.

Whatever made me glance in the backseat of my car, I don't know, but there was the white bag I'd plucked out of the bushes in the parking lot last Friday night. Back inside Jewel Bay Drug, I asked Polly if Claudette had bought anything that afternoon.

"No. But that Angelo. What a jerk. Had a prescription the pharmacist wouldn't fill and he got all huffy and stalked out. Almost didn't pay for his merchandise, but I nabbed him."

Despite her good nature, I bet neither shoplifters nor her kids get away with much.

"What did he buy?" Not that it mattered.

"Stupid kid stuff. Said it was for his nephews. Gordy's not in—he could tell you what was up with that prescription."

Angelo's purchase didn't prove my theory that he had spotted Claudette heading for the Festa, followed her, and stabbed her. Those little white bags were all over the place.

Every answer raised more questions.

"Thanks, Pol. You ever want a new job, you call me."

The sound of her Tinkerbell laughter followed me out the door.

With Claudette's memorial service scheduled for one o'clock, we'd be closed most of the afternoon. I put a note on the Merc's website and made a sign for the front door.

Myself, I refuse to wear black to funerals. Not that I don't grieve. I'd rather celebrate the life than the loss. In Claudette's case, that meant a festive look, so I'd chosen a blue-and-green batik print maxi dress with a grass green cropped cardigan and three-strap cork-soled sandals.

Tracy's outfit sprouted from that same philosophy: a gauzy red peasant blouse over a tiered red-and-orange skirt with a wide orange leather belt. Red earrings peeked out from behind her flowing chestnut hair.

"Snazzy belt," I said.

"Two dollars at a garage sale," she said, "and fifty cents for the chili pepper earrings."

But what surprised me most was her morning can of Diet Coke. She'd fashioned thin foam rubber into a thermal sleeve decorated with the Merc's logo. She squeezed the can and, miracle of miracles, no metallic twang. "If you like it, we could sell them."

Takes a lot to stun me speechless, but that did it. I hugged her. I suspected this day should have come with a "sudden emotion ahead" warning.

Meanwhile, I had questions. If Angelo's name wasn't really Angelo, what else about him wasn't right? "Trace, do you remember when James Angelo came to town?"

She poked a straw into her Diet Coke, twisting the tab over the opening so the holes lined up and held the straw in place. "I met him when he rented that little house next to Claudette's. He started at Chez Max as a sous-chef, but it didn't work out."

"Didn't I hear he cooked at the golf course, then started his Italian line and catering?"

"Yeah. After Max fired him. Claudette said he tried to persuade Max and Applause! to drop Fresca's products and let him make some of their stuff, but no chance."

The tomato and pepper sauces, pastas, and other items Fresca made for our commercial accounts were critical to the bottom line. Local sourcing allowed restaurants to cut prep time and boost their "brag factor." Angelo's interference was relevant history I hadn't known. "Which set him on a collision course with Fresca. Anyone go with him?"

"No. Seems crazy to launch a business, then behave so badly you alienate the movers and shakers."

"My impression is you have to be a real jerk not to get along with Max, but you also have to be a real cook. His menu's more demanding than Ray's." I started a pot of Rick Bergstrom's Wheat Coffee and got out the sample-sized paper cups. Spotted a purple wrapper from the huckleberry chocolates in the wastebasket. Tracy was right—we needed a replacement soon.

I added a mental note about Angelo to my list of things to discuss with Fresca.

Had that misstep sparked his fight with Claudette? Seemed unlikely—she'd left the Merc months ago, so why would she care now? With Dean's deception, she'd had plenty of new problems on her mind.

Or had she known his secret, whatever it was? What would he have done to protect it?

"Wonder if Dean and Linda will show their smarmy faces at the memorial service," Tracy said, twisting a lock of hair.

"They have to, if they don't want everyone in town talking about his affair." Or suspecting them of murder. "Sometimes you have to show up, to shut people up."

"I told her not to go to Las Vegas."

"Must have sounded like an adventure. Claudette loved to have fun."

She teared up and I fetched a box of tissue. "I told her," she said, "never move for a man just because you're afraid of being alone. She said don't assume she was making a mistake just because I had, that Dean wasn't like Mitch. She said not to begrudge her happiness and now she's dead. And she came back and she didn't tell me or call me and I never saw her alive again."

At least Tracy'd had reason to be angry with Claudette. I'd been ticked at my dad over some teenage tantrum, some "no" I hadn't wanted to hear.

I hugged her and handed her the tissue box. Anger plus sudden death equals longtime guilt.

Tracy opened the shop, and Fresca came in to prepare the funeral food we'd promised. First, though, she read me the riot act for not telling her about the spaghetti sauce incident, and made me promise to install a security system at the Merc. I didn't bother pointing out that it would not have detected vandalism in the parking lot.

I snuck upstairs to see if any of Claudette's friends had responded to my message. Several had. No surprise—they'd all loved her, couldn't believe the news. None expressed any fondness for Dean. One called meeting Claudette the highlight of the class. I printed that message to share at the service.

How is it, wrote a man whose profile picture bore an uncanny resemblance to the King, *that a dud of a dude winds up with such a dandy girlfriend?*

I'd never thought of it quite that way. Apparently as undistinguished an aspiring Elvis as he was a healer, Dean had attracted two fun-loving, sparkly women. Who had little else in common, besides being foodies who couldn't cook. Claudette had been sweet, if unreliable, and Linda was a harpy. Of course, Linda's husband had run off with another woman in a very public way. That would mess up anyone's mood.

She must really love him, to take him back and to defend him. In protecting him, she was also protecting their daughters. Linda Vincent as noble protector was a hard one to swallow. Keeping "Dr. Dean" off the stage and in the chiropractic office benefitted her financially as well.

The final message snagged my eye. *So sad. Hanging out with Claudette by the pool, it was obvious things weren't going the way she hoped. Too bad Dean couldn't appreciate her—but what else could you expect?!!?*

Meaning what? I replied, saying Dean had resumed his practice while waiting for a job offer.

A call to the College of Impersonation got me nowhere. "We don't discuss our students with anyone except potential employers, and then only with a release. Privacy concerns," said a woman who sounded eerily like Bette Midler.

I understood, but we were talking about how well a guy swiveled his hips and mimicked classic rock and roll, not state secrets. And whether the school had observed any trouble "at home." This was murder, after all.

"We're sorry. We simply can't comment. And we already told the detective—what was her name?"

Ah. Kim and I may not be sharing pages, but at least we were on the same one.

I flipped back to FB before shutting down. Dean's classmate had replied to my message: *Delusions of grandeur. Hound dog.*

Enough said.

·*Twenty-two*·

We were twenty minutes early, but Pine Meadow Lodge was already two-thirds full. Rows of chairs filled the middle of the large room, ringed by tables. French doors stood open to the glorious afternoon.

Fresca and Chiara delivered the fruit skewers and tortellini salad to the serving area, while Tracy and I found seats. Up front, Jeff sat with an older couple—probably his parents—and a petite woman with hair like Claudette's. Her sister? Ian sat at the end of the row. Thank God his grandparents hadn't come for a double funeral.

The minister who'd knelt with me in Back Street stood before us. He had the gift of making people comfortable even before he spoke.

"Claudette would want us to celebrate," he said. "To laugh and play. To throw a party she'd hate to miss." Jeff's father told a side-splitting story about meeting her the first time. Her sister, who shared her size and fashion taste, described shopping together in the juniors department and

Claudette's response to the clerks who assumed they were shopping for their daughters. Some stories were poignant, and few eyes stayed dry when Jeff spoke about their years together and their love for Ian.

The minister invited the rest of us to share a few words. I glanced at Fresca, but she gave a quick, decisive shake "no." This part of a service always unbalances me. Like I was sixteen again, with every weepy high school girl who'd ever had a crush on my dad acting like she'd be marked forever by his death, and every teenage boy whom he'd coached shuffling his feet, having no words for what he felt.

There had been no room for my words.

Which meant I needed to speak now. I rubbed my tattooed stars and cleared my throat. "Claudette was a friend to my family in more ways than I ever knew when she was alive." I told a story about going to dinner at Claudette's with Fresca once on a visit home. The power had gone out, so she tried to bake the lasagna on the grill, with results anyone else would have predicted, and everyone laughed. "One of her new friends, from Las Vegas, told me that meeting her was the highlight of the trip. I'm sure we all know exactly how he felt."

The service closed with a prayer, and friends of Ian's played a guitar and flute duet that reminded me of the first songbirds of spring. Fresca gripped my hand and I reached for my sister's.

Jeff's father invited everyone to stay for lunch, to celebrate life as Claudette had, with friends, food, and laughter. And with color: Each table held clusters of potted pansies for us to take home.

I joined Chiara in the buffet line. "Killers often go to their victims' funerals," I whispered. "So watch for anyone suspicious."

"I don't need to," she whispered back, "and neither do you. That's why Kim's here."

I followed her gaze to Kim. Today's ensemble—black slacks and a black-and-white houndstooth jacket—complemented her short blond hair. Coincidence that she was watching us at that moment? Yeah, right. I waved.

If the killer were here, he'd blend in well—half the village had come. I spotted Heidi and Kathy standing together, Sally standing alone, the owners of Applause! chatting with Mimi and Tony from the Jewel Inn, Serena from the salon, and almost every other shop and restaurant owner. The Taylor and Fontaine families were all accounted for, including Wendy's itty-bitty half-blind grandmother.

Linda and Dean Vincent stood at a tall table in the corner. He'd dressed doctor-casual today, and Linda wore a surprisingly appropriate peach linen dress, though her Roman sandals with four-inch wedge heels marred the effect. They seemed to be watching everyone else the way we were watching them. Was he wondering which classmate I'd talked to? Let him.

As I watched, two slender girls with long blond hair joined them. Linda slid an arm around one girl and kissed her on the cheek. "Their daughters?"

"Cassandra in the green dress, Jessica in blue. They just graduated. Jess is going to the same art school I went to," Chiara said. "I don't know Cassie's plans."

As I reached the round table where Fresca sat with Ted and Old Ned, Heidi stopped me, hand on my arm. "No restaurants are listed," she said. "I asked around, but no one, not even my broker friend, knows of any for sale on the QT. Sorry."

"Thanks," I said, and pulled out a chair next to the Redaways. I'd always viewed Ned as a straightforward guy, and his encouragement of the Merc's new direction seemed genuine. So why did they want our building? Not the time to ask.

"Girlie, your little car okay?" Ned said as I sat. "What is going on in this town?"

"The fingerprint powder was worse than the tomato sauce. But nothing soap and water couldn't fix."

Ted seemed a shadow of his hearty self. I smiled in sympathy. Claudette had been his friend and coworker, too.

"Ned, Friday night, you were out front greeting people, right?" He nodded, fork halfway to his mouth. "Did you see Dean and Linda Vincent arrive?"

He thought a moment, then shook his head. "Couldn't say, girlie. Too many folks milling around—they all run together."

"No crashers? No strangers?"

"They wouldn't dare."

"True."

The gathering almost felt like any other party in a town full of parties. To my relief, no one seemed worried about eating Fresca's food—meaning no one suspected her in Ian's illness.

Angelo stood alone, cradling a cup of coffee. Like most of the men here, he wore khakis and a sport coat that would probably hide any sign of a knife on his belt or pocket, even if I were close enough to check.

Fresca gave me the signal to leave. At the door, Jeff and Ian accepted hugs and condolences. Cassie Vincent stood behind Ian, one nail-bitten hand on his shoulder. Were they dating?

"Sweetie, you had us all so scared." Fresca kissed Ian tenderly. Eyes wide, skin damp and flushed in all the wrong places, he avoided her look and said nothing. Cassie's grip on his shoulder tightened. Aside to Jeff, Fresca asked, "Any word yet on what it was?"

"All I can say is, thank God the dose was too small to kill us. Either he didn't know what he was doing, or he just meant to scare us."

"He?" I said.

Jeff shrugged. "Or whoever. Thanks so much for coming."

* * *

We got back to the Merc too late to bother opening. I sent Tracy home and got a wet rag to wipe a few stray tomato splatters off my car. When I came inside, Fresca had donned her cooking clothes and begun transforming the kitchen into Production Central. She handed me a large stainless steel bowl.

"Put those eggs in here to come to room temperature, then set up the drying racks." She snapped the dough hook into the mixer with a satisfying thunk.

"You're making pasta now? I was hoping to show you Liz's sketches for the courtyard." *And find out more about your history with Claudette, and that box of recipes in the basement, and what on earth you've been doing the last few days, besides avoiding me and my questions.*

She crouched to retrieve the pasta roller from its cabinet. "Later, darling. It's time I got back to work."

"But you could be here all night."

"Better than staying home and throwing myself another pity party. The shelves are empty, and Max wants fettuccine for his weekend specials."

Had Claudette's service triggered a change in mood, or was Fresca taking her own advice to act as if she felt like whipping up a storm of spaghetti? Didn't matter. I did as directed.

But then I pushed my luck. "So now will you hire a lawyer?"

"No reason, darling. Get out of here. I have herbs to chop."

The first batch would be ready before long, and there's nothing like brand-new fettuccine boiled briefly and drizzled with freshly grated Parmesan and butter or olive oil. But I'd been dismissed.

On the side street, around the corner from the Merc, is a tiny hole-in-the-wall where Jewel Bay's resident herbalist keeps a treasure trove of natural remedies. Sixty-fivish, with neatly trimmed gray hair and the slight stoop of a tall man who's been leaning in to listen to shorter folk all his life, Bill Schmidt was not your typical hippy herbalist. A world-renowned authority on wild foods and medicinal plants of the Northern Rockies, he often closes shop to spend the day foraging, regardless of weather, if some plant or another is ripe for the picking. I'd been thrilled when he agreed to share his expertise at the Merc.

The smells of earth and spice enveloped me the moment I stepped inside. Bill emerged from the back room, a bundle of moxa sticks in hand. "Ah, Erin." His voice held gentleness, as though his hours in the woods had worn off the edges. He gripped my hand and met my gaze with clear, patient blue eyes. "I trust you're well."

"Just here to confirm our plans for Friday afternoon's walk and demonstration, and find out what supplies you need."

"Depends what nature's grocery and pharmacy is offering this week. Let's go check out my other office." He gestured toward the door.

One of Jewel Bay's many glories is the Nature Trail, aka the River Road, above the Jewel River. Originally the homesteaders' road into town, it had long ago been replaced by the Cutoff, the narrow highway on the other side of the river, and fell into disuse. In my kidhood, volunteers—including my dad and his brothers—worked out an easement with the power company and reclaimed the unpaved trail for a foot and bike path. Bill had permission to harvest there for educational purposes.

"How's your mother today?" he asked on our way up the hill behind Dragonfly Dry Goods.

"She's been in a funk since Claudette's death, but she seems to be coming out of it."

"She's a good, strong woman. Let her feel what she feels, and she'll be fine."

Was there something more to his comment than neighborly concern?

He pointed. "*Lomatium dissectum*, or desert parsley. A tincture is nature's best antiviral. Belongs in every flu kit." It grew in a sunny spot among the rocks, below a shaded hillside covered in lupine.

I fingered the lacy fronds and remembered spotting wild roses last night while searching for Sandburg. "We're mainly after edibles. How about wild roses? We could make rose petal jelly. And rose water." Candy Divine had mentioned using rose water in her Turkish delight. I imagined a class, in August when the apples and apricots ripened.

We found a bank of deep pink blossoms, and I drank in their soft, fresh scent. Plenty for a demo—everyone could take home a small jar of jelly. I whipped out my phone and made a note.

Bill took out his knife and sliced off a quarter-sized piece of birch bark. "Too dry. Too bad. In spring, when the sap is running, this is nature's energy drink."

Again with the knife. Did every man in town carry one?

Several wild mints and sages were ready to pick, and so were sorrel, watercress, and wild lettuces. We picked our way down the steep bank to the river and, in a swamp stinky with decay, found a patch of wild onions.

Back on the trail, I saw plenty of dandelion greens. We'd steam those, and sauté a few of Jimmy Vang's morels.

As we retraced our steps, I borrowed Bill's knife to cut some wild lupine.

"Careful with that *Lupinis*," Bill said. "The wild form is a natural insecticide, and useful for treating vertigo, but it can be toxic. There are some edible varieties, though, and the garden hybrid's safe." As we walked, he stressed that even toxic plants had medicinal qualities and could be consumed, if the right parts were used and prepared properly.

At his shop, Bill waved me to his consultation area. Two oak armchairs burnished dark from age and use flanked an ancient black lacquered desk accented with red and gold. I pulled one out and sat while he wrote out a list of things we needed.

I decided to pop the question that had been bugging me. "Bill, what would cause headache and nausea, with blurred vision and a slow, irregular pulse?" I summarized Ian Randall's symptoms, without naming him, but the wariness that crept into Bill's eyes told me he knew.

He looked at me intently as he handed me the supply list. "Be careful, Erin."

I didn't point out that he hadn't answered my question, or ask, "Careful of what?" I got distracted. On the shelf behind him, next to a copy of his text, *The Field Guide to Mountain Medicinals*, was Deputy Kim Caldwell's card.

Screaming "danger."

· *Twenty-three* ·

On my way home, I stopped at the grocery store for canning jars and ingredients for the jelly, and a few other supplies Bill requested. I rounded the end of the baking aisle and saw Adam Zimmerman, swinging a basket, on his way to the checkout lanes. Intriguing as he was, I didn't have the heart for any conversation that might trigger my emotions. I stepped back, letting him clear the door without spotting me. The day had been too full—I needed to retreat to my cabin, away from all demands and suspicions.

First, though, my poor little Subaru needed a bath, so I drove through the car wash. As the sprayers circled, squirting soap and water, I closed my eyes and tried to imagine who might have put a jar of poisoned pesto in Claudette's refrigerator for her son or ex-husband to find. Poisoning seems like a cowardly crime. A dangerous crime, no matter what the intent.

Why? Who benefitted?

I flashed on the Vincent twins with their parents at the memorial service. Dean was a prime suspect. How could harming the Randalls help him defend himself? Did chiropractors take the oath to "do no harm"?

What would Linda do to deflect suspicion from him—or herself? I didn't seriously believe she would hurt her daughter's boyfriend, or his father, on purpose. But Bill had pointed out that different varieties of a single plant might have greater or lesser toxicity. What if she fed them a small dose of something sickening, just to scare them? And point to my mother.

What about Angelo? My theory of a blowup between him and Claudette gave him no reason to go after Jeff or Ian. Unless one of them knew his secret and threatened to expose it. But if that were the case, he'd have left a calling card, to send a clear message of silence.

A few clicks on my iPhone gave me Linda's address. Just a quick detour before heading home. I drove my sparkling clean buggy to a subdivision up the hill behind the high school, where neat, tidy houses sported white trim and front porches that were smartly decorated but rarely used. The development backed up to the road where Claudette lived. The Vincents and Randalls had practically been neighbors, making it easy for their kids to see each other.

If I had the timeline right, the parents' affair had begun last fall, just before Ian left home. Maybe their kids' connection had brought Dean and Claudette together.

I drove by Linda's house. No cars or other signs of life. No doubt the Randall family gathering had migrated to Claudette's cottage. Cassie and Jess might be there, but what about Linda and Dean? Other than Claudette's affair with Dean, I knew little about the two families' relationship.

I circled the block and pulled over, giving myself a view of Linda's driveway but staying safely out of sight.

A few minutes later, a dark gray Suburban approached from the other direction and parked in the driveway, next to an older Subaru. Dean headed up the sidewalk and let himself in. Hardly a shock, whether he and Linda were back together or not.

Another car came up the street and the garage doors opened. A red Cadillac sedan, so new it still bore paper tags instead of real license plates, turned in and entered, Linda's platinum head visible on the driver's side and a girl in the front passenger seat.

Was the car a "forgive me" present?

Those superclose Montana connections made investigation both easier and more difficult. I ticked off the ties between our murder victim and our—well, my—suspects: Claudette dated Dean. Dean was married to Linda. And their daughter Cassie might be dating Claudette's son, Ian.

Claudette lived next door to James Angelo. Linda hired Angelo to cater—

A baritone disrupted my accounting and I practically flew out the sunroof.

"Spying on my family?"

Someone ought to bottle the restorative powers of pinot gris.

Oh, wait. They had. In fact, I was relishing those powers on the back deck, recovering from my encounter with Dean Vincent. I'd parked in front of a house with a FOR SALE sign on it, so I told him I was meeting a friend for a showing, but my pal must have gotten held up, or maybe I had the time wrong, and did the Vincents like the neighborhood? Dean had scowled, then muttered indecipherables and stepped away from my open window. Not wanting to give his suspicions any weight, I made a show of checking my phone for a text or voice mail from my imaginary friend before starting the engine and driving away.

Truth be told, he'd startled the bejeebers out of me. But my bejeebers were returning, thanks to the tart-but-fruity wine, and an appetizer of olive tapenade on Montana Gold herbed crackers. I'd channeled my burst of adrenaline into re-creating my mother's endive, radicchio, and romaine salad, topped with quarters of hard-boiled egg and slices of lightly pickled roasted golden beets. Sandburg had enjoyed a tasty treat of canned tuna, and fallen asleep in the other chair.

But I could not stop trying to unweave the strands of suspicion that entangled my mother. What was I missing?

First thing Friday morning, I met my brother-in-law at his office to review options for a security alarm and camera system for the Merc. We could stream a live camera feed to the office computer. He and I could also access it remotely with our phones. I hated the idea, but as he said, you never knew what they'd show—and I wouldn't have to check it unless there was a problem.

Then time for the Village Merchants Association's weekly breakfast meeting at the Jewel Inn. Most weeks, the biggest challenge was what to order. I adore their Greek omelet, with a homemade English muffin and potatoes. The Ranch Scramble always hits the spot, and their crepes are to die for. Chiara can be counted on to order the Veggie Benedict: avocado, sliced tomatoes, and two poached eggs on an English muffin topped with killer Hollandaise. Many a customer claims to gain weight thinking of breakfast at the Inn.

As usual in summer, the front of the house overflowed. When Chiara and I entered the banquet room, coffee and juice had been served, and other members compared notes on the first week of tourist season.

Long tables formed a rectangle, a moose rack draped with Mardi Gras beads overseeing one end of the room and an elk mount in Groucho Marx glasses the other. Wendy hadn't been a regular since opening Le Panier, but she and Linda huddled together in the far corner. Linda shot me a look that said Dean had relayed our little conversation, and neither of them believed a word I'd said. Which, I hated to admit, showed good sense.

"To the Queen of the Festa." Kathy, the Association chair, raised her cup in a toast.

A creature of good habits, Chiara gave her order, then it was my turn. My eyes popped at the sight of our new young waitress. The Vincent girls weren't identical, but after seeing them once, I couldn't be sure who was who.

"The crepes, please. And are you Cass, or Jess?"

"Cassie." She smiled shyly, looking far more like her mother than her dad.

"I think we all agree," Kathy said, "that the Festa di Jewel Bay was a rousing success and should be an annual event."

Cheers of agreement circled the room. I had my doubts, chiefly whether the Festa would be remembered more for murder than for good food, music, and profits.

"The Food Bank director tells me donations were twice what she hoped for," she continued, "although I think we can attribute some of that to the tragedy."

Linda reported on Saturday night's ticket sales, also above expectations. "And Jody Fisher says count him in for next year. He loves playing in Jewel Bay."

"We did nearly double the business this weekend over last," Ray reported. "Our Italian specials sold out."

Is this how a parent feels when her baby brings home the first report card with all A's, or cracks the first home run? Chiara squeezed my hand. "Good job, little sis."

"Sunshine always helps," Ray added with a chuckle. I made a note to track weather along with sales.

"Food lovers not only love to eat out," Heidi said, "they love to cook. And they love to shop. I've reordered glassware, bakeware, and utensils I thought would last all summer."

"Well, they don't buy children's clothing, that's for sure."

"Sally," Kathy said. "That can't be true. I saw so many Puddle Jumpers bags walking around town, I thought they'd grown legs and escaped."

Everyone laughed. Sally pursed her lips.

"So it's not too early to start planning for next year. Especially if we want to get the highway merchants more involved."

Good luck with that.

"Erin, this was your brain child," she continued. "You'll lead the committee for the Second Annual Festa?"

"Second the nomination," Old Ned said in his gravelly baritone.

Wendy shoved back her chair and stood, head bowed. Behind her, about to serve a plate of blueberry waffles, Cassie made a quick save. "I nominate Linda Vincent as committee chair. She arranged all the volunteers for Saturday night, and the food contributions and musicians." Wendy rearranged her coffee cup and water glass. "We need fresh blood." She sat as abruptly as she'd risen.

Eyes wide, Kathy scanned the room. "Do I hear a second for Linda?" No one spoke. She trained her gray eyes on me. "Erin, will you accept the nomination?"

Criminy. I didn't want the job, but I sure as heck didn't want to say no and end up with Linda in charge by default. Especially of something so important to the Merc. If her welcome speech at the Gala indicated things to come, she might leave us out entirely.

Chiara kicked me. "Say yes."

I cleared my throat. "I'd be delighted. My first act as chair is to ask Linda to reprise her excellent job on the Saturday Night Gala."

"Hear, hear," Old Ned said.

"Nice one," Chiara whispered, but I'd just done the thing I'd been determined not to do. Hate when that happens.

"Sorry we're late. Busy out front." Mimi George slid in next to me, breathless, her husband, Tony, beside her.

"Cassie, you're a doll. Coffee when you have a moment. I love summer."

"Aren't we going to vote?" Linda said, her voice rising almost to a whine.

"Erin hit a home run her first time at bat. Why change the lineup now?" Tony George had had a cup of coffee or two in the major leagues twenty years ago, and baseball lingo peppered his speech.

"There's only one valid nomination," Kathy said. "No second on yours." Linda scowled and cast a sharp look at Wendy.

"Erin agreed, if Linda would organize Saturday night. Sounds perfect," Ray said.

Kathy called the question. Like a lot of small groups, we follow Robert's Rules of Order only if we can't reach consensus, and even then, we use the short form. Bob's Rules. Only Linda voted nay. Wendy abstained. She hadn't touched her waffles and seemed to be trying to slide underneath the table.

Time for other business. Time for food. My crepes were perfect and I told Mimi so. She beamed.

We approved July's advertising campaign and heard a report from the Chamber director on the 35th Anniversary of Summer Fair, the art festival in early August. The crew from a popular TV show, Food Preneurs, planned to film the main event, a steak cook-off featuring local chefs.

I was beginning to share Mimi George's excitement.

Except for the little problem of murder and the fingers pointing at my mother.

We dispatched the rest of the agenda to the tune of knives and forks, and the murmurs of satisfied eaters. Cassie handled the room efficiently, and I complimented her to Mimi.

"We'll miss her when she goes to college in Seattle this fall. Hazard of the business—get 'em trained, and off they go."

Seattle. Where Ian lived.

A commotion arose across the room. "I don't know why I bothered to come." Linda Vincent threw down her napkin. "The same old clique calls the shots. No one else has a chance to do anything different."

"That's not true," the frame shop owner said. "Erin's new. The Festa's new."

"She's a mouthpiece for her mother. You all blame my husband for Claudette Randall's death. Give Fresca Murphy a closer look. I guarantee you won't like what you see."

"Foul ball," called Tony George.

"Now hold your bucking horses one minute there, sister," Old Ned said, voice booming. "I've known Francesca Murphy for thirty-five years. She didn't kill nobody. The slime that did it should hang, but it weren't her."

Cassie Vincent stood motionless in the back of the room, eyes big as the tray she carried. She'd come in from the kitchen in time to witness her mother's tirade.

Across the table, Kathy looked stunned, uncertain how to regain order. Serena Travis, a tall, elegant salon owner, stepped into the void. "Linda, why don't we get some fresh air?" She gathered up Linda's purse, took her by the arm, and led her out the side door.

"Adjourned." Kathy tapped her spoon on her water glass, the tinkling barely audible above the murmured comments.

I crossed the room to where Cassie stood, shocked. "Sit a moment. Mimi won't mind." I led her to the chair her mother had vacated, and I sat in Wendy's still-warm seat. Mimi brought her a glass of water, then took the tray and began clearing the tables. "Take a little drink and a deep breath."

As she did, her heaving chest slowed and her breath calmed. "I can't believe she said that. About you, and your mother."

"She's upset. Don't worry."

I could imagine her confusion: Her father ran away with her boyfriend's mother, then called it off and came home, and now the mother was dead. Her boyfriend had been poisoned, and her own mother had created a very public ruckus. All this as she and her sister were graduating and heading out into the world themselves. My teenage years seemed placid in comparison.

"How's Ian?"

"He's been so angry." Her eyes watered. "Last Sunday, he was supposed to meet me for breakfast before my shift, but he went racing by and didn't even stop. I know it's all so awful, but he's been so mean and nasty."

And then the poisoning. That can turn a foul mood downright rotten.

"What happened? How long have you been dating?"

She took a sip of water, then coughed. "Almost two years. Since the start of my junior year, right after his parents got divorced. Last night, at his mom's house after the memorial service, he said he didn't want to see me anymore." Tears rolled down her splotchy cheeks and she sniffed noisily. "I think he thinks one of my parents killed her."

"Oh, honey." I touched her shoulder, not willing to tell her I thought so, too, and so did half the town. The other half blamed my mother.

Did the Randalls suspect one of the Vincents of leaving the poisoned jar, too? I could hardly ask.

"My dad's a jerk," Cassie said. "My mom's not bad—she's just ticked at him. I wish he'd stayed away."

Time to go in for the kill, so to speak. "Cassie, when your dad left, was it for good—or was he coming back?"

She shook her head. "He told us he had a job lined up as Elvis. But I think he got there, to Las Vegas, and people found out he was scamming them. So now he's calling it a vacation to cover his sorry butt."

The peaceful harmonies of home life for a tribute artist. Not even one's children appreciate the sacrifices made for art.

"Those Elvis outfits of his are—well, form-fitting. I

couldn't help but wonder the other night where he keeps his keys when he goes out in costume."

"He tucks them in his boot. In a special pocket."

Ah. A guy could hide a knife in an ankle boot, reach down, whip it out, and stab someone in one swift motion.

"My mom never hated Claudette. People think so, but she did suggest it would be a good time for Claudette to move for good. Make a real break. She had friends in Missoula she thought might hire Claudette."

Not many women would have helped their husband's ex-lover find a new job in another town. Linda deserved credit. Of course, if Claudette quickly moved on, that would have helped ease the embarrassment for them both.

I was beginning to wonder why one of them hadn't offed Dean.

"It's got to have been hard on her, seeing him with someone else."

More sniffing and nodding. "But Mom and Claudette were friends first. We were all friends. And now no one is friends, not even me and Ian."

I squeezed her hand. "This is a hard time for him. He needs his friends, whether he knows it or not—and whether you stay together or not."

Mimi approached, looking sympathetic but ready to return to routine. "Let's get you cleaned up and back to work." Cassie nodded. I told her again how sorry I was, and what a good job she'd done that morning.

I hurried through the pine-paneled bar, away from the watchful eyes of stuffed wildlife, and out past the Inn's bustling dining room. After the morning drama, the clear mountain air startled me, and I blinked against the sunshine.

"Hey." Ted Redaway stepped out of the Inn's shadowed side.

"Hey yourself. What are you doing here? Everybody else is long gone." Split like peas, in my father's phrase.

"Just wanted to make sure you were okay."

"Why wouldn't I be?" I started down the steps. When I reached the sidewalk, he fell in beside me.

"Well, she did rip into your mother, and you."

I'd been so focused on Cassie that I'd almost forgotten her mother's tantrum. I shrugged. "You can't let talk bother you. Fresca taught me that long ago."

"Nice of you to comfort her kid. She all right?"

"You saw that?" His interest was touching.

"I bet she's pretty upset, with all that's gone on. Probably talking off the top of her head. I guess the kids are close."

"Actually, she seemed pretty rational, despite the tears. I thought Claudette intended to start a restaurant here in town, but Cassie says Linda encouraged her to move. If it were me, I'd have wanted to kill her." Cassie had said the plan was Missoula, safely a hundred miles away. Oh—Angelo had cooked there. Had Claudette been asking him about opportunities? But why would that lead to an argument?

I glanced up at Ted. Beneath his Harley ball cap, his forehead was creased and his heavy reddish eyebrows tightly knit. "Why so worried?"

He startled. "Oh, nothing. 'Cept maybe Dad's right and town's going to—whatever."

That's when I noticed. "You're not wearing your knife anymore. You've worn a knife since eighth grade. What happened?" His recent weapon of choice had been a six-inch blade in a tooled leather sheath snapped on his belt.

"Only an idiot would walk around wearing a knife in a town where a woman's just been stabbed."

"How do you know she was stabbed? Kim wouldn't tell us, and the paper didn't say."

Something across the street caught his eye. "She told my dad."

Odd. Or maybe not. Maybe standard operating procedure to be close-mouthed with suspects and their families. But very little seemed standard around here anymore.

Suspicious minds.

· *Twenty-four* ·

In between working with customers, Tracy and I double-spiffed the Merc for the wild food demo and the weekend ahead. We brewed up pots of both our standby Cowboy Roast and the surprisingly drinkable Wheat Coffee.

Early afternoon, I slipped out for a trip down the lake to the vineyard. In other regions, April showers bring May flowers, but here, we get about six weeks of spring sunshine, followed by three weeks of heavy rain. Then, in the second or third week of June, all glory bursts forth. We were right on schedule. I drove past old homesteads guarded by lilacs, their blooms fading, and rows of iris, peonies, and poppies. You can tell what's safe to plant by what's withstood decades of browsing deer.

A few miles south of town, a single light sped toward me. It zigged and zagged across the center line as though the object were to weave in between the slashes, not stay to the right of them.

"Criminy." This motorcycle rider acted like he had a death wish. I slowed and hugged the fog line, eyes peeled, not wanting to be the driver who helped him get it. He used the full lane and then some—not smart on these roads, with their slim shoulders, fallen rocks, and darting wildlife. As the bike careened closer, the driver leaned forward so far he seemed to grow out of the handlebars, a cloud of road dust behind him. I closed my window. When he passed me, going at least ninety, I sighed in relief and accelerated to highway speed. Bad as our roads can be in winter, summer is worse.

Wine making in Montana had long been limited to cherry and other fruit wines. But new short-season hybrids sprouted several vineyards along the lake, where soils, slopes, and warm winds combined with the other essential ingredient: gutsy people willing to work hard and pour everything they had into a dream.

Love those people.

I parked in front of the main building, a vintage Quonset hut that Sam and Jen had cleaned and dressed up by adding a facade of aged yellow stucco, red roof tiles, and a bell tower topped with a cross. From the outside, a visitor would never know it wasn't an old Spanish mission. Spanish explorers never reached Montana, but who's quibbling?

Smiling and sun-burnished, Sam emerged from between rows of vines and spread his arms. "Another day in Paradise."

"Heavenly spot, for sure. Glad you could spare some wine for us. It's selling well." He opened the arched wooden doors and I followed him inside. The giant fermenting tanks stood empty now, but yeasty smells blended with oak permeated the air year-round.

"You need it, you name it. The Merc's a godsend. Making wine in country that can frost twelve months a year's easy compared to selling it." He wriggled a dolly under a stack of cartons emblazoned with the Monte Verde name and logo—the pseudo-mission outlined against the mountains, the rising sun behind them.

"I don't mean to pry, Sam"—or maybe I did—"but how's business?"

"Lots of interest, and everyone who tours the place buys at least one bottle. But we need more retail outlets." I popped the hatchback and he began sliding boxes in. "We fell into that trap, you know? Sold a nice place in California, plunked the profits into our dream, and here we are, treading water. Shoulda bought a buffalo ranch—you can always eat 'em. You can't live on Viognier alone."

I flashed a quick grin. "Might be fun to try."

He brushed back a stray lock, brown flecked with gray. "Yeah, well, the bankers won't take wine and CDs in lieu of cash."

"Folks are skeptical of products they don't associate with Montana. But I can give you a list of potential outlets. And connect you with the wine buyer at SavClub." A small outfit like this might not meet the production minimums, but it was worth a shot.

His eyes lit up. "Fantastic. Hey, I don't see an invoice—let's check in the office."

No luck, so Sam called Jen down at the main house. We chatted while we waited.

"Sam, you and Jen were at the Festa on Friday night. Did you see Dean and Linda arrive?"

"Oh, yeah. Linda came over to say hi, made sure we were set for playing Saturday night, too."

Made sense. "What about Dean?"

Sam cocked his head, remembering. "He said hi, grabbed her, and they headed for the bar. I picture him coming from my left—must have come in the back gate. Like he'd dropped her off and gone to park."

But he'd insisted they parked out front and come in together. Why lie?

"Seemed like you two were in and out quite a bit. Setup always such a pain?"

His brows furrowed and he glanced at his watch. "Where is she?" He riffled back through the stacks of papers he'd already checked.

A few minutes later, Jen arrived, face flushed, her wavy brown hair coming loose from its braid. She found the invoice, in the file drawer in a folder labeled MERC.

"Why would you file it, when it goes with the order?"

"I just got ahead of myself, okay?"

I hate hearing couples squabble. "Thanks, guys." I headed out. Behind me, I heard Sam say, "What took you so long?"

"Sorry," Jen replied. "The bank called again. That guy from California who called Friday afternoon."

Friday afternoon, when the Krausses were prepping for a gig. Sounded like a lender who forgot the rule against giving bad news just before the weekend—or who wanted to make his borrowers sweat. The reason Jen looked rattled on Friday?

"They want to see the books. They want proof of a turnaround." That could be good, or bad, depending on the size of the loan and how delinquent they were. If the hole was too deep, even a SavClub promotion might be too little, too late.

"Erin, wait," Jen called, and I stopped. "We've got something we want you to try." She led the way to the tasting room and uncorked a bottle, hiding the label with her hand, and poured three short glasses.

I raised the glass to the light and swirled the deep red liquid, watching it slide down the sides of the glass. "Good color." Sniffed it. Blackberry and spice, with a hint of leather. Took a sip and let it move around my mouth. "Cabernet. A nice one."

"First bottling from the experimental plot. It won't be ready to sell for a year or so, but I think it's got potential."

Could they hang on that long? "Me, too, if the price is right. As Sam and I said earlier, people don't expect a fine local wine, so they aren't willing to spend a lot on that first bottle. I call it 'adventure pricing'—high enough to seem competitive in quality and to give you a profit, but low enough for buyers to take a gamble."

She poured us each another couple of fingers. "See, that's what I like about you, Erin. You work with vendors, you give us advice, but you don't treat us like idiots. And you don't keep changing your mind, like Claudette. She drove me nuts."

A shaky business could not afford an unreliable retailer. But a retailer could not afford a disorganized vendor in financial trouble. I'd have to step carefully.

"Thanks. Claudette did great with the artistic side and with customers, but as you know, there's a lot more to running a successful business." In truth, she blew like the wind and had been a disaster as a manager—more than Fresca had realized.

A few minutes later, I reached over the counter to set my empty glass by the sink. A case of wine stood on the floor, a knife on top. I closed my eyes briefly and pictured Sam: He carried a Leatherman on his belt, at least when he worked the vines. This must be Jen's. Everyone, everywhere, seemed to keep a blade close at hand. Except me, the lone woman out.

As I drove home, the afternoon sun dappling the road, I remembered Sam's certainty that Dean came in Red's back gate. No doubt Dean lied to divert attention from himself, thinking no one would know when he'd come in, or where, except maybe Linda. Who had plenty of reason to protect him.

That meant he either beat Claudette and her killer to the gate, or he met her there and killed her. Could I pin down the time of his arrival more precisely?

A third scenario: He'd seen Claudette meet her killer, and kept his mouth shut. Out of character, but not impossible.

The musicians had been in and out that back gate, hauling in their equipment. Had Jennifer dashed out for a forgotten cord, run into Claudette, had words, and let loose?

Or worse?

Was Jen's stress from financial fear—or criminal guilt?

A whitetail buck jumped out of the borrow pit onto the road. I braked hard and he dashed into the woods. My heart thudded against my rib cage.

Easy, girl. Eyes on the road. People are counting on you—and that load of wine.

· *Twenty-five* ·

At three thirty, eighteen people gathered at the entrance to the Nature Trail, not counting Bill, Fresca, and me.

"Welcome. I'm delighted to see so much interest in gathering and cooking with native foods. I'm Erin Murphy, manager of the Glacier Mercantile. Many of you know my mother, Fresca." She smiled and waved, crisp and summery in tan crops and a coral tank with a white visor. Only my mother would go for a walk in the woods in white Keds, though they were scrubbable leather.

"Bill Schmidt is our fearless leader today. Bill's been a working herbalist for I don't know long."

"For so long," he said, "that I was in the first class to graduate from Hogwarts." Laughter rippled the aspen leaves above us.

We hadn't expected so many people, but I'd learned at SavClub to never cringe at a good turnout. Just make sure people get what they came for. "With the size of the group and the roar of the river, it may be a little hard to hear at times. But don't worry." I held up my pocket recorder. "I'll record Bill's comments and your questions, and upload the audio to the Merc's website."

Bill gave a short introduction on the value of knowing our edible and medicinal neighbors. Recorder in hand, I watched the rapt audience. Funny to see the relentlessly stylish Heidi wearing hiking sandals with her black jungle print dress, scribbling notes. I recognized two women who'd come in the shop this morning and seen the poster.

"A few principles of wild crafting," Bill said, scanning the crowd and projecting his voice, "then we'll take a walk."

I turned my attention from Bill back to the gathering in time to see three stragglers join us. What on earth were Jeff, Ian, and Cassie doing here? Jeff joined the group, clearly listening, but Ian held back a few steps. Cassie glanced from one to the other, uncertain what to do. She spotted me and gave me a shy wave.

"Never eat or use anything you're not sure of. You've heard that about mushrooms and berries, but be aware that many safe plants have toxic look-alikes. A hybrid in your herbaceous border may be perfectly safe for you and your children to touch, and even for a canine nibble or two, while its wild counterpart may be quite dangerous."

The "record" light seemed to flash like strobes on top of a speeding sheriff's car. I couldn't pull Bill over and pelt him with questions. Was I right in thinking that whatever the poison was, and whoever had put it there, Claudette had grown it herself? At the edge of the circle, Fresca gave Jeff a hug and kissed Ian's cheek.

We retraced the route Bill and I had taken the day before. I handed out paper bags, and we plucked rose petals and picked dandelion greens. "Before you curse the dandelions in your yard, remember your pioneer grandmothers saved the seeds and carried them out here," Bill said. "In drought years, they may have been the only greens some homesteaders had, and they're a rich source of vitamins. Too many medicinal uses to mention. And the roots make an excellent coffee substitute."

Could we create our own? Something earthy and unexpected, with a bit of spice. What about a traditional roasted barley drink—gluten-free? I envisioned The Glacier Mercantile's line of locally prepared beverages: a dandelion root mix, herbal teas, and of course, a signature coffee, blended and roasted to our specifications.

"It's not the seeds' fault that the plant is so well suited for every kind of soil, or that it's fallen out of favor," he said lightly.

"Dandelion wine is always in favor, and we've got an easy recipe for you," Fresca added.

About halfway, Ian and Cassie stopped to rest on a rock ledge. Jeff left the group as well, wandering down a deer-and-dog trail toward the water. I handed my mother the recorder and followed. "Good to see you," I said. "Ian's looking much better."

"He's on the mend. I thought he could use a little fresh air—we didn't know about the herb walk, but it's always good to see Bill."

"How do you know him?"

"He helped Claudette lay out her herb garden, and gave her advice on medicinal plants." Bill, that sly fox, hadn't said a thing. "She treated all of Ian's childhood illnesses herself."

Which made it even more likely that something she grew had both beneficial and harmful properties. "Surprised to see Cassie. She told me this morning that Ian broke up with her last night."

Jeff tossed a small river rock from hand to hand. "He's pretty mixed up right now. She brought him lemon custard from the Inn, his favorite. They're good kids, and good together, but they're so young."

That they were. "I'm sure you tried to keep your nose out

of Claudette's romantic life, but any idea why she got involved with Dean?"

He scratched his head. "That puzzled me, too. It wasn't like her to break up a friend's marriage, so I'm guessing he made the first move. She could be gullible. If he said he and Linda were kaput, she'd have believed him." Consistent with my mother's theory that she'd succumbed to his flattery.

We caught up with the group a few hundred yards down the trail. Bill pointed out the wild asparagus and fiddlehead patches, past their prime. Those of us with waterproof shoes dug wild onions.

Bags and notebooks full, we worked our way back to the trailhead, pausing as Bill pointed out other useful plants and answered questions.

Cassie, Ian, and Jeff lagged, the two kids a few steps behind, deep in conversation. I waited for Jeff. "You're all welcome to come to the Merc and watch weeds turn into food and wine."

"Thanks," Jeff said with a shake of his head. "The Merc meant a lot to Claudette. But I think we need to get Ian home for a rest."

"You bet." I gave him a quick hug, waved at the kids, and zipped down the hill.

Back at the Merc, Tracy and Fresca served iced wild mint sun tea we'd made earlier. A student trimmed wild onions at Bill's direction, while two others rinsed the greens and rose petals. Love those deep sinks. Love our commercial kitchen. Love watching other people cook while I sit back and salivate.

Fresca set the rose petals to steep for ten minutes. "I like to freeze a few in ice cube trays, then add them to lemonade. Or use them to garnish a fruit salad or vanilla ice cream."

"The petals and hips are both excellent sources of Vitamin C," Bill added.

"I get my vitamins at SavClub," a student said.

"Better to get them from food," the woman next to her said, "than from synthetic chemicals. And it's prettier."

"Color is a good guide," Bill said. "The more colors on your plate, the more vitamins and minerals you'll get."

The first woman picked up a pottery plate showing a long-eared red rabbit romping through green grasses dotted with pink, yellow, and orange flowers, a rainbow in the background. "So if I eat chocolate cake off this plate, it will be good for me?"

So nice to hear laughter fill the Merc, after all the tears.

The front door chimed and I turned to greet the customer. My smile stiffened. Impossible to tell, from Kim Caldwell's dress or demeanor, whether this was a personal or professional call. Betting on the latter, I met her at the front counter.

"For a woman who never eats, you have an amazing talent for showing up when we're cooking," I said in a teasing tone.

"You're always cooking up something, Erin."

I ignored that. "Any developments?" Meaning, don't arrest my mother in the middle of a demonstration.

"I have some questions for your mother."

No phalanx of deputies outside, no passel of patrol cars. She'd come alone, so no arrest. Not yet anyway.

I gestured at the crowd gathered around the kitchen counters. "Can they wait? She and Bill Schmidt are *in medias demo*."

Kim nodded and followed me to the kitchen. I poured iced tea for her, and we watched Fresca strain the rose petal tea and start it to boil, adding lemon juice, pectin, and sugar. Two students sterilized jelly jars and lids. Bill prepared the morels, discoursing about mushroom hunting, safety, respect for the land, and vitamins as he chopped. He managed to make it all sound so appealing that I half convinced myself I'd get up early in the morning and traipse up to a swampy area up behind the orchard and search out—

No way. I love the woods, but I also love snuggling with Mr. Sandburg, and coming to work clean.

Bill sautéed the morels and set them aside, then sautéed the boiled dandelion greens, wild onions, and seasoning. The mouthwatering aromas did their trick, and when Tracy and Fresca handed out small plates of wild veggies, sprinkled with a touch of grated Parmesan, we all fell on them. "Mmm," they said, or "I never imagined," and "if I don't tell my kids what it is, they'll love it."

Even Kim ate up. Whether that foretold good news or bad, I couldn't guess.

Finally, the jelly was in its jars and the herbs in their bags. Tracy distributed the bounty, along with packs of recipe cards. The Food Underfoot wild food and herb walk and demo was an official success. Unlike most demos, we weren't promoting our own products, so we didn't sell much—although the women who'd razzed each other about vitamins each bought a rainbow rabbit plate. But immediate sales aren't the main measure of success. The event brought in several newcomers, and I was sure they'd all be back for more Montana-made food and drink. And the things that go with it.

If seeing Kim bothered Fresca, she'd done a good job hiding it. When I locked the door behind the last customer and Kim hadn't left, we had to face the music. Fresca retreated momentarily into her own personal yoga class, releasing a long breath, relaxing her shoulders, and standing tall. Even I couldn't tell whether she really felt steady, or was just acting "as if."

"Bill, you'll stay a moment?" Kim asked. He wiped his hands on the Merc's apron and nodded. "Tracy, you can go." Tracy's head—and her beaded earrings—bobbed in relief.

Once she left, I refilled our iced teas. Bill and Fresca stood in the kitchen, and I took a stool at the counter, facing Kim. I sipped my tea and tried to absorb my mother's calm by osmosis.

"Fresca, you harvest herbs and vegetables from

Claudette's garden for your cooking, don't you?" Fresca nodded slowly. "Have you ever harvested foxglove?"

"No. It's toxic. I take cut flowers home occasionally, but that's it." Her knuckles were white as she gripped the iced tea glass.

"Have you been out there in the last week?"

"To the house, yes. I told you I dropped off a basket. But not in the garden, not since she left." She tilted her head, chin lowered. "I'll admit, after the way she left, I wasn't sure we were still friends."

"So that's when you started buying herbs and flowers from Jo and Phyl instead?" I asked.

"I've confirmed that. Ms. Eriksen and Ms. Williams are great fans of yours. Both of you." Kim included me in her gaze. "We got the lab tests back on the artichoke pesto. It was contaminated with digitalis."

"Purpurea, then," Bill said. "Because it didn't kill him."

Kim nodded.

"What does that mean?" I asked, but their expressions made clear they were not going to tell me. "Okay. So, we know Fresca put a jar in her sympathy basket. If she didn't poison it—"

"I didn't," Fresca said.

"She was upset with Claudette," I continued, "but she had no reason to harm Jeff or Ian. Which means someone else must have poisoned a jar and left it open in the refrigerator for someone—anyone—to find."

"Why?" Fresca asked. "What would anyone hope to gain from that?"

"I think," I said, "someone planted that jar to divert suspicion from someone else by casting suspicion on you. Maybe Linda did it, to protect Dean. Or one of the girls—Cassie's in and out of that house regularly."

"Using a plant from Claudette's own garden. Oh, that's vile." My mother's face darkened. "To make it look like I did it."

"Who knew you picked Claudette's herbs and flowers?"

"Lots of people," Fresca said. "I never hid it."

Kim turned to Bill. "Have you talked with anyone recently about digitalis?"

A frown creased Bill's forehead. "I treat all consultations as confidential."

"You're not a doctor. The privilege doesn't apply."

"And if you get a court order requiring me to testify, I will. But until then, I owe it to my patients to preserve their trust." His tone was firm and clear.

"Bill, are you saying you know who might have poisoned that jar, but you won't tell us who?" I didn't understand his logic.

"I'm saying I treat all consultations as confidential, until a court tells me otherwise."

"But if you know something that will help us—help Kim—find the poisoner, or the killer—"

"The killer? What does the poisoning have to do with Claudette's murder?" Fresca asked.

"It's a double frame, Mom. Someone wants us to think you killed Claudette, then poisoned Ian." Kim's poker face irked me. Was she betting on an ace in the hole? "The killer tried to shift Kim's attention to you, but when she didn't make an arrest, he or she had to act again. To force her to focus on you."

Fresca blanched. Bill didn't move, but something unspoken passed between them.

"And if we don't find the person soon, he could strike again. Please, Bill," I said.

"Darling, if Bill says he has a good reason, we need to trust him."

Was he protecting her? From what?

It was looking more and more like the killer had gone after Claudette to set up my mother. The rumors in town assured that Fresca would be blamed. Then, when she wasn't arrested, the killer had to up the stakes. First, scare her by smashing the Merc's front window. Then, leave the poison for Ian or Jeff to find.

The only thing that didn't fit was the spaghetti sauce on my car. The note made that personal.

Who harbored so much hatred or resentment of my mother? Even if my theory was wrong, there was a killer in town, who might not be finished with us.

Twenty-six

"You still on duty?" I asked Kim after Fresca and Bill left. "Burger and a beer, my treat?"

She eyed me warily. "Promise no fishing for info?"

I nodded, fingers crossed behind my back.

A row of Harleys parked outside Red's drew lusty whistles from passersby. "Nearly collided with a crazy-man biker on the Eastshore today. Surprised you weren't called to the scene of a major wipeout."

"Road pizza," Kim said. I made a face. "Cop humor. Keeps us from going nuts."

As usual in summer, music spilled out Red's open front door, the air heavy with grease, beer, and Friday night sweat. The satellite radio mix tipped heavily toward the 1970s and 1980s, as Bob Seger wrapped up "Fire Lake" and Pat What-was-her-name sang "Hit Me with Your Best Shot." Seemed a little early for that tune, but what I know about the bar business wouldn't fill a shot glass.

We ordered burgers and fries at the kitchen window, then elbowed our way to the courtyard bar. Ted reddened when we approached. I love odd couples, but could not picture the polished detective hooking up with the big lug bartender.

He snapped his bar towel. "Ladies, what'll it be?"

We carried our beers to a table near the stage, quiet tonight. My glass was a touch full, so I sipped as I walked. At that odd angle, I couldn't help noticing all eyes on Kim. She noticed, too, and called out, "Carry on—I'm off duty."

The stage reminded me of Sam's comments. I told her Sam had seen Dean and Linda arrive separately, and presumed Dean came in the back gate.

"The musicians all said they hadn't seen anything unusual. I need to interview them again, and get more specific."

"But it makes sense, doesn't it? If Dean was the last person to come in the back gate, then either he didn't see her—so he wouldn't have had any reason to lie about where he parked—or he killed her. They had words, he pulled a knife out of his boot. She was stabbed, wasn't she?"

"You said you wouldn't fish."

I shrugged.

Kim sighed, resigned. "Yeah, she was. But we haven't found a weapon."

"He'd have ditched it by now, for sure."

Our food came. Kim squirted her fries with mayonnaise, a disgusting habit she'd picked up in high school to keep other kids from stealing them.

How easily we'd slipped back into our old roles: stubborn Erin; calm, cool Kim. We'd stayed friends despite being competitors because each of us cared more about different things. Like barrel racing. In a fluke, I won the last race senior year with enough points to snare the title. "How nice after the tragedy," everyone said, like being crowned Miss Teen Rodeo made up for my dad dying. It was like we had switched roles; Kim had lost interest despite being far the better rider, and I had gone for broke.

"Kim, you have no evidence against Fresca. First"—I

gestured with a fry—"Claudette didn't know about the dinner Friday night until I invited her. She hadn't been back in town long enough to catch up. She was genuinely surprised. Second, she insisted she didn't spread any rumors. You should have seen how furious she was. And no matter what else people say about Claudette, no one calls her a gossip or a liar."

Kim raised one eyebrow. "So what's your point?"

"The point is, that disproves any theory that she was coming to the Merc to confront Fresca." I whetted my whistle with a long swig of Scapegoat Pale Ale. "Yeah, she called Mom, and me, so she had something on her mind. Who knows what? Maybe she wanted to apologize. Or get her job back. Or ask for help in her quest for a restaurant—Fresca always knows what's going on in town." Even if I couldn't convince Kim of Mom's innocence, I hoped she'd at least start questioning her own theories.

"Third, you say Fresca disappeared for a few minutes right before I found Claudette. Not being able to pinpoint exactly where she was exactly when isn't exactly disappearing. But nobody puts her in the alley, right? No one says they saw Fresca leave and go around back."

"Hey, Erin. Hi, Kim." Polly Paulson danced up to our table. "Girls' night out?"

"Hey, Polly, the other day you said you saw me talking to Claudette outside the drugstore, right?" She nodded and I looked at Kim, as if to say, *See, I was there—I didn't make it up.*

"Something I thought of later, after you interviewed me," Polly said. "I closed up at five thirty, and on my way home, I drove through the village to drop off my daughter's library books. And I saw that fellow who was talking with Claudette at the drugstore—what's his name?"

"James Angelo," I said. "Yeah, he said he went kayaking Friday evening."

"Not likely, not in those stupid chili pepper pants and a

white cook's jacket. Stomping up Front Street like he meant to kill somebody." Polly's husband called her name. "Ooh, nachos. Gotta go—I'm starving. You girls ever want to go dancing, call me."

"Tell me you haven't been going around town interviewing everyone," Kim said.

"Not everyone. Not yet." I recapped what I'd learned from Polly and Wendy, and what I'd uncovered about James Angelo, aka Jay Walker. Though Dean seemed like the guy, I told her my alternate theory about Angelo, arguing with Claudette at her house and again in the alley. Wendy witnessed the first argument; the second was speculation, but it fit.

"You keep telling me somebody else could get hurt, but if you keep sticking your nose into this investigation, it could be you."

"I'll take that chance."

The old song "Sad Eyes" came on. Perfect reminder of the Dean-Claudette-Linda love triangle. "Both Angelo and Dean lied to you, about where they were and their relationship to the victim."

"Lying doesn't make them guilty of murder."

"Agreed. But I wish I knew what Angelo is hiding."

"Everybody has secrets, Erin."

I'd promised not to dig, but her refusal to share any info irritated the heck out of me. "So what's yours?"

She pushed back her chair and threw a tip on the table. "Thanks for the burger and beer." She wasn't wearing her usual bracelet. The handmade silver and onyx bracelet I gave her for Christmas senior year. When we were still friends. The one she'd been wearing earlier in the week.

"Why did you come to the Merc today? You didn't come to arrest Fresca. You wanted information." Digging.

"Look, Erin, I don't want the killer to be your mother any more than you do, but I have to find the truth. And she and Bill aren't helping. Ask yourself why, and see if you like the answer."

I sat alone, finishing my beer. Ted cleared our table and offered me another, but one was enough. "Kim leave?" he asked.

"Yeah. She's hot on the trail of a killer."

His eyes widened. "Not Fresca?" I nodded. "No. No." His worried tone touched me. "You're smart, Erin. You show her, it was Dean Vincent. Or his wife—they could have been in it together. Or Jeff."

"He and Ian were in Seattle, just back from China."

Ted's face fell. Someone called his name. He opened his mouth to say something else, then closed it and left me alone.

Oh, what a tangled web we weave, when first we practice to deceive. Not Shakespeare, as my high school English teacher insisted, but Sir Walter Scott. She hadn't liked my proving her wrong. Nobody did. Including Kim.

What had she said as she left? To ask myself why Fresca and Bill weren't helping her. On the one hand, Bill believed he needed to preserve his clients' trust. On the other, shouldn't he voluntarily speak up, to help find a poisoner—who might also be a killer?

That's the kind of philosophical dilemma best left to lawyers. Meanwhile, what did Bill know? It had something to do with the poison. Had someone consulted him about it? Obviously, they wouldn't have told him what they intended to do with it. But if someone asked him about medicinal uses and potential side effects, they could have used that info any way they wanted. Or misused it.

Claudette had been knowledgeable about medicinal plants. My mother knew very little—her approach to all but the severest childhood illnesses had been chicken soup and rest. Linda didn't seem the type, either. A woman willing to sprinkle iodized salt on chocolate-covered almonds from SavClub and call them handmade wasn't likely to delve deeply into herbal remedies.

Was Kim suggesting that Bill's secret might implicate Fresca? There might be more between them than simple friendship, but I didn't believe for one minute that they shared evidence of crime. No matter what Kim thought.

The crowd had gotten beerier. Polly Paulson belted out "Born in the USA" along with Springsteen. I waved good night as the Rod Stewart song "Do You Think I'm Sexy?" came on. I crossed the alley, turning to face the row of businesses. Some, like Red's and the Merc, had courtyards with fences. Others, like Le Panier and Chez Max, and the liquor store, had back doors that opened directly onto the alley. I searched for cameras. No doubt Kim and her deputies had checked any security video. But if no cameras captured the altercation between Claudette and her killer, or showed the killer arriving, then the killer must have come from a direction outside the cameras' scope.

Polly put Angelo coming from the south. Where had Dean parked? Like he'd tell me. He'd already caught me scoping out Linda's house—no reason to confront him until I had more evidence.

"Ned," I called to my neighbor as he zigzagged between cars. "What are you doing here?"

"Weekend nights, I come in to check on things. I'm Red, after all." He grinned and rubbed the remains of his faded hair.

"Ted seems to have the place under control." Except maybe for Polly's singing.

Ned peered over the top of his glasses. "Not all chips fall far from the block."

I squinted until his meaning came into focus: Ted lacked his touch. Fair enough. But his comment raised questions. "Ned, are you saying Ted isn't taking over the bar? So why do you want to buy our building?"

"What the bleep you talking about, girlie?"

I explained that Ted had made an offer to buy the Mercantile building, and I assumed Old Ned approved. Intended to bankroll it. Naturally, I did not tell him how I knew.

"That is plum crazy, by jingo. Even if we had any notion

of putting you out of business—and don't you think that for a moment—why would we want more space? Red's is purt' near perfect the way it is."

Yup. Sticky floors, sticky plumbing, and all.

"I'm going in there and give that boy a piece of my mind."

I grabbed his arm. "Ned, wait. Don't. Don't collar him when you're upset, and not in front of customers. It'll become gossip, and we've all seen this week how damaging that can be."

He heaved a sigh. "Right you are, girlie. 'Sides, with what you got going on in that old Merc, you'd be better off taking over our space than t'other way around."

"Thanks." I kissed his cheek. "But no thanks. I've got my hands full enough."

And that, by jingo, was the truth, and nothing but the truth. But I still hadn't discovered the whole truth.

· *Twenty-seven* ·

When nothing is as it seems, then what? Take another look from another angle. Stand on your head if you have to.

Or go home.

An older maroon Subaru had parked in my driveway. I pulled in next to it. Ian Randall leaned against a front porch post, while Cassie Vincent sat on the steps, petting my little cat.

"Hey. What brings you guys out here?"

Ian straightened and Cassie stood, giving Sandburg a last quick ear tug.

"I—uh. Umm," Ian said, blinking hard, then staring off into the trees above my head.

"Tell her," Cassie said.

"I—we—I came to apologize. I'll talk to the sheriff if you want."

My brow furrowed. "About what?"

"Umm. Your window." Finally, he ventured a glance at me. "At the shop."

I scooped up Sandburg. "Are you saying you threw the Playhouse paver through the Merc's front window?" He nodded.

Holy cow. "I think we all need to sit down. Iced tea? Fizzy water?" Cassie said yes and Ian said no. I took the cat inside and returned with three glasses and a bottle of Pellegrino. I took the red willow chair and gestured for them to sit. Cassie perched on the edge of the other chair, and Ian sank onto the top step. It's an odd thing to realize that a whole generation sees you not only as an adult, but intimidating to boot.

"Why don't you start at the beginning?"

Ian let out a ragged breath and told the story, with a little prompting from his girlfriend. He and Jeff had gotten the news of Claudette's death Friday evening, in Seattle. They'd driven partway back that night, and rolled into Jewel Bay around noon Saturday. Although Detective Caldwell had not identified a suspect, Ian heard the talk and zeroed in on my mother. Sleepless and furious, he'd left the house in the wee hours Sunday morning, eventually finding himself in the village. Both Ian and Cassie were Children's Theater veterans—they'd started dating while in a play together—and Ian had sat on the park bench behind the Playhouse, staring at the lake, seething. The same bench I'd sat on during Sunday's festivities.

The longer he sat, the hotter he'd raged, until he grabbed a paver from the stack behind the theater and dashed down the street.

"Honestly, I don't know how I got there. I don't remember any of it. The next thing I knew, I was standing in front of the Merc, my hand empty, the window smashed." He stared into space, seeing it all again. "Scared me to death. I took off."

"That's when I saw him," Cassie said. "Running past the Inn."

He'd gotten angrier when he saw me in Claudette's

garden on Monday evening, and when Fresca dropped in for a sympathy call. But the more he'd seen of us that week, Ian realized how genuinely we grieved his mother's death. He confessed to Cassie, who talked him into coming clean.

"Thank you for telling me," I said.

"Maybe we should have gone to your mother," Cassie said. "But she's kinda scary sometimes."

"That she is," I said wryly. I refilled my glass—they'd barely touched theirs. "Now, my turn. Ian, sorry as you are about the window, you wouldn't be here if you thought my mother killed Claudette, or poisoned you."

They exchanged nervous glances. Finally, Cassie spoke. "The whole mess is kind of our fault. Our parents wanted to break us up—"

"'You're too young to be so serious,'" Ian added, mimicking adult concern.

"And we figured if they got to know each other better, they'd stop bugging us. Turned out my dad and his mom hit it off a little too well." Cassie's gray eyes filled with regret. I remembered the newspaper photo of Dean and Claudette, cheek-to-cheek and starry-eyed, in the community theater musical.

"The best-laid plans," I said. "But that doesn't make you responsible for their affair, or anything else. They're adults."

"What if my dad killed her?" Cassie said, trembling. Worry lines creased her smooth face. Ian put his hand on her knee. He looked anxious, but wisely said nothing. "He's just so gone off the last couple years. Pretending he's Elvis, trashing his chiropractic practice. Acting like Jess and I don't even exist. And then what he's done to my mom."

"Is his interest in Elvis new?" He'd mentioned collecting the furniture over the years.

"It was just for fun. He didn't let it run his life."

Who wouldn't want to be king for an evening? Classic midlife crisis, in not-so-classic fashion.

"Does your dad have a temper?" I asked.

She swallowed hard. "He throws things. But he never hit us, or Mom."

Still, when it came to evidence tying Dean to Claudette's murder, they had none. Cassie had never seen her dad carry a knife. There had been no blood on his stretchy white jumpsuit—and Dean was fastidious about his costumes. All they had was strange behavior that had gotten stranger over the last few days.

"Do you suppose," I said, "that your dad is acting weird out of guilt? Not for killing Claudette, but for putting her in the situation that caused her death? Like you feel guilty, because you introduced them?" Like I did, because I'd invited her to the Festa.

"You mean, if he'd been a better fake, she would never have come back to Jewel Bay and gotten killed?" Ian said.

"Sounds kinda goofy, but remember he's not thinking straight." Criminy. Listen to me defending Dean Vincent. "Combine that with guilt over hurting your mother and you girls, and grief over Claudette's death, and anybody's bound to act a little crazy."

Not to mention having made himself look like a bit of an ass—running off to Vegas to steal the show and getting sent home instead.

"It's worse than that." Cassie's voice wobbled. "What if my mom poisoned Ian?"

I gaped in astonishment. Linda's candy tasted awful, but not deadly. If the killer used a toxic plant from Claudette's garden, he—or she—was likely to be knowledgeable about herbs and plants. Someone without knowledge might pick marigolds, thinking if they stink, they must be poison—not only not true, but some varieties are actually tasty, especially in salads. *Focus, Erin.*

By all accounts, Linda wasn't a gardener or an herbalist, and certainly not much of a cook. I pictured her house and yard: the barest minimum of developer landscaping and nothing more. Certainly no perennials. "No love lost between me and your mother, but do you honestly think she could do that? To Ian?"

"I don't know anymore. It's all so screwed up." Her fists clenched and unclenched. "I saw Fresca bring her basket. Ian and his dad don't like red peppers, so I took the jar of roasted pepper sauce home. My mom saw it and decided to make a basket of her own."

My phone buzzed with a text and I stole a look. Rick Bergstrom saying, *Check your e-mail for the scoop on Jay. Later.*

"Cassie, did your mother put a jar of artichoke pesto in her basket?"

Her face darkened and scrunched like a constipated baby's. "I think so. She has jars and jars of Fresca's stuff. She loves it. And she knows Ian loves the artichoke blend—he's always eating it at our house. What if—what if first my dad killed Claudette, then he poisoned the pesto to kill my mom, but she gave it away instead and it nearly killed Ian?"

Ian reached up for her hand. "But it didn't. I'm fine."

"It could have, if you'd eaten more. It could have been anybody—my mom, or my sister, or me. Your dad, your aunt."

But how could we prove that the poisoned jar had come from Linda's basket, not my mother's? No doubt Kim would send it for fingerprinting, which might help identify who'd touched the jar, though it wouldn't eliminate Fresca, who still filled and labeled every jar by hand.

My head reeled. Cassie's fears put a whole new spin on things. I believed Dean to be a first-class conniving heel, but all this? Still, Dean did have a key to Linda's house. "Let's sort this out." I handed Cassie her no-longer-fizzy water and made her take a sip. "You told your mom about my mom's basket, and she decided to send one of her own. How did she act?"

"Happy. She likes making things. She's not that great at it, though. Her basket looked punk next to Fresca's."

"Other than thinking you and Ian are too young, how does she feel about him?"

Both kids colored. "She likes him. Or did. It all got weird after Dad and Claudette ran off. But she never blamed Ian."

I asked her to tell me more about Linda's reaction to the affair. Linda, it seemed, had been of several minds herself. Self-righteously angry, alternating her fury between her man and the woman who stole him. Mortified, for being played a fool—which made her angrier. And Cassie admitted, she even seemed relieved at times. "They fought a lot. It was more peaceful when he was gone." She gave me a crooked grin. "But the new car's hot." Would they get back together now? Cassie couldn't guess, but both she and her sister looked forward to leaving home. Which made them feel guilty.

More than enough guilt to go around.

"What now?" Ian said, his voice betraying his anxiety. This no doubt seemed like the worst week of his life. With any luck, it would be.

"You're worried, but you have to trust that everything will be okay. The truth will come out, and you'll survive it." They looked unconvinced, and I hardly blamed them. "I'm really glad you talked to me. Ian, promise you'll call Deputy Caldwell in the morning. If I don't hear from her by noon, I'll call and report you myself."

They walked to Cassie's car hand in hand. I wondered whether their relationship would survive this.

I watched them drive off, then went inside. When I touched the antique door handle, I remembered the feeling that someone had been in the cabin earlier in the week. Had I been overtired, imagining things?

No matter. I clicked the door firmly shut. All would be well.

· *Twenty-eight* ·

"What do you think you're doing, talking to Ned Redaway? What gives you any right to interfere in my decisions?"

After the kids left, I'd checked my e-mail. Comparing the high school class photo with the shot of Jay aka James on his Facebook profile, and the man he spotted at the Grille, Rick was sure he'd correctly identified Jay Walker. And his parents and older sister had given him a little more info on the family, shedding some light on why Jay had wanted to remake himself, while staying close enough to help his mother when his father went on drinking binges, blowing what little money they had. I began to feel a little sympathy for the fellow.

And then my mother barreled in.

"Whoa, Mom. Easy. Calm down."

"Do not tell me to calm down. I am calm." My mother stalked into the cabin and tossed her bag on the couch, barely missing the sleeping Sandburg. I closed the front door and followed her into the main living area. She paced the narrow aisle between couch and kitchen island, heels rapping angrily on the pine floor.

I poured two glasses of wine and set hers on the island. As she walked, her hands flapped like a drunken hummingbird. I inched her glass back a bit.

"How did you even know Ted made an offer on my building?"

In her present mood, I didn't dare admit listening to her phone messages. The dents her heels made in the floor would be the least of my worries. "Last Monday, Ted tried to convince me to move the Merc out to the highway. Touted all the pros, ignored all the cons. I realized he'd been talking to you, and put it together." The partial truth.

She glared, skeptical, but slowed her stomping long enough to take a sip. "And you had to mention it to Ned."

"I assumed he knew. And what do you mean, 'my building'? You always said it was our building, that you owned it in trust for the family. You called it the Murphy legacy." A faint tremble crept into my voice. I was unbelievably peeved, and unbelievably sad.

"Don't talk to me about decisions and legacies." She wagged her finger at me.

"I've been waiting for you to tell me. Don't you think I had a right to know?"

She stabbed her chest. "I've had to decide everything. For fourteen years, ever since your father . . ."

"You asked me to come home and work with you, to run the Merc, and I did. And you always say, Murphy girls don't quit."

We were shouting. My mother and I had never shouted at each other in my thirty-two years. If this was a rite of passage into a new stage of adulthood, I did not like it one bit.

"Oh, darling." My mother looked at me, lifted her hand slightly, then let it fall back to her side. "I am so sorry. None of this is your fault. And you do have a right to know." Glass in hand, she slipped off her black sandals and made for the living room. I scooped up Sandburg and deposited him safely in his cat bed, but Fresca ignored the couch and sat in the Morris chair in the corner by the stone fireplace. I curled up in the big leather chair.

"What happened? I thought you were having dinner at Bob and Liz's."

"Lovely evening. But on my way out, Ned called on my cell—I'm starting to hate those things. He'd discovered Ted's plans from you, and gave Ted what for, then called me to apologize."

I should have known Old Ned would blow his top sooner rather than later. The old song "On Top of Spaghetti" started looping through my brain.

"Hear me out, darling. This may be the perfect opportunity. Chiara and her family are cramped in the old homestead. They can take over the main house, and you can live in theirs. Nick will be fine on his own."

What was she saying? That she might sell? And leave Jewel Bay? Go where?

And what about me? What would I do here if she closed the Merc? Go back to Seattle? Friends in other companies had tried to recruit me. But I did not want to be "in transit," like poor, pink, rootless Candy Divine. Or indecisive Claudette. Or James Angelo, who'd walked away from his past but still felt it nipping at his heels. I'd been afraid that coming home was an admission of failure. But leaving now would be worse.

"This town can be a little claustrophobic," she said. "The talk, the merry-go-round."

"You can't leave. You can't make them right. Even if you aren't charged with killing Claudette, they'll still think you're guilty—of all the things the rumor mill says. And they'd tar me with that brush, too."

My mother looked sadder than I'd seen her in years. "That's what I'm most afraid of."

"I don't understand."

"Darling, you are the only person besides the killer who knew Claudette was coming to the party."

"You mean you think she suspects me? Kim?" My one-time best friend and partner in crime. An unseen weight crushed me. I felt like an idiot. My mother was trying to protect me. Again. Even if it made her more of a target. But while challenging her over protecting me too much all those years ago had been high on my list of things to talk about, the need to identify the killer—and convince Kim Caldwell—had leapfrogged to the top.

I fired up my iPad, flew to the cloud, and grabbed the Spreadsheet of Suspicion. "I have two theories. Suspect Number One: Dean Vincent." I showed her the screen and recapped my reasons. No need to relay Cassie's suspicions, though I did tell Fresca that Ian had confessed to the vandalism.

"Oh, that poor boy. Don't press charges, Erin."

I shrugged. "Not up to me, Mom. I did think Linda might have been involved, but now I suspect she's reached the same conclusion we did: She's afraid Dean's the killer, and wants to divert attention from him to you, with rumors and indignant talk. And she may have left the poisoned pesto." I summarized what I knew.

"The protection racket," Fresca said.

"Exactly. Second theory, James Angelo. You said I'm the only person who knew Claudette was coming to the Festa. Of course, I had no idea what entrance she'd use. But I think Angelo knew, too. He may have overheard me, or she may have told him. They argued earlier in the day, then talked at the drugstore, after I invited her."

I opened a package of shortbread Scottie dogs—emergency treats—and refilled our glasses. "And then he spotted her. Polly saw him downtown, walking toward Back Street. So that's opportunity. What we don't have is motive."

"Any idea what they were arguing about?"

"Maybe her restaurant plans, but I keep thinking it has something to do with his past. He's not who he says he is."

She snorted. "You mean, he's not a real chef. I know all that."

"Worse than that." I explained what I'd discovered about his real name and family background.

"He's reinventing himself. Nothing wrong with that—it's the great Western tradition."

I showed her the picture I'd found, and the e-mail from Rick. "He's made a new life on this side of the mountains, but he can still get home in a few hours if he needs to. For his mom, the Bergstroms think. He's been spotted there a few times. Compared to the rest of the family, he was an angel." The source of his pseudonym?

"Odd that you couldn't find anything about him under his new name, either. As if he's determined not to be found."

"Not to be noticed," I said. "As if he doesn't know how to make his dreams into reality. Haunted by being Jay Walker, bullied child of the town drunk and butt of the family jokes."

"The victim has become the bully." She seemed to be replaying a scene in her mind.

I set the iPad aside and picked up my wine. "What were you two talking about on Tuesday? I know he called you."

"He called to gloat," she said. "To tell me he's cooking for Ray now, and that over the weekend, his Italian food had 'em lined up out the door. Ray is expanding their gourmet food section and I should watch out."

"Ray did say this morning that their Italian dishes were a hit. That's good. He's got what, two shelves of imported cookies and jams? If he expands that, great—he's selling things we aren't carrying. And if he starts offering Angelo's stuff commercially, that increases interest in locally made products. No sweat."

"Right." She bit the tail off a Scottie.

But there had to be more to their conversation. She

wouldn't have gotten so angry over Angelo's sixth-grade antics. I waited.

"I never told you," she said, "how he sabotaged me last winter. When he tried to get the other restaurants to drop my products and use his. He told Max I'd decided to quit the business—Max got so upset I could hardly understand a word. How could I quit without telling him, weren't we friends, did I need a better price? I finally realized what had happened. He did the same thing with the Inn.

"So I called my friend at the culinary program in Missoula for the scoop. Jay had basic skills and a bad attitude. You can be a prima donna after forty years of high heat, but not after six weeks of an introductory class."

"When he can't compete fairly, he plays dirty instead."

"It will come back to bite him, I know—karma and all that—but in the short run, it could be ugly."

My jaw cramped. "So he may come after you again. With more than words."

This time she paced in bare feet, so no worries. "Don't you see, darling? That's one more reason to close the Merc and sell the building. Because of all this trouble."

I did not see. "Trouble happens everywhere, Mom. You can't let it stop you. You never have before."

She stared at the empty fireplace, contemplating something I couldn't see. But I had more questions. "Mom, that note of Claudette's. I found it in her personnel file, after you said you couldn't find it. What gives?"

"I'm embarrassed to admit, I didn't behave like a grown-up when I found it. I crumpled it up and threw it in the garbage. Then dug it out and stuck it in a cookbook to flatten it out." She rolled her eyes. "But then I couldn't remember which one, and I had to plow through the office shelves to find it. Turned out it was *Larousse Gastronomique*, one of my cooking school texts."

A doorstop of a book. We burst into giggles.

But the mention of cooking school raised another

possibility. "Mom, do you suppose Angelo spread the rumors about you stealing Claudette's recipes and firing her to make room for me? She found out when she got back to town, and that's what they argued about?" Except that the box in the basement had me wondering if those rumors really were false.

"Two slime bags, Jay and Dean. Which one attacked her?"

"Maybe Old Ned's right and Jewel Bay is going to the dogs."

She whirled on me. "Don't you believe that for one minute. This is a great town."

I stared, wary, teeth clenched. "So why are you thinking of leaving?"

She didn't respond. How could she brush aside my future so easily? But if I solved the murder, and removed the threat to the Merc, I might convince her not to sell.

Worry about that later—after snaring Claudette's killer.

"So maybe Claudette confronted Angelo about the rumors, and he stabbed her," I said. Had he meant to kill, or exploded in a fit of rage? Didn't matter. "Now, he has to cover up his involvement. I'm surprised he's still in town. But he's smart enough to know leaving would only make him a suspect."

My mother glanced at her watch, a silver Brighton cuff with enameled flowers. "Too late to call Kim."

I sat up and slammed my feet to the floor. "We are not calling Kim. First, we have to gather more evidence against Angelo so we can convince her he's the killer."

"Erin Murphy, that is ridiculous and dangerous. Don't you dare go after that man yourself."

"Mom, Kim thinks you killed Claudette. She won't believe anything either one of us says without proof."

"What's gotten into you? Of my three children, you've always been the one I never had to worry about. Who buckles her seat belt without fail and knows where all the airplane exits are. Who plans and plots every step, and never did a reckless thing in her life."

I guess I'd never told her about bungee jumping off a bridge in British Columbia. Over a stretch of river a lot like the Wild Mile.

"And now this. It's downright foolish," she continued. But she didn't pull out her phone. She paced in front of the fireplace, glancing back at me every few steps, as if to see whether I'd come to my senses.

On one of her turns, her gaze swept the room and she stopped on a dime. Stared at the open shelves in the kitchen. "What . . . is . . . How . . . did . . . you . . .?"

A lot of strange things had happened in the last week, and seeing my mother stunned speechless topped them all. I'd completely forgotten I'd set the dusty recipe box on the shelf, out of the way.

This was the night for unexpected conversations.

Fresca crossed the room with what looked like a mix of reverence and fear. She lifted the box off the shelf as if she were a priest raising the chalice, and I swear, when she caught her breath, my own almost stopped. She carried the box—a boy's shop class project—to the coffee table, and perched on the couch. Anticipation filled the air like garlic on pesto-making day.

I knelt on the floor next to her. "I know you didn't kill her, Mom. I never thought that. But the recipes. Are they hers? They're typed. You never typed."

She shook her head slowly, a tear rolling down her cheek. "Your father wanted to help me, when I first started to cook professionally. Long before Claudette came to town. He transcribed all the recipes—my notes and scribbles, and your noni's."

My turn to be stunned. Of all the possibilities in all the world, I had not imagined that one.

"He had a computer—remember that old Mac? But it wouldn't print on recipe cards, so he typed these. They fit perfectly in this box your brother made." She turned it over and traced Nick's initials with her finger, then slid a card out of the box and held it up. "We had to do a lot of testing. Grease spatters—carbonara." She pulled out another, smiling at the memories. "Tomato stains."

I sat back on my heels, picturing my father pecking away on his ancient Smith-Corona, with the cartridge ribbon. I had no idea what I'd thought he was doing, but not this.

The anxiety I'd been shoving under a mental rug since finding the box eased, but questions remained. "So why was the box in a crate in the basement of the Merc? With the Christmas decorations?"

"I've developed new recipes since then, and revised these—they're all in three-ring binders now—so I didn't need to keep the cards out. But I couldn't bear to toss them." Her voice cracked, and another tear fell. "The box was in the kitchen at the Merc. I must have put it down there one January, and it got mixed in with the holiday things."

Made sense. And once in the basement, there it stayed, until I started digging.

"Are they dated in some way?" I said. She gave me a quizzical look. "If we can prove that they're yours, that they predate Claudette, then we can show them to Kim and put the rumors to rest. Later, when we're ready to make our case."

She flipped to a divider near the back of the box and pulled out more cards. "See? These are my handwritten versions. Your dad kept them, in case he mistyped something and I needed to check a measurement or ingredient." She pulled out another card, yellowed, the very formal handwriting faded to a spidery blue. "This is my noni's recipe—my grandmother's—for gnocchi."

I took the card carefully. I'd never known my great-grandmother—always referred to as "Mynoni," as if that were her name—but I felt her presence now, as I did in every plate of potato dumplings.

Fresca sped through the typed recipes. "Here. Here's the proof. Nobody uses my secret ingredient." She handed me a card for Fettuccine with Minted Tomato Sauce. I scanned the list of ingredients. Found it: toasted walnuts, sprinkled on top of the chopped tomato mixture, with fresh Parmesan. I knew this wasn't Claudette's recipe. I'd eaten it since childhood—not every Sunday, but often.

And so had Kim Caldwell.

·*Twenty-nine*·

I stared at the ceiling like Sandburg staring at a spider, tracking every move. For me, it was not spiders millimetering across the planks, into the crevices, and back out the other side, but images from the past and present, impossibly intertwined. My mother at the stove, my father at the typewriter, in the orchard, in the grave. The recipe box, Claudette in the alley. Red boots and silver bracelets. Chefs' knives, table knives, jack knives, folding knives. Flashing lights, blinking, warning, off on off on off.

My future—and my family's—demanded I untangle the web of signs and symbols, so I stared. The cat snored softly on the pillow next to me, while I stared and stared.

"On Top of Spaghetti" still ran through my brain as I drove into the village. I needed an antidote song, but nothing came to mind.

"Make it a triple shot," I told Max a few minutes later, wishing Le Panier made triple *pain au chocolat*. I ignored the question in his raised eyebrow. My late night was none of his business. Across the street, my sister unlocked Snowberry's front door. "And my sister's usual."

"We can't let her sell," I told Chiara a few minutes later. "There has to be another way." We sat in the gallery's back room, on rolling stools flanking a low worktable. Mat corners in dozens of colors hung on a wooden rack, while frame samples clung to a Velcro-covered stand. Flattened gift boxes lay atop colored tissue, and a pile of sturdy packing cartons teetered by the back door.

She listened to the abridged version of my conversation with Fresca, occasionally rattling her double iced vanilla latte. She squinted at my spreadsheet, then scrounged in a giant straw basket for a sketch pad and colored pencils. In moments, she created a diagram with circles and arrows connecting the names on my list to each other and the three categories: motive, means, and opportunity.

"Like that?"

To me, her drawing resembled a Spirograph on a sugar high. A fresh point of view can shed new light—or look like squiggles.

"So Ted wants to expand the bar, and his dad doesn't," she said. "Thanks for the coffee, by the way."

"Right, and you're welcome. What exactly he has in mind, he never said."

Chiara clicked her tongue. "Beats me. Ted's never seemed that interested. But I don't think we should interfere in Mom's decision."

"But it affects the whole family. Selling out the Murphy heritage in what amounts to blackmail—that's wrong. Besides, it's not her building." My hands spun like propellers. *Slow down, Erin.* "I mean, it is, because Grandpa gave the Merc to Dad, and Dad died. But he meant it for us."

"I don't want to be tied down by a leaky old building, and Nick sure doesn't. Do you, honestly?"

Honestly, I did. I love the place. I love the stone walls in the basement and the courtyard, the brick front, the sticky brass door handle. I cherish the wide plank floors and tin ceilings. The creaky plumbing gives me fits, the heating bill gives me hives, the roof is a pain in the backside. The whole darned enchilada is a truckload of trouble, and I adore every inch of it.

"Yes," I said.

"But I'm still confused. You're saying Ted is spreading rumors to damage her reputation and force her to sell?"

I nodded and sipped my latte. I'd briefly wondered about Angelo, but when Mom and I talked about Ted's attempt to force her to sell, it had become clear that he was the rumor monger.

"Okay." She drew an arrow connecting my name and Fresca's, then another linking us to a Monopoly building she labeled MERC. "So your mission, should you choose to accept it"—and her tone implied no doubt—"is to convince her to see things your way. Let you control the building, not just run the business."

I wanted that opportunity, yes, but so soon? And how to persuade her? What would Hank the Cowdog do? Solve the crime, and save the ranch. Easy-peasy.

She stabbed the air with a red pencil. "But rumors never bothered her before. Angelo's attempted sabotage only ticked her off. If one of us got a bad grade or didn't make the starting lineup, she always said, 'Don't get mad, get better.' I get that she's tired of trouble. But it's not like her to give in. Why now?"

"She said she was tired of making all the decisions." A spasm of pain shot through my jaw. After the urge to hyperventilate passed, I forced myself to speak calmly. "Do you suppose she's ill?"

Chiara's dark eyes widened. "She hasn't said a thing. Not a clue. Not a hint."

"All week, she's been off schedule—disappearing, not showing up when she said she would. I blamed the murder."

And the vandalism and the rumors. "But what if she's been going to Pondera to see a doctor?" No calls to the shop from doctors' offices, and none that I had seen on her phone. But if she wanted to hide it . . .

"She said she didn't need to consult a lawyer to defend herself. Because she's ill? Because she's been seeing doctors instead?"

Consulting. The word triggered a mental chain reaction. "I won't tell you how I got here," I said. "Too convoluted. But what's up between her and Bill Schmidt?"

"Bill?" Chiara's head tilted, her expression puzzled. "Nothing that I know of."

"Is she consulting him for herbal remedies and Chinese medicine?" She'd suggested the herb walk, and I'd expanded it from medicinals to wild foods. Maybe the idea had come up in their consultations.

"She trusts him. Everybody trusts him."

The mental lightbulb flashed. "Which is why he won't talk to Kim. He's not protecting a killer he gave advice to. He's protecting Fresca, because she's ill."

It can be disconcerting to see your own face on someone else. My sister's expression no doubt mirrored my own: shock turning to horror, then fear. And because we are Murphy girls, determination.

"Your mission," I said, "is to talk with her."

Chiara bit her lip. "She'll talk with us when she's ready. You run the shop, so you have a stake in the building. But her health is personal. We have to trust her, not interfere." She didn't look as convinced as she sounded.

"No," I said. "We have to help her."

She glanced at the clock. "Time to open. We'll talk more later." She folded our white bakery bags and laid them on top of the already-full recycling box.

"I'll take that out for you. Tracy's opening the Merc."

"Thanks. What a week. I just want everything resolved, so we can be a family again."

That reminded me. "Oh, geez. I'm supposed to go for a hike tomorrow, but now I really don't want to miss family dinner. I'll tell him we'll go another time."

"Him? Who?" Her face brightened as mine heated. "That cute guy Adam? Are you seeing him?"

I shook my head. "It's just a hike. He works a lot, especially in summer. Every guy I meet works too much." Like the airplane engineer I dated for nearly a year who got a promotion and a transfer and lost my number in the move. Or the software engineer who got a promotion and no transfer but lost my number anyway. Or the guy at SavClub who chased me for months and we finally went out and had a perfectly nice time until he told me he'd accepted a job with a competitor out of state. I didn't bother giving him my number.

She cackled. "The pot calls the kettle black."

I stuck out my tongue. "Tell me the minute you find out what's going on with Mom."

Chiara opened the gallery's back door and I carried the loaded box toward the garbage and recycling bins that served this side of Front, two doors down, behind Kitchenalia and Puddle Jumpers. She might be right about me working too much. How else did you get what you wanted?

The raised lid kept me from seeing who was using the bins until I rounded the corner and found myself box-to-box with the chef formerly known as Jay Walker. Criminy. Did the man wear the same pants every day? Weren't professional chefs maniacs for cleanliness? Or was he aiming for a signature look?

"Hey, Jay—James." Subconscious slip of the tongue, or what? How can you keep a secret like that? But I had to. I raised my box and let the paper slide in. Angelo set his empty box on the ground and bent to pick up a container of glass, mostly red wine and beer bottles, by the smell of it.

Glass. Glass jars. Bingo, by jingo, as Old Ned would say. "It was you. You poisoned the jar of artichoke pesto, didn't you?"

He sneered. "You're crazy. Your whole family's crazy."

Ah, pots and kettles. Talk fast, girlie. "One tainted jar, two targets. After you and Claudette argued Friday, you left her the poisoned jar. You wanted her to get sick but put the blame on Fresca. Neat trick."

Half-bent over the box of glass, he straightened, eyes wide. "Who says we were arguing?"

"You of all people know you can't hide anything in a small town."

His face darkened and I was acutely aware that I was standing in an out-of-the-way spot with an angry man, maybe armed, who had already done vicious things to protect a secret. An empty box was no protection.

"Or a second possibility. Kindly next-door neighbor takes a jar of poisoned pesto to a dead woman's grieving family. Puts it in the fridge, where anyone can dig in. Are you that heartless?" *Shut up, Erin, before you make him mad.* But I finally had a chance to find out what really happened.

"You don't know anything about it."

Jackpot. "Either way, you cast blame on Fresca. After that, no one would ever buy her food again. Am I right, James? Or should I say, Jay? Jay Walker?"

He blanched. Channeling the Cowdog, I plowed on. "What an irony. You tried to eliminate the competition for your food by serving up poison. To make your name—your false name—by ruining someone else's. You are pathetic." I slipped the phone out of my pocket, my other hand holding the box like a shield.

"That Bergstrom kid recognized me, didn't he?"

His tone worried me. Could my mouth get me out of the trouble it had just created? "I'm sorry, Jay. I know what your dad was, and that of eight kids, only you and your sister avoided prison. You bucked the odds. Good for you."

His right hand twitched. The flap of his cook's jacket covered his hip. Knife or no knife?

"I got nothing to do with those losers. I've had to make

my own way. People like you and Golden Boy, born with everything handed to you—you don't know what hard work is."

I scraped the gravel with my foot and snapped my head to the left, pretending to see something. He followed my lead and I glanced down, frantically pushing buttons behind the box.

The brief distraction increased his agitation. When he turned back to me, he was practically vibrating.

"We all have to make our own way, Jay, regardless of what we're born with. I admire your determination, but you went about it all wrong. You get ahead by hard work, yes, but also by helping other people. We're all in this life together."

"Like your mother helped Claudette Randall? By stealing her recipes, then stealing her job and giving it to you?"

"None of that's true, Jay. It's all talk."

He shrugged. "Like you said, in a small town, everyone knows everything. The queen of pasta is a phony."

"Says a guy living under a fake name with a fraudulent résumé. You never ran a restaurant in Missoula. You were a prep cook, chopping and slicing all afternoon. And you didn't get a Culinary Arts certificate. You dropped out of a night course. You aren't even Italian. Nothing wrong with working your way up, Jay. Just do it honestly."

"Right." He snorted. "You waltz home and take over the family business, then act like we should all follow your rules. You conjure up this stupid Festa dinner, then you and your mother won't even let me participate."

Ignore the barbs. Keep him talking. "That had nothing to do with you, Jay. We planned the dinner to showcase the village restaurants. Saturday night was for the caterers." Except that dear Linda excluded my mother. "Help me understand. You thought Claudette disliked Fresca as much as you did and resented me. So why kill her?"

"I didn't kill her." His features twisted like a face in a

funhouse mirror and he took a half step toward me. Why hadn't I bought one of those knives at SavClub?

"She said she'd help," he said. "The point was to disrupt the dinner. Her part was to sneak stuff into the gift baskets. She said she'd do it—after I swore no one would get hurt—but Friday, she changed her mind."

"That's when you argued, over whether you would be the cook for her new restaurant."

"Yes. No—I don't know anything about her and a restaurant. I met her downtown before the dinner Friday night. I tried to give her the stuff, but she thought it was stupid."

"You meant to sneak the poisoned pesto into one of the prize baskets." The posters showed a basket brimming with local goodies, and proclaimed "a lucky winner at every table." "But what other stuff?"

He spotted my confusion. "Ha. You're not so smart after all." He looked ridiculously pleased with himself. "Fake toys, like a dead mouse in vomit, something the cat threw up. My dad and brothers stuck one in my goulash when I was a kid and I couldn't eat for a week. Garbage like that."

The guests were all adults. They'd roll their eyes, wonder how the toys got there, and laugh it off. But he'd been serious. And if he wasn't part of her restaurant plans—

"The white bag. You gave her the toys in the white drugstore bag."

"She mocked me. She threw them down the riverbank."

And crumpled up the white bag and tossed it in the bushes above the riverbank, where she and I had both parked.

Their agreement, and Claudette's change of heart, explained why she tried to call me Friday. When she missed me, she called Fresca. Because she knew what James aka Jay didn't know: You can't burn a bridge with my mother. Even on high heat.

But Claudette's reaction to his juvenile prank escalated his desire for revenge—and gave him a second target. Still, from plastic toys to poison was a big leap. If Fresca Murphy's Law was, "Don't get mad, work harder," then Walker's Law must be, "Get mad, and get mean."

"So when you saw my mother take a basket to Jeff and Ian, you saw another opportunity. You snuck in and left the poisoned jar in the fridge." I was right about the poison, but he'd had to change his plans.

He nodded. "People think my dad was drunk when he hit that other car and killed those people. Yeah, he had alcohol in his system, but he always did. Didn't mean he was drunk. He had a heart attack—that's what caused the crash. Never would have happened if they'd been able to afford the digitalis."

I wasn't sure that's what had really happened, but it didn't matter. "You picked the foxglove in Claudette's own garden." And I'd given him the idea, last Monday afternoon, when I told him Fresca had harvested Claudette's herbs and flowers for years.

"Idiot pharmacist wouldn't fill my prescription. So I talked to that herbalist. Told him I'd inherited a heart condition and wanted to treat it naturally. He believed me at first, but then he got suspicious. He's pals with your mom—did you know that? She turned him against me." His hand slipped in and out of his pocket. "Time for her to pay."

He flicked open the blade and stepped so close I could practically smell his stale garlicky breath. My chest and stomach got all hot inside. The big bins had me boxed in.

They were so quiet I saw them before I heard them. Kim and a deputy, drawn guns held low, crept around one end of the block, while two more deputies approached from the other end, behind Jay's back.

He grabbed for me with his left hand, and the blade glinted in his right as I jammed the recycling box over his head and darted away.

It took him only moments to stagger free and see the deputies in a half circle between him and freedom.

"Hands in the air, Angelo," Kim said.

Behind her, a door opened. Sally screamed. That split second was all Jay needed. He took off through Puddle Jumpers' open door, shoving Sally aside. The closest deputy barged in after him while Kim barked directions and the other two deputies sped back to Front Street to head him off.

Kim glanced at me. "I'm okay," I yelled. "Go." With a sweeping gaze, she sized up the situation, shouted "Stay" at Sally, and ran into the children's shop.

Sally sat on the graveled alley, feet splayed, mouth hanging open. She reminded me of my nephew Landon when he fell and waited for an adult's reaction before deciding whether to get up and go on playing—or scream bloody murder.

"What happened?" she sputtered.

"Jay—James Angelo—confessed to poisoning Ian Randall."

"It wasn't your mother?" She sounded genuinely disappointed.

"Are you hurt?" She shook her head and let me help her up. She started for her door, but I pulled her back. "It might not be safe."

"My shop!" Her shriek hit my eardrum like a mallet hitting a cymbal.

We reached Front Street in time to see a deputy muscle the hand-cuffed Jay-James into an idling patrol car. He'd be trading those chili pepper pants for jailhouse orange. I made a mental fist pump. *Yes!*

"Sorry, ma'am," another deputy said as Sally stared in her shop window. Jay-James had not gone down easily, taking with him a rack of girls' summer dresses, a shelf or two of picture books, and an entire display of hats and T-shirts emblazoned JEWEL BAY, MONTANA. Stick horses with calico heads and bright yarn manes lay scattered on the floor like Pick Up Sticks.

Sally's sobs turned to howls at a decibel level I'd last heard at a Smashing Pumpkins concert.

I leaned against the brick wall, doubled over, hooting silently. Kim managed a straight face while she told the small crowd that a suspected felon had been captured, there was no danger, and nothing to see, folks, just keep moving.

"Oh, I need a hanky," I said, tears of laughter on my cheeks. "Of all the shops in town for him to crash—it's too perfect." Sally would milk this mess and bemoan her bad luck the rest of the summer. I sympathized, from firsthand experience. But if Jay had to wreck a shop, better hers than Kitchenalia with all its glassware and china, or Snowberry's pottery and handblown glass.

"We don't get many crime-in-progress reports by text," Kim said matter-of-factly. "It came out kinda goofy, but we got the point."

"I figured if I called 911, dispatch might not realize he was confessing to a crime. So I texted you instead." I handed her my phone, glimpsing the stars on my wrist. Lucky after all. "It's all recorded."

She whistled softly. "Thanks. Oh, by the way, your young friend Ian Randall called this morning."

In the craziness at the recycling bins, I'd forgotten Ian's promise. Two crimes down, but the biggie loomed.

"We need to go to the riverbank," I said. "Angelo—Walker, whoever he is—oh, geez, you don't know." I summed up her prisoner's tangled past while we walked.

"You pieced all that together yourself?" Kim said as we crossed the parking lot. Midmorning and the summer heat was rising.

"Don't sound so surprised. Running a successful business nurtures all kinds of skills." We reached the riverbank, a sixty-foot drop-off heavy with brush, rocks, and very brave trees.

"What exactly are we searching for?" I described the stuff. She made a face and radioed for a deputy to join her.

He jogged over in minutes. "You stay put," she told me sternly, and they started down the slope.

I perched on a boulder at the edge of the cliff and closed my eyes. Growing up in an orchard, I'd learned to recognize sweet floral scents early, and caught a whiff of mock orange above the pine scent and the musky odor of river mud. I heard Kim and the deputy moving through the brush, an occasional "ow" or a stronger word when a thorny branch snagged one of them.

An osprey screeched overhead. Too close to her fish, or her chicks?

Far below, the waters of the Wild Mile raced by. Only a few hundred yards farther, they flew under the bridge, then out in to the bay and lake. A rushing river meets an irresistible force, and the vast expanse of seemingly still water wins every time. Aren't we all a bit like that? We rush and rush, running from something, then hit open water and nothing is ever the same.

"Detective." The deputy's voice broke my reverie. He stood in a small hollow at the base of a fallen spruce. "This isn't what you had in mind, but I think it's what we're really searching for." He held up a folding knife, the open blade darkened with reddish-brown spots.

Bingo by jingo. I bent over and threw up.

· *Thirty* ·

"Well," Kim said when they'd climbed back up the slope to the parking area. "That's a lot more interesting than a rubber snake."

The mistress of understatement shuddered. Bloody knives she could handle, but snakes gave her the willies.

I didn't recognize it. With so many knives around, how could I? "Any way to tell how long it's been there?"

"Not long," the deputy said. "Like it got tossed down, hit that tree, and landed in the tree well, waiting for me to find it."

Searching for one thing, you find something you didn't know you were looking for. As my business mentors liked to say, luck favors the prepared.

"So you type the blood to see if it's hers, print the handle, and voilà, there's your killer, right?" I said.

The deputy rolled his eyes. "It's tough to get usable prints off a weapon," Kim said, "except on TV." But they did handle it with care, bagging and tagging it. "That recording of yours should give us everything we need to corroborate

Angelo's confession. I don't think we need the toys, but I'll send the reserves out later to do a more thorough search."

Maybe my surveillance theory mattered after all. I pointed out the cameras on the back of the art gallery next to Red's and the liquor store up the block. "I'm sure you've checked the footage, and if it showed the killer, you'd have made an arrest. But I'm thinking that what it doesn't show might be important, too." I explained about the angles of coverage, using the toe of my sandal to draw a picture in the dirt and gravel. Not as nifty as Chiara's diagram, but you work with what you've got.

"She might be onto something there, boss," the deputy said. "There's a gap, right behind the bar. We didn't see nobody come from the north, behind the liquor store, or from the south."

"Which means it wasn't Angelo," I said, "because Polly Paulson places him coming up from the bridge. So either the killer came from the parking lot, right here where we are, or . . ." I stopped, suddenly chilled. "Or the killer came out Red's back gate." Right before our eyes.

The Merc's back door slammed shut behind me. With my face flushed and my skin drenched, I might have been the one scrambling up and down a brushy hillside hunting for evidence that might not be there and getting bitten by deer flies, mosquitos, and other nasty things. A frosty lemon Pellegrino, please, to set things right.

In the kitchen, I popped open the refrigerator door. Foamy brown liquid dripped off the bottom shelf, leaving a sticky brown slug trail. The goo slithered down the ledge.

"Tracy!" In a flash, she stood beside me. The cloying sweetness dissipated as the crud advanced.

"Geez, Erin. Is that all? I thought somebody'd died." Her hand flew to her mouth as she realized what she'd said.

"What is it?" I said.

"It's only Diet Coke." She dampened a rag, working hard to keep from laughing.

Okay, so Kim freaks out at snakes. I lose it over exploding Diet Coke. I sat on the floor and we both started howling.

When the laughter died down, we hugged and she helped me to my feet.

"I'll get bottles next shopping trip, promise." She handed me a can. "I know you sneak one now and then."

We lost it again. When we finally stopped laughing, she headed back to the shop and I took refuge in the office. Feet up, I leaned back in the Aeron chair, and rolled the cool bottle across my forehead. Touched it to the back of my neck.

I popped on the computer and scrolled through the sales and inventory figures. A well-done spreadsheet is a thing of beauty, its columns and figures comforting—if the numbers add up and trend right. Ours shone.

Fresca had worked late Thursday and much of Friday, restocking our best-selling products. I hadn't seen her yet this morning. After our conversation last night, she deserved a morning off. I had not shared with anyone my fear about what the recipe box hidden in the basement might mean, so there was no one to share my relief now that I knew the real story. Or the sweet sadness that story evoked.

At least my sister shared my ongoing concern about her. I crossed my fingers and rubbed my stars, praying that we were wrong and she was fine.

Then I pulled up the Spreadsheet of Suspicion and scanned what I knew—and didn't know. Angelo's arrest for the poisoning closed out that column. I shaded it gray. That left the murder. His story combined with the camera coverage probably ruled him out.

The rumors were still circulating. I could disprove the recipe theft. Claudette's note disproved the theory that Fresca had kicked her out.

But even with all that, Kim might not drop her suspicions

of Fresca unless we produced solid evidence incriminating someone else.

Fresca feared Kim would focus on me. I didn't believe that for one minute. But an outsider, looking at the facts and implications of my spreadsheet, might disagree. Kim wasn't an outsider, but the last week had demonstrated that I no longer had any idea how her mind worked.

Which made hard evidence even more important.

The killer had to be Dean. Sam had seen him come in the back gate. That area wasn't shown in the security footage. But the footage from the liquor store didn't show him coming from the north, and his absence on the gallery film meant he hadn't approached from the other direction. If I confirmed that he'd parked in the back lot, entering the alley and courtyard from the east, we'd almost have him nailed.

Almost.

Who else might have seen him? Easy to spot in that white jumpsuit.

Kim had the resources to quiz everyone who'd been at the dinner—guests and staff—but I didn't. Still, if I got lucky, we wouldn't need to. I reached for my phone, then remembered I'd given it to Kim. So I scribbled out a list, grabbed my bag, and headed downstairs.

"Darling." Fresca gripped my shoulders, gave me a long gaze, then kissed my cheek. "Thank God you're safe. I don't know whether to be thrilled that you caught Angelo or furious that you put yourself in danger."

I may not have given chase, but I had caught him, hadn't I? The TV shows don't make clear that detecting is more about taking advantage of the situations you find yourself in than boldly putting yourself in harm's way. "Now maybe everyone will agree that the recycling centers are a good idea."

"Except Sally," Tracy said with a giggle.

"When she cools down, I'll buy Landon a stick horse as an apology," I said.

Fresca smiled. The fine lines around her mouth seemed

a little deeper, her eyes less peppy. Drained from our late night, the weight of suspicion, or illness? I felt a stab of guilt for adding to her burdens, and for not having seen the effect.

I could handle the Merc just fine without my mother. Point was, I didn't want to. My old boss predicted pitfalls—and they're out there—but I like the family part of running a family business.

Tracy went to greet a customer, leaving Fresca and me alone.

"About last night, Mom. Please don't make any decisions yet. We have a lot to talk about."

"You took the words out of my mouth, darling. Now look at you. You're filthy. Go home and clean up. Tracy and I will handle things here."

Ah, yes. The real Francesca Murphy was back.

Village life was in full swing. I held the front door open for a spry, silver-haired couple in their eighties. He pointed at the carving on the threshold. "Murphy's Mercantile. I came here as a boy on summer vacation."

I bowed. "Erin Murphy, at your service."

"From your description," his wife said, "I pictured a dusty old joint with canned Spam and Veg-All. But this is a delight." She headed for the jam and jelly display in the ancient Hoosier. He winked.

Before heading home, I had more investigating to do. First, my sister.

"Erin, thank God. You got him." She hugged me tight, then released me with a scowl, channeling our mother. "What were you thinking? You should have called 911 right away."

Her kid might only be five, but she had all the contradictory instincts firing.

I asked if she'd seen the Vincents arrive Friday night, but no such luck.

"You know, you're filthy," she said. I gave her my Teen Rodeo Queen smile and waved good-bye.

"I am amazed," Heidi said when I popped into Kitchenalia, "at your quick thinking. Texting and recording that slimeball's confession."

"I'm amazed at how quickly the story's made the rounds."

"Sally can't stop talking. On the one hand, you saved her life. On the other, you put her in mortal danger. On the other-other, you caught the killer."

I hadn't actually done any of those things, but why quibble? Though if villagers let their guard down, thinking the killer was behind bars, and more tragedy struck—well, no point going there. I had trouble enough without borrowing more.

I posed my question about the Vincents, and Heidi cocked her head, searching her memory banks, before slowly shaking no. "But that new red Caddy of hers may have circled a time or two. I bet he dropped her off, then found a spot. No telling where."

Parking problems are a mixed blessing. You like a full town, but if tourists anticipate a problem and stay home, business can wither up and blow away like a prairie tumbleweed—with about as much chance of changing course and coming back.

Next on my list were Kathy Jensen and the Georges, at the upper end of the village. Kathy had arrived at the Festa dinner late, shortly before the chaos, and couldn't shed any light on the Vincents' movements.

Tony George swore the Vincents were already in the courtyard when he and Mimi walked down from the Inn. "Funny, Kim Caldwell was just here asking the same questions."

On the same track, at last. I headed for my car, cutting through town on the side street. Bill didn't usually open the herb shop on Saturdays, but his lights were on, so I tried the door. It gave with a creak.

"Hey, Erin. Come on in. I'm putting some remedies together. Nice work this morning."

So much for thinking Bill stayed out of the village loop.

"Your mother told me," he said, responding to my unspoken question. "We were having coffee when it happened, and she called me later." He paused, studying me over his reading glasses. "Our coffee dates are becoming a regular thing."

Knock me over with a moxa stick. I pulled out a client chair. He would hardly discuss a patient's illness with her daughter, if confidentiality kept him from answering a detective's questions about a crime. But now that Angelo had confessed to the poisoning, maybe Bill would talk about that, at least. We'd leave the personal stuff for later.

How had Angelo gotten the poison? I needed to know, to alleviate my fear that I had inadvertently sent him down the poison path. But more important, I didn't think he had killed Claudette. If I could trace his movements Friday afternoon, maybe I could figure out who had.

And besides, Kim would never tell me.

"James Angelo told me he came to you for herbs for his heart condition."

"His nonexistent heart condition. I knew right away that he wasn't experiencing the symptoms he described. The MDs call it drug-seeking behavior, but nothing he wanted provides euphoria. That roused my suspicions."

"Good instincts. He ended up picking foxglove out of Claudette's own garden to poison her family."

"Lucky no one died. It would have been worse had he gotten hold of chemical digoxin. He should be charged with attempted murder."

"You sound like a lawyer," I said with a laugh.

He wrapped a label around a bottle. "You can take a guy out of the courtroom—but not very far." He saw my surprise. "Didn't you know? I practiced law for years."

I surveyed the tiny space, crammed with mysterious bottles labeled in Chinese, homeopathic remedies, rows and rows of glass jars that held his herbal pharmacy. Shelves of books on all variety of natural medicine, but nary a law tome in sight.

Bill put the bottle on his desk and sat, a softness in his eyes. "Nearly thirty years ago, my wife died. Complications of a Caesarian. I sued for medical malpractice, and lost. Everyone agreed it was a tragedy, but no one would say her doctors had done anything wrong. I felt like a double failure."

I'd had no idea. "The baby?"

He smiled. "Alicia. I put everything I had into raising her. And into my second career, in natural medicine. A few years ago, I discovered Jewel Bay." He gestured at the strange brews and potions, the curious ingredients of an herbalist's work. "I wanted to make a direct impact on people's lives. The law is important—don't get me wrong. But this—this work is such a gift."

For the second time today, I realized you never know what secret pain people carry. Or what secret joy. How had Bill been able to convert tragedy into triumph, while Jay Walker turned humiliation into cruelty?

"Why tell me?"

Another gentle smile. "I'm sure you've figured out that I care for your mother very deeply."

His admission acted like Drano on my plugged-up fear. "Is she sick? Fresca, I mean. I know you take confidentiality very seriously, and I respect that. But she's been acting weird all week, and we—my sister and I—we know she's been consulting with you. Is she ill?"

A cloud fell over his sky blue eyes, and my heart sank. We'd guessed right. "I'm still a lawyer, Erin, though I don't practice."

Was I dumb as a post, or what? Finally, I got it. "Meaning, while I've been trying to convince her to see a lawyer, she's been talking to you. But not telling me."

He pursed his lips. "I believe in justice, Erin. And I know your mother is innocent."

So much for the late-night heart-to-heart and this morning's sweet concern. My mother had kept more secrets than I ever imagined. Did she think if I knew she was getting legal advice from Bill, that I'd pick up on their relationship—and disapprove?

She had dated over the years, though never seriously. But she should have somebody special in her life. Somebody who treated her well, as Bill would.

"Naturally, she's concerned about her children's reaction. We intended to go public at the Festa, but at the last minute, she popped around the corner to say no because she hadn't had a chance to tell you girls yet. Then the murder happened, and she thought it better to wait to tell you after the criminal investigation."

So that's where she'd gone when Kim thought she'd snuck out to kill Claudette. Made sense. Made me a little dizzy. "What about your daughter?" On the shelf behind his desk sat a framed snapshot of Bill with a small blond girl, on a trail by a mountain lake, fishing rods in hand.

He picked up the bottle on his desk. "I need to deliver this. You'll like Alicia. She lives in Portland. I'll tell you more about her tomorrow, at dinner in the orchard."

Dang. I really was going to hate to miss that one.

I blew out a horsey breath. "Just treat my mother right."

We parted outside the shop, my mind swirling. "All will be well," I muttered. "All will be well."

But as I pulled out of the parking lot, I spotted Bill, medicine bottle in hand, headed for the back door of the Merc.

One more stop on the medicine trail.

Polly's morning greeting had fallen a notch or two on the cheerfulness scale, and she didn't move quite as spritely as usual. Rocking the night away will do that.

"Pol, you said Angelo bought stupid kid stuff for his

nephews, but you didn't remember what." He'd told me this morning he wasn't in touch with his family. "Any chance it was stuff like fake vomit and toy dead mice?"

She wrinkled her nose. "I was so mad at him for trying to sneak past me without paying, I hardly noticed. But yeah, that sounds right." She led me to the boy toy aisle and an impressively disgusting collection of lifelike snakes, giant spiders, and all manner of rodentia.

I picked up a small black rubber object. "Shrunken heads. Didn't know they still made them."

"Gad. Remember Ted Redaway wearing one of them on a shoelace around his neck? Maybe fourth grade."

"He always had style. You said Angelo argued with Gordy over a prescription. Is he in?"

"Yeah." She waved me back to the pharmacy counter. The Springers had been pharmacists in Jewel Bay as long as the Murphys had been grocers. Gordy was a few years ahead of us in school. His dad led the wave of moves to the highway in the 1970s; now Gordy's wife ran an antiques shop in the old drugstore building, a block up from the Merc.

I hadn't seen him since last Friday, when we crouched alongside Claudette's lifeless body. A tall, homely man with a fringe of dark hair and the eyes of an eager puppy, he unlatched the pharmacy door, descended, and wrapped his long arms around me.

"Rough week," he said. "I usually lose my customers to natural causes."

"Gordy, you heard about James Angelo's arrest?" He nodded. "He said you refused to fill a prescription for him last Friday afternoon. What happened?"

"You look close when a first-timer you don't know brings in a scrip from a pad. Most are electronic these days. And it looked funny—faded ink, kinda crumpled, and the date might have been written over. Like, to change it, which is weird."

Old and crumpled. What did that mean?

"We routinely ask all new patients for ID. He said James

Angelo was a professional name, and showed me his driver's license, in the name of Jay David Walker. But the name on the prescription was David J. Walker. It was all just strange enough that I wanted to call the prescriber, so I said fine, but he'd have to wait his turn."

According to the elder Bergstroms, Jay's dad blew the drug money on booze. I bet Jay had done as my mother did with Claudette's note, and I with the note on my car—crumpled it up in anger, then thought better. A prescription seemed like an odd souvenir. But then, Jay Walker was an odd duck.

"That's not something you need to report?"

He rested an elbow on the counter. "No. Digoxin isn't controlled. I only call the sheriff if somebody's fishing for narcotics. Sometimes we hear about a guy making the rounds. I mean, it doesn't produce a high, so it's an unusual drug to forge a request for. Sounds like self-prescribing."

Or poisoning. "So you refused. Then what?"

"He threw a fit. Practically gave himself a heart attack." Gordy chuckled. "Ranted and raved about the state of health care in this country, how hardworking people can't afford it, we're all in cahoots to bleed the people dry. I told him he was no longer welcome, and he should leave."

"He thinks anyone working a family business had money handed to them on a silver tray."

Gordy rolled his eyes. "Ten minutes with my accountant would dispel that notion."

"Thanks, Gordy."

Polly helped me pick out a squeaky duck toy for Tracy's dog Bozo. On our way to the register, I spotted a display of Fourth of July decorations. There at the front was a foot-wide red metal star—perfect for the back gate.

Then I remembered my other question, and headed back to the pharmacy. "Hey, Gordy, when you came to the Festa dinner, any chance you saw Dean and Linda Vincent arrive?"

"Sure did. He must have dropped her off out front, then parked out back near me. We walked in Red's gate about the same time." Gordy ran a hand over his thinning hair. "Made it a double shock when you found Claudette out there a few minutes later."

And with that, I was back at square one.

· *Thirty-one* ·

If hanging a red star on the back gate would enhance the Merc's fame and reputation, then I wanted it up there toot-sweet.

If red star energy would help protect my mother, I'd hang a whole constellation.

I wanted a word with her, even if my pants weren't clean. Bill had neatly sidestepped my questions about her health. But when he said he had a prescription to deliver, he'd headed for the Merc.

An Audi with Arizona plates pulled out of a parking spot right behind our building, and I grabbed it. My lucky stars were on fire today.

Even though the killer was still on the loose—and Gordy Springer had just eliminated my prime suspect.

I slipped the star's wire loop over a nail on the gate. Its rustic style coordinated nicely with the weathered planks and dark iron latch and hinges. Liz would approve. But we'd need to clean up the weeds in the alley, haul in some dirt, and plant a few shrubs. Why did every project seem to take on a life of its own?

I itched to get going on the courtyard remodel. One more reason to get this murder solved, and soon. Crime is big-time distracting.

So why did I all of a sudden feel panicky and fearful? *Shake it off, girl. It's just the morning's adrenaline metabolizing.* Maybe Dean wasn't the killer, but I sure as heck knew it wasn't Fresca or me. With Angelo in custody, and Ian's confession, we were all in a lot less danger.

And if my mother was ill, it couldn't be serious, could it? Plus, she had an herbalist, and a lawyer, and a potential boyfriend—all in one. That was weird. But I liked Bill—his Zen seemed a good match for her zing. Everything would be fine.

Still, it already seemed like a very long day, even for solstice.

The gate between our courtyard and Red's stood open. That latch popped again, darn it. I'd take a look later, and talk with Old Ned about a replacement—and about making sure his boys kept it locked. We can't let bar customers traipse through our courtyard, especially if we turn it into retail therapy space. Imagining the safety and liability issues gave me the creepy-crawlies worse than any fake snake or shrunken rubber head.

What might Ted do to our courtyard if Fresca sold?

No way, José.

I opened the screen door. If Liz is right and space holds energy, then the Merc's back hall had been unplugged. I took a step forward, listening to the quiet.

Nothing.

"Mom? Fresca?" Another step. I paused at the foot of the stairs, but heard no one in the office.

"Tracy?" The kitchen to my left, the shop ahead, both radiated deathly stillness. My jaw and throat tightened.

A muffled sound caught my attention, then stopped.

Where was it? *Breathe, girl. Pay attention here.* Shop lights on, nobody home. No sign of Tracy, Fresca, or a customer.

I reached for the phone in my pocket. Damn. Kim had it.

One landline phone was upstairs, the other up front. Before I could decide which to go for, I heard a scraping sound.

I stepped into the kitchen and grabbed the biggest, sharpest chef's knife we had. Knife in hand, I reached for the basement doorknob. Should I call for help first? What if Tracy had fallen down the steps and hurt herself?

The first aid kit. No. Get it later. Get to her first.

I gripped the old, dented brass. How many times had I turned that knob, had a Murphy turned that knob?

It turned a quarter inch each way, no more.

We never lock that door.

The lock was original to the building, keyed on both sides. We kept a key on top of the door frame, just in case we needed to lock it. No sign of it. I reached up, probing, hoping. Dust only.

I rattled the knob, then listened. Tracy? I couldn't tell.

Criminy. We so never lock that door that I didn't know where the other key was. My desk drawer? I bounded up two steps, then remembered. No. Check the old cash register.

I dashed to the front counter and punched the register drawer open. Lifted up the cash drawer. Grabbed the brass barrel key, and prayed I could make it work.

I ran back to the door. *Steady, Erin. Breathe.* The key slid in okay, but the latch mechanism balked. Locks and I never have gotten on well. Tracy must have gone downstairs for something, then gotten locked in by accident, though that didn't explain the missing key. The sounds from the basement increased: a banging. A muffled voice—or two voices? A rattling, like a pipe. The pipes were in the ceiling. Tracy could never reach them, unless she dragged something over to stand on.

I set the knife on the floor, then turned the key slowly

with my right hand, twisting the knob with my left. My curled fingertips rubbed the stars on my other wrist by accident, and the door popped open.

Tracy crouched on the landing, her left hand gripping a rock in the wall.

"Erin, it's you," she said, eyes wide, face red, hair wild with panic and cobwebs. "Thank God. We were afraid he was coming back."

He who? We who? And then I noticed.

Behind her on the steps stood Rick Bergstrom.

·*Thirty-two*·

A war of words erupted in my head and spilled out my mouth.

"Are you okay? What were you doing in the basement? How'd you get locked in?" And to Rick, "Why are you here?"

"We're fine," Rick said. "Did you see him? Did you call the police? We have to catch him."

"Catch who?"

"Ted," Tracy said, her voice anxious and thready. She staggered up the last few steps. One earring hung askew; the other had gone missing. "He came in here all riled up, looking for you or your mom. Stalking around the store, like you were hiding behind the jelly jars. Then he started yelling at me." She blinked back tears. "Grabbing my shoulders and screaming."

"They were in the back hall when I got here," Rick said. "I shouted 'let her go' and sprinted toward them. Somehow he got the basement door open—I didn't even know it was there. We fought, and I ended up on the wrong side of the door. Then he shoved her down the stairs, too, grabbed the key from on top of the door frame, and locked us both in." A look of terror struck him. "Geez, you scared me with that knife."

I'd picked it up without thinking. I put it back in the kitchen. "Are you hurt? Did you call the sheriff?" I asked Tracy.

She shook her head, one hand pawing through her hair. "I tried to pull Ted off Rick. The landline was up front, and my cell's upstairs, in my purse."

"And I'd left my phone in the car," Rick said.

No blood or visible injuries. I dashed to the front counter and grabbed the landline. It's a lot easier to call in a crime than to text one. Even if you don't exactly know what the crime is. I flipped the OPEN sign to CLOSED and locked the front door. No key needed, thank goodness.

"Water first," I told Tracy. "Wash down that shock. Then you can drink all the Diet Coke in the world. And ping the can if you want."

Her laugh teetered on the edge of hysteria. I knew the feeling—the fear and anger that rise up after physical danger ends. Things were starting to make more sense. I'd been looking in the wrong direction, and Ted had pointed me there.

He was less of a doofus and more of a coward than I'd thought. If you're mad at me, have the guts to yell at me, not my employee. Kim arrived while Tracy and Rick were sitting at the kitchen counter, telling me the story. Fresca had left with Bill for a late lunch. Ted barged in from the back. When he couldn't find my mother or me, he'd turned on Tracy, telling her, "Make them see. Make them understand."

"What did he mean?" she asked.

"He wants us to sell him the Merc. I couldn't figure out why, but now I think I know. Claudette used to run Red's kitchen." I felt a flash burn inside me. Had it been Ted in my house earlier this week? And watching me in the woods last

Saturday? "Trace, did he say—had he been following me, maybe gone to my cabin?"

She nodded. "And to your mom's house. Claudette loved working at Red's. And she did a good job. She only left because your mom needed help. Erin, don't sell."

I covered her hand with mine. "Don't worry. When the move to Vegas fell apart, Claudette confided in Ted, and he suggested she take over Red's again. To sweeten the deal—and prove his worth to his father—he promised to expand the kitchen into a full-scale restaurant. For that, he needed more space."

"The Merc," Kim said.

"The Merc," I agreed. "But Fresca refused to sell. So he spread rumors, to disgrace Fresca and at the same time, create sympathy for Claudette by suggesting that Fresca built her success on Claudette's recipes and management."

"I can't believe Claudette had anything to do with that," Tracy said.

"She may have intended to help him by encouraging Fresca to sell," I said, remembering some of the Facebook messages, "but his rumor campaign made her furious. She told him no. He confronted her in Back Street on Friday night. And he stabbed her."

Tracy yelped and began to sob. Rick draped an arm around her shoulder in a reassuring hug. A natural gesture, a protective response after the ordeal they'd been through. It didn't mean anything.

I turned to Kim. "Ted was with us in the courtyard while the caterers and musicians were setting up. I remember because I was irked at him for standing around and not pitching in. I didn't realize he'd left, but when we were all gathered in the courtyard waiting for you, Ned told me he'd put Ted on guard duty out front, as payback for showing up late."

Kim flipped through her notebook, searching. "Ted said

he arrived after the body was found and came in the front door."

"Ted never comes in the front unless he parks his Harley out there to show it off. But Red's was closed for the Festa, so Ned parked his '57 Chevy out front to keep the Harley crowd away."

"He came in the front," Kim said, "because he knew what he'd find out back."

Claudette, sweet doomed bird, dead.

"I think the blood on that knife your deputy found will match hers, and if you can lift any fingerprints, they'll be his." I told her about my conversation with Ted after I'd noticed he wasn't wearing his knife. Had that been only yesterday? So much had happened so fast.

"And the prints on that spaghetti sauce jar," I said. Crimminy. "He went to my place at least twice. First Saturday. Tuesday, at the Merc, he tried to convince me to move the business out to the highway, and I brushed him off. And he kept calling Fresca, increasing the pressure. Then Wednesday, he went into my cabin, then came back here and he tried to scare me by vandalizing my car." I was speculating about his presence in my cabin, but every instinct said I was right.

"Taking advantage of the atmosphere of fear in the village," Kim said.

I nodded. So much made sense now. No doubt he'd been watching me at the cabin, maybe other places, like he'd waited for me after the meeting Friday morning to keep an eye on me. I shivered. "Right. But that incident didn't fit the pattern, because it was aimed at me. And he kept it up. Friday afternoon, the crazy motorcyclist I nearly hit on the highway—I bet that was Ted, coming from the orchard, pressuring Fresca."

"Who's pressuring me?" my mother said. "Why are you closed with the front door locked? What's happened now?"

None of us had heard her come in, we'd been so focused on working out Ted's movements. Her eyes flitted from me to Kim to the others, and back to me. Bill stood beside her, one hand resting protectively on the small of her back. Kim gave her a quick rundown. Her dark eyes widened with amazement, then narrowed with anger, as she realized, along with the rest of us, how much danger we'd faced from someone we never suspected.

"But I don't understand what you were doing here," she said to Rick.

"Uh, well." His broad Nordic cheekbones flushed handsomely. "I planned to drop in, see how you and Erin liked the product samples I'd left, see about placing an order. But truthfully"—his eyes on me were intensely blue—"I wanted to see Erin again."

My turn for hot cheeks.

"Erin, you left the produce cart outside." My mother kicked into command chef mode. "Bring it in and cut up some vegetables. Finger food is best, I think. Tracy, open some tapenade and slice some bread. Bill, you're in charge of beverages." She, of course, was in charge of all of us. That would never change.

Other deputies arrived to start the search for Ted. Kim kept tabs while taking statements from Tracy, Rick, and me. My mother fed us all, even the deputies.

I showed Kim my timeline and the Spreadsheet of Suspicion.

"Not as fancy as your murder board," I said, "but retail managers have skills, too."

"I hope you understand," she said, "why I focused on your mother."

"We'll have to agree to disagree on that."

"Oh. Almost forgot." She pulled my phone from her pocket and set it on the counter. "We copied your text and the recording of your conversation with Angelo. Good work." She extended her hand, and as I shook it, I noticed the bracelet on her arm.

"Thanks."

* * *

There was no point reopening that day. After Kim and the deputies finished up, Bill took Fresca home, where a deputy would stand guard. Another deputy took Tracy home and would keep watch over her. No word on Ted yet, but while we couldn't rule out more trouble, I figured we'd all be safe. Put a desperate man on a Harley, and he's long gone. I'd misjudged him, but I didn't think he'd intended to kill Claudette—or to terrorize the rest of us. She'd frustrated his plans, ill-conceived as they were, and he'd reacted impulsively. After that, he'd attempted to misdirect or stymie the investigation by pointing fingers at Dean and Linda Vincent, and scaring me so I'd stop asking questions. Selling might have convinced some people of Fresca's guilt, but he'd seemed genuinely horrified to hear that Kim had threatened to arrest her.

Time to think about all that another day.

I glanced around my beloved, beleaguered Merc, site of too much work and not enough play. My eyes filled.

Rick's gaze followed mine. "It's a grand old place. Don't let this incident spoil your memories. And don't let anyone take it away from you."

"I don't intend to." I turned to face him. "I'm so sorry you got caught up in it. Not quite the reception you'd hoped for."

"I like a woman who's full of surprises. And one who can rescue me from my own stupidity."

"Ted had the advantage of surprise. And desperation. Plus he knew about the key." I smiled wryly.

It didn't seem right to just send him away, after he'd been trapped in the basement by a madman mad at me. But Kim had ordered me to go home and stay home, and had assigned a deputy to trail me until Ted was caught. Plus, if I knew Liz and Bob, they'd be watching me with hawk eyes until all danger had ended.

Which didn't mean I couldn't invite him to the cabin, or the dock. We'd be amply chaperoned.

But as appealing as Rick was, and apparently interested—at least before said madman came on the scene—I wanted to be alone. To relax, and think, and spoil my cat.

From the window display, I grabbed a basket filled with the Merc's goodies and held it out. "For the road. Come back anytime for a refill."

He gave me a long, understanding look, followed by a smile. "You bet."

· *Thirty-three* ·

A soft, warm touch brushed my leg. I opened my eyes slowly. A pair of eyes stared back at me.

Yellow-green eyes with almond-shaped pupils.

"You slept in." Sandburg's tail swished across my skin again, and his eyes closed. "Good boy. Too wet out for cats or mice."

Sunday morning's deluge had the feel of an island off the Northwest coast, or the heart of a jungle forest, all gray and green, the only sound rain pelting the roof. Even the squirrels were napping.

Thank heavens for my warm house and full pantry.

I left my sweet little guy curled up on the cool cotton sheets. While the coffee—extra-strength—brewed, I found my phone. Might be time to rethink the policy against carrying personal cell phones on the shop floor.

"Take the day off," I told Tracy.

"But you always say rainy days bring people off the lake and the golf course into the shops." In the background, Bozo the Harlequin Great Dane gave a rare bark.

"Nobody needs the Merc today. And you and your dog need some quality time together."

Then, crossing my fingers for voice mail, I made another call.

"Adam Zimmerman," the message said. "Talk to me." I took a rain check, literally. Too much had happened, and I was not ready to put my emotions on the line. Not until Ted was behind bars, rumors were squelched deader than any field mouse who'd ever crossed Sandburg's path, and all my questions about Dean, Linda, Claudette, and my mother were answered.

I rubbed the stars on my wrist.

Soon.

"You stop stopping cree-me-nals," Max said Monday morning, "or we go broke giving you free breakfast."

I scooped up my latte and *pain au chocolat*. "Thanks, Max. You're a prince."

"Ehh." He waved a hand. "I am but a chef."

"You are the real thing," I said with a wink.

Wendy emerged from the back room, smiling. She stepped around the counter and wrapped her arms around me. With my hands full, I couldn't return her hug, so I brushed her cheek with mine and smiled back. "I thought he killed her," she said, "I thought if he—Angelo—knew I'd told you, my grandmother might be in danger. But I know now, it's better to talk. To trust the people you've always trusted." She looked happier than I'd seen in ages. "I'm so glad you're running the Merc. I'm so glad you came back to Jewel Bay."

My jaw tightened and my own eyes grew damp. "Me, too."

By mutual agreement, there'd been no family gathering at the Orchard on Sunday. We all needed the extra day to rest. It worked—I was raring to go today.

Almost ten and no Tracy, so I set up the cash box, swept the sidewalk, and refreshed the produce cart. The Monday morning opening ritual is fun, signaling to the world that the Merc is ready for business.

I was about to call Tracy when she charged in the back, wearing a white open-weave sweater over a sunshine yellow tank dress, matching seed bead earrings that brushed her shoulders, and an impish expression.

"Time off agrees with you."

She set a large round cookie tin on the kitchen counter, and gave it a pat. "A surprise for later." At my wary look, she clarified. "A good surprise."

A new variety of dog biscuits, no doubt.

If it's made in Montana, it must be good.

More customers than we expected—more of that crime-is-good-for-business effect—kept us hopping. Fresca roasted peppers for a batch of Summer Red Pesto, and I set out the demo sign.

"What would you think about retiring the artichoke pesto?" she said.

"Don't you dare. Why not add CLAUDETTE'S FAVORITE to the label instead?"

Her eyes filled and she gave me a long hug. "You're brilliant, darling. Where did your passion for this business come from?"

I gestured around me: tin ceiling tiles, pine doors milled when the town was young, oak floors smoothed by a century of feet. "It's in my blood."

"Murphy blood," she said. "I'm fond of the place, but not like you are. I think it's time you took full control of the building as well as the business. Consult me when you want to, but make your own decisions."

"Mom. Seriously?" I took a step back. Then I remembered. "Are you ill?"

"What?" Her brow furrowed. "No. Whatever gave you that idea?"

"We—Chiara and I—wondered, when we realized you'd been consulting Bill. Never imagined he was giving you legal advice. But Saturday morning, he made up some formula, then delivered the bottle to you and, well, I'm worried is all."

She grabbed an oven mitt and slid the peppers out of the oven. The hot skins snapped and popped when the cool air hit them, and I breathed in the sweet-sharp smell.

"Darling." She put one gloved hand on her hip, gesturing with the other. "There is nothing to worry about. He made me a calming remedy. I've been a little anxious, with Ted's pressure, then Claudette, the vandalism, the accusations. But I'm fine. Bill and I . . ." She paused, blushing, unsure how to tell a grown daughter about a new relationship.

When Sparky the Border collie died, my parents jokingly asked who would tell them what to do. I felt a bit like that now. But no worries—Fresca would always be part of the Merc.

I touched her hand. "I'm glad, Mom. I like him. Especially if it means you won't be leaving town." My father lived on in all of us. Nothing would change that. "Be happy."

The front door chimed and a gaggle of customers entered. "Back to business," I said. "Now that I know we still have a business."

"There have been Murphys here since this town began, and you and I will not be the last. Besides," she said with a laugh, "I can't sell. My buyer's on the lam."

Just before noon, Fresca, Tracy, and I stood at the front counter, making plans for the week. Old Ned came in, aged a decade in two days.

"Girlie," he said to me, "I am so ashamed. I knew Ted was greedy and irresponsible. Maybe if his mother had lived . . ." He shook his head. "But I never imagined anything like this. Can you ever forgive me?"

For all his gruffness, I realized now that Ned had coddled his son. Would he have come up with the money for Ted's expansion scheme, as Ted had counted on, despite his protests to Fresca and me? No way to ever know.

"Don't blame yourself, Ned," Fresca said. "Our children have grown up. They make their own decisions."

"Nothing to forgive," I said.

He shook his head. "I raised a killer. Whether it was pre—prima—what's the word?"

"Premeditated."

"Premedicated or not don't matter. Nothing can bring Claudette back, but if I can make up for what he did to you girls, you just tell me."

"Ned, that's sweet," Fresca said, "but there's no need—"

"I have an idea. Lend us a couple of your employees for the afternoon. We've got a basement to clean out." And neither Tracy nor I were in any rush to go back down there. Maybe the boys could find her lost earring.

"You got it, by jingo."

Right then, Kim Caldwell arrived, natty in a navy blazer and matching slacks with a silky red T-shirt. "Good to see you, Ned. I have some news. Highway Patrol stopped Ted outside Deer Lodge." My eyes widened at the irony of being arrested outside the town that housed the men's state prison. "A tricked-out Harley and an inexperienced rider aren't a great getaway combo. He'll be arraigned this afternoon, and sent back here."

My mother clasped a hand to her chest. Ned paled, but his expression remained stern.

Angelo would be charged with attempted deliberate homicide for the poisoning. The prosecutor was investigating possible charges for presenting an altered prescription and whether he'd violated any laws by using a false name. I hoped his sentence included a psychiatric evaluation and therapy. And maybe community service, teaching basic cooking skills in a shelter or halfway house.

"Ian and the window?" I asked.

"No charges, if you agree."

I nodded. His reaction had been extreme, even irresponsible, but I understood. He would always feel marked by losing a parent so young. No need to complicate it further.

"Ned," Fresca said. "I think you and I should pay a visit to Jeff and Ian. It won't be easy, but it will do us and them good." She took his arm, and they left.

I wondered whether I ought to follow their example and apologize to Dean and Linda for suspecting them.

Nah.

"Got a minute? Coffee?" Kim nodded and I poured, then we retreated to the courtyard, soon to be radically improved.

"So what's next for you?" I took a deep, slow breath, letting the scent of caffeine work its magic.

"Paperwork." She grimaced and I laughed. "Witness statements, lab reports, photos, all supporting a formal report that goes to the prosecutor. It'll take days."

"Why Claudette? She was so much fun. So sweet and generous, a great friend to my mother. And yet, in her confusion or distress, she agreed to do some nasty things. To her credit, she backed out, but the wheels were already in motion."

"And neither Ted nor Angelo could stop. Or should I say Walker? Thanks, by the way. Would have taken us ages to identify him if it hadn't been for you."

"Give Rick Bergstrom credit for that." He'd earned it, and I genuinely looked forward to seeing him again.

"Another witness I need to call." She made a note. "I talked to Dean Vincent. He admitted lying about where he parked because he knew he'd be a suspect. People—they only make things worse when they try to cover up."

"And Linda? Did she think Dean killed Claudette? Or hope to divert attention from him long enough for the real killer to be found?"

"A little of both, I suspect. Murder's never cut and dried. Every victim has a good side. But they're often the folks who live on the edges, and find themselves on the wrong side of luck."

I let that sink in. It explained a lot. "You know, despite all this, I'm really happy to be back in Jewel Bay." I barged on, determined to clear the air. "When my dad died, I thought you didn't want to be friends anymore. Like I'd done something wrong. But I realize now his death had nothing to do with it. It was a total fluke that I beat you in that last barrel race. I showed you up in something you took seriously, that I just did for fun."

Her mouth hung slightly open, but she didn't speak.

"That must have been hard," I said. "I'm sorry."

"Yeah. The things we think matter at seventeen . . ." Her voice trailed off and she gazed at the dirty brick walls, the cracked, dusty concrete. "Seems silly now."

"Maybe we can go for a ride some evening. I'm out of practice, but I'm ready." I stuck out one red-booted foot.

She flashed me a grin. "You'll pick it up in no time. Once a Rodeo Queen, always a Rodeo Queen."

Back inside, I worked with a few customers and made a deal with a man selling duck and quail eggs. Then I remembered my conversation with the Krausses on Friday, and headed up to my office. I called the wine buyer at Sav-Club and made the pitch for a promotion in the Northwest stores. The idea intrigued her, so I called Jen and passed the word.

"Oh, wow," she said. "We owe you big time. If this comes through, we'll plant an extra row of Viognier vines just for you."

Music to my ears.

The door chime sounded as I came back down.

"Hey. I just heard what happened this weekend. You okay?"

The depth of concern in Adam Zimmerman's eyes touched me. "I'm fine. Sorry about canceling our hike."

"No worries—not after all you've been through. Plus we'd have gotten soaked. Next weekend? If you're not off investigating something."

I laughed. "Yeah. I think I'm done with this Cowdog stuff."

The reference puzzled him, but he smiled when I explained. "I look forward to meeting your nephew. And the whole family."

What could I do but grin and nod?

I had book work to take care of, and Tracy had deliveries to shelve, but that surprise of hers had me intrigued.

"So what is in that tin?"

Beaming, she handed me a napkin that read WILL WORK FOR CHOCOLATE. Then she pried off the lid to reveal a treasure trove of black gold. I gasped.

"I've been experimenting," she said. "I needed that free afternoon yesterday to get the filling exactly right. But I think I've got it."

I picked up one gemlike, dark chocolate truffle, and admired the smooth coat and classic swirl. Then I bit into the rich, toothy chocolate, perfectly balanced by the sweet-tart fruit cream. Dark and light danced on my tongue as I savored the best huckleberry chocolate ever.

"By jingo," I said. "I think you do."

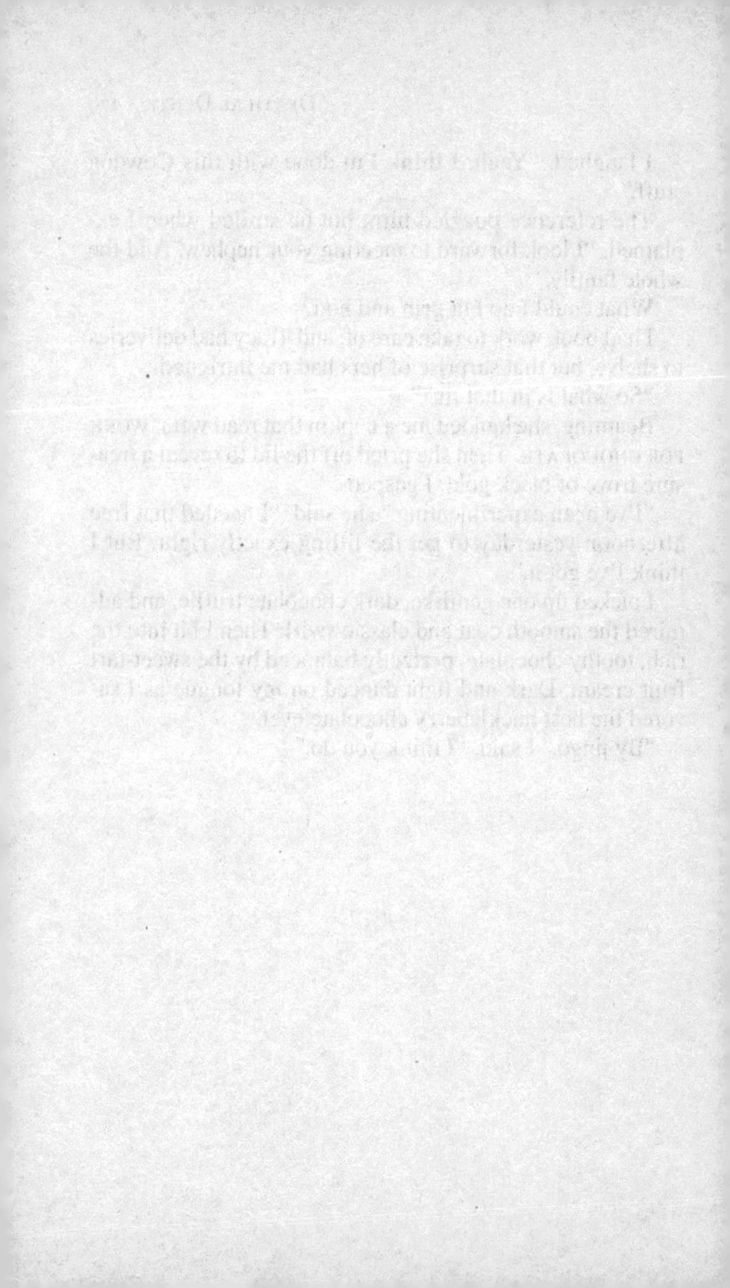

Create Your Own Festa di Pasta

Appetizers

Erin could make a meal of appetizers—and often does!

Caprese Salad

Serve this as an appetizer or a salad course, with a loaf of crunchy bread.

ripe tomatoes—any round, meaty variety will do
fresh mozzarella
fresh basil leaves
fruity olive oil
coarse sea salt and fresh-ground pepper—optional

Slice the tomatoes and mozzarella about ¼ inch thick. Arrange the tomato slices on a salad plate or an appetizer tray. Top each tomato with a slice of cheese and a basil leaf. Drizzle with olive oil. Season if you like. How many you need depends on whether you're serving other appetizers, but these are a guaranteed hit!

Fennel and Shrimp Prosciutto Wraps

Unusual and tasty!

1 fennel bulb
8 large shrimp, preferably tail-on
8 thin slices of prosciutto

Preheat oven to 400 degrees, or heat your outdoor grill. Trim the fennel bulb, cut it in half lengthwise, and core it; cut each half into four spears. Wrap each spear in a slice of prosciutto; one wrap is fine, two are even tastier. Wrap the shrimp.

Place the fennel spears on a baking sheet and roast at 400 degrees until fennel is tender and prosciutto is lightly browned, 15–20 minutes. Add the shrimp about halfway—they cook more quickly. These can also be grilled outside.

SERVES 4, ALTHOUGH ERIN HAS EATEN AN ENTIRE RECIPE HERSELF WITH NO REGRETS.

Stuffed Mushrooms

1 pound (18–20) medium-sized button mushrooms
2 tablespoons butter
2 tablespoons olive oil
1 clove garlic, minced or pressed
2 tablespoons fresh flat-leaf (Italian) parsley, chopped
½ teaspoon salt
¼ teaspoon dried thyme leaves or 1 teaspoon fresh thyme
¼ teaspoon dried oregano or 1 teaspoon fresh oregano leaves
¼ teaspoon nutmeg
¼ teaspoon black pepper

¼ cup bread crumbs (standard crumbs work better than Panko-style)
¼ cup Parmesan, grated

Preheat oven to 400 degrees. Wash, trim, and stem the mushrooms. Set the caps, hollows facing up, in a lightly greased or sprayed shallow 9-by-18-inch baking pan.

Chop the stems finely. In a medium sauté pan, heat the butter and oil over medium heat. When the butter is melted, add the chopped stems and cook, stirring, until juices evaporate and mushrooms are lightly browned. Mix in garlic, parsley, salt, thyme, oregano, nutmeg, pepper, and bread crumbs. Remove from heat. Spoon stuffing into the mushroom caps and sprinkle with Parmesan.

Bake, uncovered, at 400 degrees for 20–25 minutes, until the cheese is lightly browned.

If these don't disappear the night you make them, they can be eaten at room temperature or reheated—briefly, under 10 seconds—in the microwave.

Olive Tapenade

Erin adores her mini (2-cup) food processor—perfect for the home-size version of Fresca's best-selling taste treat.

1 cup pitted Kalamata olives (Nicoise olives work well, too—the flavor will differ)
2 cloves garlic, peeled
2 tablespoons olive oil
2 tablespoons fresh oregano leaves
2 tablespoons fresh flat-leaf (Italian) parsley
2 tablespoons fresh lemon juice

Combine all the ingredients in the food processor and pulse until just pureed. The spread should be textured, not smooth. It will keep up to a week, covered and refrigerated.

Morel Sauté

morel mushrooms
butter
shallots
fresh flat-leaf (Italian) parsley
red or white wine

Wash morels thoroughly and slice or chop. Sauté with butter and shallots and parsley to bring out the meaty earthiness, and a dash of wine to deglaze the pan and emphasize the natural sweetness.

Serve tapenade or morels with thinly sliced fresh bread, crostini, or crackers. Make your own crostini by slicing a baguette thinly, brushing the slices with olive oil, and toasting lightly. (Erin loves Lu brand Flatbread Crackers, both Herbes de Provence and Pain Rustique varieties.)

For a crostini tray, add a small bowl of creamy goat cheese mixed with herbs—fresh chives are an early-summer favorite—to impress even the hard-to-please.

• • • • •

Salads and Vegetables

In summer, even Northerners can forgo the old standbys and go fresh and local with vegetables. Try a mesclun mix, tossed with late asparagus, fresh beets—now available in gorgeous yellows and oranges as well as deep reds, new carrots, all lightly steamed, and sugar snap peas. Serve with a vinaigrette. If you don't mind turning on your oven, roast the beets for extra sweetness: Drizzle beets with oil, wrap in foil, and roast at 375 degrees for 25–30 minutes. Slip the skins and marinate for a few minutes in oil, vinegar, salt, and pepper.

An easy alternative: fresh spinach with a raspberry–walnut oil vinaigrette.

4 tablespoons walnut oil
1–2 tablespoons raspberry vinegar, depending on strength and preference
1 teaspoon Dijon mustard
coarse salt and freshly ground pepper

Place all the ingredients in a wide-mouth jar. Tighten the lid and shake to emulsify. (Erin keeps an old jelly jar with an opening wide enough for grinding pepper—without peppering the kitchen counter.)

•••••

THE PASTA COURSE

Pasta makes a lovely main course in summer, as at the Festa. Choose your dish based on the size of your crowd. A short, sturdy noodle such as rigatoni with a Bolognese sauce, or a baked dish such as lasagna, which can be made ahead of time and served buffet-style, works well for a larger Festa like Jewel Bay's. For a more intimate Festa at home, Erin and Fresca prefer a long pasta with an easy-to-make sauce. Assemble your ingredients in advance, so you can mingle with your guests, then dazzle them as you make the sauce while the pasta cooks.

Pasta Primavera aka Spring Pasta

Is this the dish Botticelli's models ate, as some claim—or a 1970s New York City restaurant invention, as others insist? As long as it's yummy, Erin doesn't care.

Get your veggies ready before you start cooking the pasta and sauce—this sauce cooks quickly.

¼ cup butter
½ pound mushrooms, sliced—a mixture is nice
½ pound asparagus; snap the ends, cut the stalks into 1-inch pieces, and leave the tips whole
1 medium carrot, thinly sliced
1 medium zucchini, diced
¼ cup slivered prosciutto (optional)
3 green onions, including tops, sliced
½ cup tiny peas, frozen and thawed
1 teaspoon dried basil

¼ teaspoon nutmeg
½ teaspoon salt
¼ teaspoon pepper—use white pepper if you have it
½ pint whipping cream
¼ cup grated Parmesan
8 ounces fettuccine or linguine
additional Parmesan and chopped fresh flat-leaf (Italian) parsley for serving

In a large sauté pan over medium-high heat, melt the butter. Add the mushrooms, asparagus, carrots, and zucchini. Cook, stirring occasionally, about 3 minutes. Add the prosciutto; cover and cook another 2 minutes.

Meanwhile, cook the pasta in a pot large enough to hold the pasta and sauce.

To the vegetables, add the green onions, peas, basil, nutmeg, salt, and pepper. Add the cream and increase the heat; cook until the sauce boils and forms large, shiny bubbles. Drain the pasta and return it to the pot. Pour the sauce over the pasta, lifting and mixing gently to coat the pasta. Add 1/4 cup Parmesan and gently mix again. Serve in a warm bowl, sprinkle with parsley, and serve with additional Parmesan.

MAKES 4–6 SERVINGS.

Spaghetti Carbonara

Fresca adds sausage to this classic. Some cooks use only prosciutto; others substitute pancetta or American bacon.

¼ pound mild Italian sausage
¼ pound prosciutto, thinly sliced
4 tablespoons butter

½ cup fresh flat-leaf (Italian) parsley, chopped
3 eggs, well beaten
½ cup Parmesan, grated
pepper
8 ounces spaghetti
additional grated Parmesan for serving

Bring salted water to a boil and start the spaghetti cooking.

Chop the sliced prosciutto. In a large sauté pan over medium heat, melt 2 tablespoons butter. Add the sausage and half the chopped prosciutto and cook, stirring, until the sausage is lightly browned and the prosciutto is curled, about 10 minutes. Stir in the remaining prosciutto.

Drain the pasta well and add it to the meat mixture. If you'd like to be dramatic, à la Fresca, transfer it to a large bowl and complete the operation at the table. Otherwise, finish it in the pan. Add the remaining butter and parsley to the pasta mixture; mix quickly to blend. Pour in the eggs; quickly lift and mix to coat the pasta well. Stir in the ½ cup Parmesan and a grind or two of pepper; mix again. Serve with additional Parmesan in pasta bowls.

MAKES 4 SERVINGS.

A tip from Erin: *If your deli or specialty grocer sells prosciutto in bulk, ask that ends be saved for you. They're less popular, because the slices are smaller, so some grocers will give you a killer deal—and they work beautifully in this dish.*

Fettuccine with Minted Tomato Sauce aka Fettuccine à La Fresca

(Francesca's nickname, Fresca, means "fresh" in Italian.)

A great vegetarian option—something Erin and Fresca like to include in dinners for large groups.

½ cup walnuts, coarsely chopped
2 large ripe tomatoes or 1 15-ounce can chopped tomatoes (not a seasoned variety)
¼ cup dry white wine
1 tablespoon fresh basil leaves, chopped
¼ fresh mint leaves, chopped
¼ teaspoon salt
¼ teaspoon pepper
⅓ cup olive oil
1 small onion, finely chopped
1 clove garlic, minced or pressed
8 ounces fettuccine
additional grated Parmesan for serving

Toast the walnuts in a shallow pan at 350 degrees for about 10–12 minutes. (Don't wait until they look dark, as they will continue cooking after being removed from the oven.)

If you're using fresh tomatoes, peel, seed, and chop them. In a medium bowl, mix the tomatoes with the wine, basil, mint, salt, and pepper.

Heat the oil in a medium sauté pan over medium heat. Sauté the onion until soft and just starting to brown; stir in the garlic and cook briefly. Add the tomato mixture and cook at a gentle boil, uncovered, about 5 minutes. Stir occasionally.

Meanwhile, cook the pasta and drain well. Place in a warm serving bowl and spoon in the sauce, lifting to mix. Sprinkle with toasted walnuts and serve with a bowl of Parmesan.

Alternatively, make nests of spaghetti in individual bowls and spoon sauce into the middle of each nest.

MAKES 4–6 SERVINGS.

If you like bread with pasta, go ahead! Erin and Fresca readily mix homemade dishes with tasty commercial products. Wendy's ciabatta, baguettes, and French country bread complement these pastas beautifully.

• • • • •

DESSERT

Because everyone deserves something sweet—even Dean and Linda Vincent!

Grilled Peaches with Balsamic Vinaigrette

Try this version Erin and Wendy cooked up.

3 tablespoons white sugar
¾ cup balsamic vinegar
2 teaspoons freshly ground black pepper
2 large, firm peaches
Optional garnishes: crumbled blue cheese, goat cheese, whipped ricotta, mascarpone, vanilla ice cream, cookies, mint sprigs

In a small saucepan over medium heat, dissolve the sugar in the vinegar. Add the pepper, and cook at a low boil or simmer, stirring, until reduced to about half volume. Remove from heat.

Halve and pit the peaches. Oil the grill. Grill the peaches, cut side down, about 5 minutes, until soft and carmelized. Turn and brush with vinaigrette, and grill about 2 minutes more. Place each peach half on a small plate and drizzle with the remaining vinaigrette.

Optional: Fill peach cups with ice cream or soft cheese, or garnish with crumbled cheese. Serve with a cookie and a mint sprig.

For the Festa, Wendy garnished the peaches with freshly baked palmiers from Le Panier. Another option Erin enjoys: Tuck in a simple yummy cookie, such as biscotti, shortbread, or Pepperidge Farm's Chessmen.

Palmiers aka French Sugar Cookies

¾–1 cup sugar
1 sheet frozen puff pastry, thawed

Preheat oven to 425 degrees. Line two baking sheets with parchment paper or a silicon sheet.

Sprinkle your work surface with 1–2 tablespoons sugar. Lay the thawed puff pastry on the surface. Sprinkle with 2 tablespoons sugar. Roll into a 10-by-14-inch rectangle. Sprinkle ½ cup sugar, stopping about ½ inch from the edges. Lightly press the sugar into the pastry, using your hands or the rolling pin.

Use a knife to score a very fine line across the pastry, starting in the middle of the long side. Start at one short side and roll up the pastry tightly, stopping at the score line in the middle. Repeat from the other side. Cut into 3/8-inch slices and lay the slices 2 inches apart on baking sheets. Sprinkle lightly with 1 tablespoon sugar. Bake at 425 degrees for 12 minutes. Turn the cookies over and sprinkle with 1 tablespoon sugar. Bake 5 minutes or until golden brown and glazed. Place on wire racks to cool.

MAKES ABOUT 24. AT THE MURPHY HOUSE, THESE GO FAST. STORE ANY LEFTOVERS IN AN AIRTIGHT CONTAINER.

An easy alternative: Affogato, *a grown-up sundae. Top a scoop of vanilla ice cream or gelato with a shot of espresso or strong coffee. Garnish with a cookie, a dusting of cocoa powder, fresh raspberries, or sliced strawberries—or not, as it's perfectly wonderful on its own. A splash of liqueur is nice, too.*

• • • • •

WINE SUGGESTIONS

In summer, Erin loves a light, crisp pinot grigio or pinot gris, or a sauvignon blanc. The citrus tones and hint of smoke pair well with the fresh flavors of summer and starry evenings on the deck. Guests who choose a pasta with a tomato-based sauce may prefer a less tart white, such as a Viognier, a non-oaky Chardonnay, or a light pinot noir.

Lately, Erin's been drinking A to Z Oregon Pinot Gris and Al Fresco Pinot Grigio. She also loves Zenato Pinot Grigio Della Venezie, Waterbrook Sauvignon Blanc (Bob and Liz's favorite), and A to Z Oregon Pinot Noir. And she will never refuse a glass of Santa Margherita Pinot Grigio—unless she's driving!

If you're in the mood for red wine, let Fresca pour you a glass of DaVinci Chianti.

FROM *NEW YORK TIMES* BESTSELLING AUTHOR

JENN MCKINLAY

THE CUPCAKE BAKERY MYSTERIES

Sprinkle with Murder

Buttercream Bump Off

Death by the Dozen

Red Velvet Revenge

Going, Going, Ganache

INCLUDES SCRUMPTIOUS RECIPES!

Praise for the Cupcake Bakery Mysteries

"Delectable . . . A real treat."
—Julie Hyzy, national bestselling author of the White House Chef Mysteries

"A tender cozy full of warm and likable characters and…tasty concoctions."
—*Publishers Weekly* (starred review)

jennmckinlay.com
facebook.com/JennMcKinlaysBooks
facebook.com/TheCrimeSceneBooks
penguin.com

M1212AS1112

THE WHITE HOUSE CHEF MYSTERIES FROM ANTHONY AND BARRY AWARDS WINNER

JULIE HYZY

Introducing White House executive chef Ollie Paras, who is rising—and sleuthing—to the top . . .

"Hyzy may well be the Margaret Truman of the culinary mystery."
—Nancy Fairbanks

"A must-read series to add to the ranks of culinary mysteries."
—*The Mystery Reader*

STATE OF THE ONION
HAIL TO THE CHEF
EGGSECUTIVE ORDERS
BUFFALO WEST WING
AFFAIRS OF STEAK
FONDUING FATHERS

M546AS0812
P.O. 0003633837

RET